Love is the...

Sweetest venom.

mia asher

Sweetest venom.

Love is
the sweetest
venom!

Mom and Dad, This one is for you.

preface.

Revenge.

What an intoxicating thing…

prologue.

As we look at each other silently, sadness fills me from within, sorrow gripping my heart with its sharp nails. A gut feeling tells me that this is the last time that we'll see one another, and I'm not ready for that.

A knot forms in my stomach. "So is this good-bye?"

He stares at me and, without a word. I already know the answer. I can see it in his eyes.

chapter one.

Ronan

"Where are you going, baby?"

I'm looking for my underwear when I hear Ana speak. I turn to look at her, half naked on her bed. She's all hair, perky tits, and no brains. "I gotta go. My boss' assistant just called to let me know that I need to pick him up in Midtown in an hour. I'll call you, 'kay?" As I stare at Ana with her blue eyes and swollen lips from having sucked my dick, I hate myself even more because I can't stop myself from wishing she were Blaire.

"But why? You told me you were free for the day."

I hate this shit. I run my fingers through my hair. "Yeah, sorry about that, but the other driver had a family emergency."

She huffs, crossing her arms. "There's always an excuse with you, Ronan."

"Ana, we spoke about this. I thought we were clear. We're having fun."

"You're still not over that girl I saw you with at that bar, are you?" She frowns. "The one who looked like she thought she was above us all."

5

"Let it go, Ana," I warn her.

"I knew you two didn't belong together the moment I saw her. You're too good for a bitch like that."

I walk toward the bed, lean down and kiss her aggressively, my mouth fucking hers. Ana responds instantly, deepening the kiss, and for a moment I forget that this woman who looks exactly like Blaire isn't her. I kiss her as though she's the woman who is everything and nothing to me—the woman I can't forget.

With the kiss coming to an end, I brush her black hair out of the way and then grab her chin between my fingers, lifting it and forcing her to look at me. I know my hold is growing painful because she winces in pain.

"If you ever speak of her like that again, I won't be responsible for my actions. Good-bye, Ana." I let go of her face and watch her fall backward on the bed.

"Wait, Ronan, don't go! I'm so sorry. I didn't mean…"

I finish getting dressed in my usual black suit and walk out of her bedroom, never looking back. Riding the elevator, I lean on the wall and close my eyes momentarily, the anger and resentment I feel leaving me emotionally exhausted.

I knew you two didn't belong together the moment I saw her.

Ana's words haunt me. Maybe she's right. Maybe I was just too blind to see it.

Or maybe I created someone in my head that never existed in the first place.

I wait for Lawrence to get in the Rolls Royce before I close the door behind me and make my way to the driver's seat.

"Where would you like to go, sir? Back to the office?" I ask, staring at him in the rearview mirror.

He answers without raising his gaze, his eyes focused on a file that's opened on his lap. "Actually, no. Take me to East 34th Street."

Shock courses through me as my mind registers his words. I clear my throat before I repeat the address, as if by doing so it will become a mistake. I'm sure I've heard him wrong. It can't be.

Lawrence looks up and our eyes connect. "Yes, that's correct."

Stunned, I nod quietly as I tighten my hold on the steering wheel and watch my knuckles turn white. "You got it, sir."

As I'm driving away from the building where Lawrence spent most of the late afternoon in a meeting, I'm overpowered by such dread that it's hard to focus on the road. My chest feels empty but heavy all at once, making it hard to breathe.

Please, no.
Don't let it be her.
Not her.

But even as I try to fool myself by chanting that empty prayer in my head, I already know the truth. I can clearly hear her voice and her cutting words …

"I fucked a man the entire night."
"And it wasn't for love."

By the time I park outside her apartment building and watch Lawrence disappear inside, I'm completely numb even though logic tells me that it isn't possible. My heart still beats in my hollow chest. Blood still flows in my veins. My lungs still breathe the air that once tasted like her, her essence long gone. But as I remember her last words to me there's this darkness, this hatred, taking over, seducing me with its bitter freedom. Slowly...

Surely...

I can feel it. My heart once weakened by my love for her has finally grown quiet. I touch my chest and rub the spot where that useless organ should be. There's nothing there anymore. I am free.

Calm, I see her first.

And as I watch her smile at Lawrence as she once smiled at me with that deceiving light in her eyes, I surrender myself willingly to darkness.

Yes.

I'm finally free.

chapter two.

Blaire

WATCHING ME WITH EYES that could potentially destroy me is the last man I hoped to ever see—the only man to have ever made me want more.

"Blaire?" I hear Lawrence ask, making me realize that I'm standing in the middle of the street, blatantly staring at Ronan, who's more glorious than I remembered.

I close my eyes, take a calming breath, and turn to face Lawrence. "I'm sorry. Did you say something?"

"Is everything all right?" he says, curiosity ringing in his voice.

"Yeah... I thought I saw someone I knew, but I was wrong," I lie.

Lawrence nods as he places a hand on my lower back, his touch possessive and intimate, and propels me to walk toward the car. *Toward the man who's looking at me as though I killed his dog.* When our gazes connect once more, my heart is pounding. I want to look away, yet a part of me wants to absorb every familiar detail of his features and carve them in my brain until they draw my blood. But what I see in his eyes, so full of hate, holds me hostage.

When I've had enough, I look straight ahead at the cars passing by, the street lamps illuminating the night with their glow, and pretend not to know Ronan. I ignore the man whose kisses I can still taste, whose warm hands I can still feel caressing my skin, and whose words still echo in my head. I ignore him like I ignore the tightness in my chest. I ignore all emotion and listen to my head. *As usual.*

I turn to look at Lawrence as he glances between Ronan and me. I push myself closer to him in an attempt to distract him.

"About what you said before …" I place a hand on his hard chest, sparks shooting up my arm.

"Yes?" he asks.

I stop walking and stand on my tiptoes, not worrying that Ronan is watching us, and whisper against Lawrence's mouth, "I want you, too."

He leans forward, grabs my hip possessively, and speaks in my ear, his lips grazing my neck. "Good."

Lawrence and I finish walking the short distance to the car and with mere inches separating Ronan from me, I get in without glancing his way. Out of the corner of my eye, I notice he is no longer watching me. Tears sting my eyes as I lift my chin and tell myself that I don't care.

Once Ronan is sitting behind the steering wheel, Lawrence places a hand on my thigh possessively before he orders, "To the townhouse, please."

And then it all happens at once. Ronan looks up as Lawrence pulls me in for a kiss, his fingers sliding under my skirt and settling between my legs. Ronan's gaze follows Lawrence's hand before locking with mine in the rearview mirror. Our eyes connected, he watches Lawrence claim my mouth with his demanding tongue. But when Lawrence deepens the kiss, cradling the back of my neck and pushing me harder against him, I can't meet Ronan's stare anymore. Shame corrodes my soul as Lawrence's soiled touch awakens my body.

Feeling Lawrence's mouth on mine, I think of all the events that have brought me to this moment. I once yearned for love like everyone else, but it was the lack of love that made me realize that, by opening my heart to people, I was allowing them to weaken me. I was allowing them to take parts of me until all that was left was a girl with nothing else to give, with nothing inside of her but broken dreams. I was giving them the power to rule over my emotions and my thoughts. Every tear shed, every wish wished upon, and every smile that went unnoticed hardened me and made me who I am. I swore to God that I would never give anyone that power. That I would never let anyone get close enough to take another part of me.

And that's why I had to let Ronan go.

He got too close. He made me feel too much. Ronan doesn't only have the power to break me—he has the power to destroy me.

So here I am, pressing my lips harder against Lawrence and opening my mouth wider for his tongue. I look away and disregard a pair of brown eyes that once looked at me as though I were everything good in this world.

Yeah, pretending not to care takes skills, after all.

The memory of his words whispers in my ear, trying to pull me back to him.

Don't you see it, Blaire? Don't you get it? You're in me. In everything I see. In everything I touch. You're in the air I breathe, in the water I drink, and in every dream I dream.

chapter three.

THE TRIP TO LAWRENCE'S TOWNHOUSE is a living, breathing nightmare. Everything becomes a haze of emotions and images where it all blends together. Green eyes. Brown eyes. Hate. Lust. Yearning. One big clusterfuck of my own doing.

I might be sitting next to Lawrence but my mind is in the past, replaying the last time I saw Ronan over and over again.

It isn't until we're standing inside his house, Ronan and the world left outside its doors, that I'm able to breathe freely for the first time. Without saying a word, I make my way toward the staircase. The sooner we're in his room fucking, the sooner I'll be able to freeze my treacherous heart currently thawing like an ice cap in spring once more. I place my hand on the wooden handlebar at the bottom of the stairs when I realize that Lawrence isn't following me. I turn to look at him and notice that he's standing by the front door, studying me closely. I smile at him, but even I know that it's a pathetic excuse for a smile.

He doesn't smile back.

"Why are you standing there and not here? Is something wrong?"

As I await his answer, I take a moment to admire him, to absorb his wild yet polished beauty. Lawrence reminds me of an untamed animal, magnificent as the king of his domain with hunger in his eyes and graceful movements. He's danger, inviting you to play with him as he taunts you with a tempting smile. And you know that you will be hurt for having done so, but you won't be sorry—no, never sorry. He looks like a man who was born to rule and fuck.

"Come here," he orders in his commanding voice.

Slowly, I walk to where he's standing as my pulse accelerates. Without looking at me, he raises a hand and begins tracing my shoulder blade with the back of his fingers. "Tell me …"

"Yes?" I close my eyes and tilt my head slightly to the side, exposing—offering—myself to him. When he reaches the length of my neck, he closes his hand around it, the pad of his thumb caressing the spot where he can feel my blood pulsing through me. And though the stroke of his finger is ever so gentle, a violent shiver runs down my spine, leaving me hot and cold all at once.

"Do you happen to know Ronan?" Lawrence asks nonchalantly.

Sharply, I open my eyes. His question freezes me on the spot, extinguishing the spark that was kindling inside of me a moment ago. Our gazes connect and I'm afraid of what he sees in mine. Afraid he will see how my heart yearns for a man who I can't have—my summertime in autumn.

Deep down, I know that my love for Ronan is a wound that won't ever heal, but being with Lawrence lessens the pain. And isn't numbness—a blessed oblivion—what we seek after love has done us wrong? Lawrence helps me forget him, dulling the ache with my inexhaustible want for him and his money. He's my savior and foe. My sickness and cure, all at once.

"Does it matter?" I ask, licking my dry lips. "I'm here."

In the silence that follows, tension running high, I wonder if Lawrence has figured out the truth behind my unspoken words. I don't think Lawrence would care either way. He has made it more than clear what he wants from me, and my love isn't it.

And that's perfectly fine with me.

There's something carnal in the way he's staring at me that makes me feel as though I can't breathe. I don't want him to ever stop. My heart beats wildly and my pussy grows wet with anticipation as his gaze travels leisurely across my body. With his fingers wrapped around me like an ivy vine, it would be so easy for him to snap my neck in half. The contact is dangerously divine.

"Be still," he orders, his voice full of restrained power.

Lawrence lets go of me, my skin burning from the ghost of his touch, and begins tracing the edge of the lace cup covering one of my breasts. The caress, soft as a lover's whisper, hardens my nipples and raises goosebumps along my arms. Blood rushes to my head, making me dizzy, and I breathe deeply.

I bite my lower lip when he hooks his finger around the cup, pushing the fabric aside, and watches my tit spill out, his green eyes growing midnight dark. Then he touches my nipple, rubbing the rosy tip and rolling it between his thumb and forefinger. It sends shockwaves of pleasure throughout me, focusing on the pulsing center of my body.

I'm about to close my eyes, lost in sensation, when I hear him say, "Eyes on me, Blaire."

He grabs me roughly by the waist, closing the space between us, and wraps an arm around my middle. Holding me tight in his embrace, Lawrence moves his free hand under the skirt of my little black dress and impales me with two of his fingers.

There's pain laced with pleasure as he pumps his fingers in and out of my pussy over and over again. Hard. Deep. Unapologetically. Flesh and sweat. The smell of my body's reaction to his touch coats the air—I can taste it. Leaning over me, high color on his cheeks and a searing gaze, Lawrence looks like a God sent from above to punish me or to seek my salvation.

It's hard.

It's punishing.

It's divine.

Lawrence stops his assault, his fingers still inside me, and stares at me. Before I have a chance to speak, he pulls his hand out of me and cups my cheek, his fingers wet with my essence. I lift my face as he lowers his and just like that our lips touch once again. Something basic in me, something primal makes me lift my hands and tangle my fingers in his hair, bringing him closer to me. Our open-mouthed kiss turns hungry and then it turns into a desperate fight for air, where the source of such relief can only be found in the other. Urgently, thinking of Ronan but desperately wanting—*needing*—the man in front of me, my hands go to his belt and I unbuckle him.

I push my hand inside his boxer briefs covering his cock with my hand, pumping its length and feeling it throb for me. *"So hard …"*

Take me to your bedroom," I whisper between hungry kisses.

He picks me up by the ass and I wrap my legs around his waist, grinding myself on his cock, feeling the way it swells for me, the way my body instantly ignites for him.

"No. Fuck the bedroom—I want you now," he hisses. He walks us to the wooden table sitting in the middle of the foyer. Without giving it a second thought, he pushes the grand and extremely expensive looking crystal vase off the table with the back of his hand so he can place me on it instead. I hear glass shattering as it smashes on the floor, the smell of roses rising like steam.

I glance toward the floor. "Oh no …"

"Shh, it doesn't matter." Lawrence grabs my chin, making me look at him, and quiets me with another kiss that I feel all the way to the tip of my toes. His touch a dark paradise, he palms my tits savagely and surprises me by ripping the front of my dress down to my belly button, baring my breasts to him. Laughing as euphoria runs through my veins, I grab him by the hips, spread my legs wider to make room for him, and pull him closer to me.

Hardness against softness.

Purgatory of my soul. Heaven of my flesh.

"Put your cock in me," I moan, tilting my head back as Lawrence begins to shower my neck with deep kisses that feel like small heartbeats on my skin, reviving my body with his mouth. Urgently, I take his dick out of his underwear while he pulls the scrap of lace covering my wet pussy to the side and sinks into me in one smooth and deep thrust. I gasp. He groans. And then we get lost in the cursed and prohibited pagan dance of our bodies.

Lawrence closes his eyes and lowers his head against my chest, moving his hips furiously. The harder he thrusts, the easier it is to forget *him*. The easier it is to pretend that this is what I want.

This is need.

This is cruelty.

This is hunger.

This is total obliteration.

Matching him thrust for thrust, I feel an earthquake of sensation about to shake my body from the inside out. My ears ringing and my core vibrating, I don't think I can hold on much longer.

"Oh shit, Lawrence ... I-I'm ... oh fuck," I groan.

"Touch yourself. Rub your pussy for me," he whispers, looking down to where we're joined.

Intoxicated with lust, I lean back on my elbow, offering myself to him as I slip my hand between us. And while I watch the intoxicating visual of his glistening cock pumping in and out of me, I spread my lips open with two of my fingers and begin to rub my clit in circles. I moan as the tempo of my touch grows faster ... furious ... merciless ... making me even wetter than I already am.

"Fuck ... Blaire," he breathes, increasing the speed of his thrusts. His cock becomes a blur as it leaves and enters me over and over and over again, bringing me closer to the skies.

Our bodies soar in ecstasy with the power of our orgasm, climaxing together. We stare at each other, his eyes a bright bonfire as the frenzy of our hearts slows down and our labored breathing goes back to normal. With his hardness still pulsing inside of me, Lawrence brushes the hair stuck to my cheek. "You make hell feel like heaven, Blaire."

For a brief moment, a veil is removed from Lawrence's eyes and I'm able to see a sliver of his soul—beautiful yet so full of naked yearning and pain that it takes my breath away. It shakes me to the core.

Before I have a chance to reply, he pulls out and takes a step back, his soul hidden behind a cool and calculating gaze once more.

He extends his hand, offering me help. "Let's go upstairs and get clean."

I stand, look down, and notice the sorry state of my dress. "My poor Versace," I say, meeting his gaze and smiling. "At least it died a good death."

As I watch him walking next to me, my body trembling from satisfaction and my mind confused by our exchange, I realize that he never answered my question regarding Ronan.

Tonight I let a man fuck my brains out so he could eradicate a different man from my heart. I've done it before but, this time, it didn't work. Ronan was everywhere. In every kiss and every touch. He still is.

Why did Ronan have to come back into my life and screw everything up? He was supposed to be a thing of the past. He wasn't supposed to make me doubt myself. I thought I had moved on, but seeing him again shattered all my idiotic illusions that I had conquered my feelings for him. If anything, it proved how deep he engraved himself within me.

Why?

Why?

Naked, I'm sitting up on the bed with my back against the headboard. I'm cold to the bone but I don't bother putting my underwear back on. What's the point? Clothes are a waste of time when I'm here because I'm getting paid to fuck and to be fucked. Besides, the cold feels good. It numbs everything.

I look down and stare at the unsuspecting man sleeping next to me as I try to convince myself that this is what makes me happy. But as I watch the night shadows dancing on his beautiful back, I know it's all a lie.

As I continue to stare at Lawrence, I wish for another man's kisses, my senses drunk with memories of a man who isn't here.

Suddenly an idea comes over me, making my heart beat hard and fast.

I don't know …

Trying not to think of what I'm about to do, I take one last look at Lawrence and get out of bed.

chapter four.

Ronan

Earlier that night ...

DONE WITH WORK FOR THE DAY, I walk to my usual subway station and begin the commute back to my empty apartment. I nod at Joe, the ticket seller sitting in the booth at the foot of the stairs, as I take my wallet out of my back pocket and grab my MetroCard. I swipe it through the turnstile in one swift move and try to walk through, but it seems that today isn't my fucking day. Instead of the usual "Go" appearing on the screen, it says, "Please swipe again." I swipe my card angrily; one, two, three more times.

Please swipe again.

Please swipe again.

Please swipe again.

This is just fucking great. It seems that my day is going from bad to shit-tastic. For a short moment, I wonder if the universe is conspiring against me, or having a laugh at my expense. *Probably both.* What better time to kick a man than when he's down.

Frustrated, I run a hand through my hair and realize that I'm taking out my anger on the wrong subject. I take a deep breath and, calmer, try swiping the card again. This time, the word "Go" lights up the screen and I'm able to walk through the turnstile.

A creature of habit, I go to my spot by the torn poster of a Broadway show and wait for my train to arrive. In this urban underground world where the air is humid and everyone wishes to be anywhere but here, I observe the people standing on the platform and wonder what kind of monsters they are battling. I wonder if they see me and realize that they are staring at the leftovers of the man I used to be. I doubt it, though. Who the fuck gives a shit?

As the train approaches, an image of Blaire's black hair blowing across her face as she laughed at something I said while a different train sped by flashes through my eyes. Rubbing my chest, where my heart should be, I enjoy the numbness there. It makes it easier to breathe.

I find an empty seat. Maybe my luck is turning, after all. Loosening my tie, I recline my head back against the glass and let the familiar vibration of the moving cart relax me. And as tired as I am, part of me doesn't want to go home. On a normal day, my apartment reminds me of her, but tonight, after seeing her for the first time in weeks, it will be a fucking nightmare. I can't be there. I remember my friend Edgar mentioning that he had an upcoming exhibit of his paintings when I saw him the other day. I grab my messenger bag, pull out my phone, and send him a text as soon as I have reception again.

Me: Dude. Is tonight your exhibit?

As I wait for his reply, I look up and notice that a pretty redhead is watching me. When our eyes connect, she smiles at me sweetly as a faint blush covers her cheeks, looking all sorts of lovely. Nothing like the smile of a pretty girl to raise one's spirit. I smile back and feel my phone vibrate.

Edgar: It's tonight, bro. And your pretty mug better be there. Alicia is bringing her friend, that model from Victoria's you banged last summer. Do you remember her? Apparently, she hasn't forgotten about you.

Of course I remember her. It would be close to impossible to forget the things that woman could do with her mouth. However, the memory does nothing for me. My fingers hovering on the screen, I'm about to tell him to forget about it when I realize that Blaire is probably going to fuck Lawrence at some point tonight, if she isn't already. Gripping my phone tighter, my knuckles turn white as the thought of Blaire and Lawrence together fills my entire being with pure hatred. My mind swirls with memories of us and fabricated images of them as one. I can picture her on her knees riding his cock, moaning like a bitch in heat, her long black hair touching his thighs. She throws her head back, lost in sensation, but not before her traitorous eyes lure him to believe that he's the one—the only one. And I know this because I was once fool enough to fall under that same spell.

But not anymore—not anymore.

Me: Send me the details. I'll be there.

I stand outside the gallery, smoking a cigarette, and watch a group of women and men in their early thirties opening the door and going in. Laughter and the buzz of chatter momentarily fill my ears as they walk past me, their expensive perfume lingering in the air after they've gone inside. Burying a hand inside my front pocket, I observe them getting swallowed by a sea of people standing on the other side of the floor to ceiling glass windows.

They're all gathered there with their deep pockets, ready to shell out over a million dollars per painting to celebrate the success of my friend Edgar Juarez—the man of the moment and the new darling of the art scene in New York City. The true American dream. According to a profile written about him in an acclaimed art magazine, he was born in Port Chester, New York, to a single mother, a Mexican immigrant, calling his home the four walls of the one bedroom he shared with her. His mother spent her days cleaning the houses of the rich so she could provide food and shelter for her son, and her nights, her body exhausted and full of calluses, dreaming that he would grow up to be a man with a chance for a bright future.

One day, she had to bring him to work. Edgar went with her, happy for the rare chance to spend more time with his mother. In the living room, he was sketching on a notepad when the lady of the house walked in and saw him and his drawing. A lover of art, she immediately recognized his raw talent, and the rest is history. Now, he makes more money than he ever dreamed of and, most importantly, he makes enough so that his mother doesn't have to work another day in her life.

I wonder how many of them are here tonight because they truly appreciate his work or because owning an Edgar Juarez is the *in* thing at the moment in our ever-changing, fickle society. Whatever the reason, it doesn't change the fact that my friend has arrived and isn't going anywhere anytime soon.

I'm happy for him, but feel like an intruder. And maybe a small part of me, a part whose voice keeps getting louder and louder, wishes that those people were there for me. That it was my name being celebrated and not his. Maybe if I'd had his success …

I tilt my head back as I blow smoke out of my mouth and stare at the black sky. The moon, serene queen of the night, burns brightly with its white fire that illuminates the dark cottony clouds around her. She's lovely ruling in her desolate throne yet I can't help but feel sadness when I stare at her. She's up there: always a spectator, never a participant. An outsider looking in.

Like I was.

Like I am.

Like I will be.

It seems that all my life, I've been looking in from the outside. It never used to bother me. I never wanted more. I was happy, content,

But maybe I'm not being completely honest with myself. I'm changing, and the man I used to be is becoming more of a memory with each day that passes by.

I remember waiting by the car for Lawrence to come out of the Met when I first saw her. She was wrapped in the arms of another man, a man who looked at her as though she was a thing to be owned, to be possessed. I wondered what it would be like to have someone like her in my arms—what it would feel like.

At first sight, I knew she didn't belong in my world. That women like her belonged in the arms of men like the blond man in the tuxedo. Powerful men with bank accounts big enough to buy small countries. I knew then that she was out of my league; that falling for a woman like her would only lead to my destruction. Even so, I couldn't stop myself from momentarily thinking *what if*. It was the first time I'd wanted something that I couldn't have—something unreachable. The first time I'd felt a stirring of something sinister in my chest, something that eats away at people, killing everything good inside of us.

Was it jealousy?

Envy?

Bitterness?

Yes. No. Maybe all of the above. Maybe none of the above. But what I do know is that it was the first time I resented my lot in life.

And it was all because of her.

But that's the power that women yield on poor unsuspecting bastards. We go through life sort of numb, sort of alive, sort of content, sort of unhappy. Living life as only half humans until one day we meet a woman who completes us, who gives meaning to our pathetic existence and makes it worthwhile, enriching it with her laugh, with her smell, and the taste of her body. Days and nights spent with her become a string of moments embedded in our memory, never to be forgotten. She's the air you breathe, the blood running in your veins. She is you as much as you are her, for she not only owns your body but she owns your soul. Until the day when she wakes up and realizes that you aren't enough, that she wants something that you can't offer her. So she leaves you, taking away not only your heart but your soul, too. And all you're left with is the bitter taste of heartache.

I shake my head, smiling ruefully. Nothing like having a woman break one's fucking heart to bring out the sad, pathetic poet inside all of us. I take one last drag of my cigarette and watch its tip blaze intensely before tossing it to the floor and stepping on it. Enough about Blaire and her witchcraft. Tonight, I plan to enjoy myself.

As I close the gap between the glass doors and me, there's a tall woman with long blonde hair dressed in a tight black dress heading in my direction. We both stop a foot away from the metal handle bar. This close to her, it's impossible not to admire the way her small tits outline the expensive silky material of her dress. When I lift my eyes to have a better look at her face, three things become obvious.

One: She's hot as fuck.

Two: She's watching me blatantly admire her without blinking an eye. But how could I not? It would be a crime not to. I lift a hand, running my fingers through my hair, and grin shamelessly.

And three: She's older than me and in the prime of her life.

"Going in?" I ask.

Without saying a word, our gazes lock for a second or two before she looks away, dismissing me like an unwanted thought, and reaches for the door. I see her white, slender and perfectly manicured fingers wrap around the metal handle bar. Instinctively, I close my hand over hers and say, "No, please, allow me."

She stares straight ahead and doesn't move her hand. "I don't need a man to open the door for me," she says coolly, turning her head until her eyes meet mine. "I can do it myself."

Ah. Even her voice is sophisticated like the rest of her. I'm not sure what comes over me, but I let go of the bar and reach for her hand, slowly peeling her fingers away one by one. Perhaps I just want to flirt with an attractive woman. Or perhaps she's a challenge that I want to win.

Or perhaps I'm annoyed that I was so easily dismissed and I want to put her in her place by seducing her.

Turning her hand so her palm is facing upward, I lower my eyes and begin tracing a blue vein in her wrist, noticing how pale and soft her skin is there. "No doubt. But my father taught me good manners, you see, and old habits die hard."

"What if I say no?" she asks, raising her chin as if she's challenging me to change her mind.

I lift her wrist to my mouth. "I'd do it anyway." I kiss the spot on her wrist where life flows through her veins and wait for a slap on the cheek that never comes. Instead, I feel a tremor run through her and it makes the bastard in me smile. *Not so cool now, huh?*

She stares at me for a moment and I take pleasure in the fact that she doesn't remove her hand from mine. And then she smiles. A small smile that barely lifts the corners of her mouth.

"Go ahead, then, even though I should slap you for your forwardness."

"You won't, though, because deep down you know you love it." I smile cheekily. Releasing her hand, I grab the door handle and open it. "After you, unless ..."

We hear the buzz of people talking inside, beckoning us to go in. A man excuses himself when he walks past us, but neither of us seem to care what's happening around us. Eyes on each other, we war silently.

The world stops spinning.

Time comes to a halt.

Tension crowds the air we breathe.

I watch the small bump in her throat move ever so slightly as she swallows unsaid words. Then, she licks her coral colored lips, and images of her mouth wrapped around my cock flash in my mind.

"Unless what?"

"We don't go inside and go somewhere else."

"Where would that somewhere else be?"

I lift a hand and pull her hair to the side, revealing her porcelain-white shoulder, and caress it with the back of my hand. "My apartment."

"And what would we do there?"

I lean down and kiss her shoulder. "Take a guess."

Short of breath, her chest rises and falls rapidly. "I'm not in the mood to play games."

"Yet I can practically smell you getting wet." I close the space between us until I can feel her soft and supple body grazing mine, hardening my cock, and whisper in her ear, "But if you want me to spell it out for you, beautiful, so be it. If you leave with me now, we're going back to my place to fuck. And it won't be nice. And it won't be pretty, but you'll love every second of it."

She takes a step back, putting some space between us. Placing my hands in the front pockets of my jeans, I watch her run her palms down her dress, smoothing imaginary wrinkles. It allows me to admire how graceful her movements are. With her icy beauty, she reminds me of a Russian ballerina, from the curve of her pale neck to the elegant curves of her body hidden behind black silk. Briefly, the thought crosses my mind that I'm asking a complete stranger to go back to my place to fuck, but I came here to forget and that's exactly what I plan to do. *With her or with someone else.*

I'm thinking that she's going to tell me to go fuck myself when she looks up.

"Let's go then."

After we get in the cab and I give my address to the cab driver, she reaches for my hand. She leans her head back on the leather seat and turns to face me, her features made indistinguishable by the darkness surrounding us.

"I've never done something like this before."

I squeeze her hand. "Me neither. Are you afraid?"

She nods.

"We don't have to do this if you don't want to. We can go back, go on our separate ways, and pretend like this never happened."

Waiting for her answer, I watch the lights coming from outside dance with the shadows of the night on her body as we speed through the streets of Manhattan.

"It isn't that. It's just ..."

"Yes?"

"I'm afraid of what you make me want."

"And what's that?"

"To feel," she says, her words barely a whisper.

I smile ruefully, lift her hand, and kiss it. "That's exactly what I *don't* want." *What I'm running away from.*

chapter five.

TONIGHT'S FUCK ISN'T ABOUT connecting with someone. Tonight's fuck is about seeking an emotional stupor, where I can lose myself in her body and stop living in the hell that mine has become. It's about reaching that point when I'm buried in her pussy, my cock surrounded by her warmth, pounding away my feelings for another woman in her. Where there are no emotions, no memories, no expectations—nothing. Just pure, unadulterated, and selfish ecstasy.

Beyond the few sentences we shared on the ride here, we haven't said anything. It isn't like there is no need for words—there is—but not of anything that is relevant to what we are about to do. Besides, the silence allows each of us to battle our own ghosts. I turn to look at her and take in the rich color of her blonde hair that looks as though it were spun out of pure gold, the two small laugh lines shaped like the curved brackets of a parenthesis that imprison her mouth, and the way she holds herself so upright. She reminds me of a soldier about to face his enemy. The only sign that betrays her cool and unperturbed exterior is her damp palm in mine. *Or maybe it's mine.*

Standing outside my apartment, I turn to look at her. "Last chance to change your mind," I say.

"Why do I get the feeling that you're trying to get me to change mine?" She glances in my direction, our gazes connecting briefly before she goes back to stare straight ahead. "Or maybe you're afraid that I'm—"

I pin her against the wall, my front crushing hers. "I'm not afraid. I just want to make sure that you won't change your mind, because once we walk past those doors"—I nod in the direction of my apartment—"I will fuck you. And you will love every single second that I'm inside you, fucking your pussy. Over ... and ... over ... again." *Until I numb myself and forget that I can't have her.* "Do you hear me?"

Maybe I'm being purposely cruel to her because deep down a part of me is afraid. Afraid of having this woman erase the last traces of Blaire lingering in my apartment, in my body, and in my soul.

"So I'm going to ask you one last time. Are you sure you want to do this?"

"Shhh... Don't say another word." She cups my face with her hands and brings our mouths so close I can feel the whisper of her breath hitting my lips. "I'm here because I want you. Nothing else. Nothing more."

Without saying another word, I push myself away from her and head to my door. I open it for her and watch her go in, her shoulder brushing my chest as she walks past me. When she's inside, I bolt the lock and turn to face her.

She browses my small, messy apartment without touching a single item.

I rub the back of my neck. "I have to say that I'm surprised that you're still here after what just happened."

Without looking at me, she says, "Me too. Honestly, I'm surprised that I even left with you in the first place. Throwing caution to the wind and going to a stranger's apartment aren't things I'm known for—quite the opposite, actually."

Her voice is soothing and calm, and I find that I enjoy listening to her talk. I lean my back on the door, my shoulders touching the flat surface, and cross my arms. "What are you known for?" I ask, curious about the woman standing in front of me. "You seem the type of person who never breaks rules. Am I close?"

She laughs, but it's an empty sound. "Oh, I don't know… I was groomed to be the perfect child and later on, the perfect wife. And I was taught that impulsiveness is an emotion that only the weak give into."

"Yet here you are."

"Yes, here I am."

"Are you married?" I look at her hand and notice the lack of a wedding band and wedding ring.

"Recently divorced. I'd like to drop the subject now."

I nod in acquiescence. It's odd to see a woman standing amongst my furniture and belongings once again. Elegant and aloof, she seems out of place surrounded by my shit. Turning left and right, she takes in the old leather of my second-hand couch, the paperbacks scattered like freckles on the wooden floor, and the small kitchen to the right serving as both the dining room and laundry room.

"Sorry about the mess. I wasn't expecting guests."

I watch her focus her attention on an item lying on the wooden coffee table. She bends down and retrieves the worn out picture—one that I haven't been able to throw away. I don't have to look at it to know that the colors of her face have begun to fade, nor do I have to look to know the difference between the man in the photograph and me.

Her finger traces the spot my own have memorized. "She's gorgeous."

I rub my chest. How can something hollow suddenly hurt so much? "She is."

"What happened?"

I stare at the picture in her hands. "I fell in love with her."

And suddenly I'm hit in the face with memories of *her*...

The sun was setting as we lay on the grass, its rays pint-sized torches that warmed our bodies and bathed our surroundings in amber light. The air, sweet because it smelled like her, caressed our skin. I remember she turned in my direction and looked at me with her sapphire eyes, and in that one look we exchanged an unspoken truth that she was too scared to admit and I was too eager to believe.

"Don't move. I need to take a picture of you just like that."

She laughed but let me do it, anyway. After I'd put my camera on the blanket next to me, I turned toward her and cupped her face, my thumb tracing the curve of her cheek. "He stepped down, trying not to look long at her, as if she were the sun, yet he saw her, like the sun, even without looking."

She smiled slowly. "Trying to seduce a girl with Tolstoy, huh?"

"Depends. Is it working?"

She stared at me, amusement sparkling in her eyes. "You have no fucking idea." We laughed freely but, after a moment had passed, she added quietly in that husky voice of hers, "Are you really here?" She reached for my hand, brought it to her lips, and placed a kiss so soft I could have imagined it. But I didn't. The heat, the electricity of her touch was flowing through my veins, slowly awakening my body and senses. And I had never felt more fucking alive.

I moved closer to her and propped myself up on my elbow, feeling the feathery grass blades tickle my skin. In this position, I was able to absorb the way the wild wisps of her black hair framed her face, enhancing the delicate blush spreading across her cheeks, and the color of her apple red lips.

"I am," I murmured.

"It all just feels like a dream … one that I never want to end." There was fear in her voice and sadness muting the light in her gaze.

"I'm very real, Blaire," I whispered before biting her earlobe. "And I'm not going anywhere. You're stuck with me."

"But for how long?" she asked, and there it was again. Fear lingering in her voice, in her words.

"For as long as you let me, baby."

"Forever?"

"Forever wouldn't be long enough." I leaned down, closing the space between us, and felt her body tremble in mine. I kissed the tip of her nose, her eyes, the curve of her neck, her mouth …

I kissed her deep and never ending. I kissed her until she was completely and utterly branded by me—her flavor memorized on my tongue. When we pulled apart, Blaire smiled at me and I thought life couldn't get better than this.

"What is it?"

"I'm not a complicated man, Blaire. I don't need expensive things to be happy or to validate my own worth. And for a long time, I thought my life was good, you know? I had good health, a roof over my head, food on the table. Did I ever think that things could be better? Maybe, but it wasn't something that I dwelt on. I was happy with my lot in life. But I think, deep down, I knew something was missing and I just didn't know what it was. Until I met you."

"Ronan …"

"No, hear me out. I know how this sounds, and maybe it is crazy, but for the first time in a very long time, I feel like I'm awake. My life isn't a blur anymore. No more going through the motions for me, and it's all because of you." I paused and stole another kiss. "Fuck it. Run away with me. Let's get married, for real. Today. Be mine and only mine."

Blaire giggled. "You're insane! We can't do that. Besides, you know that I'm yours."

"But are you really?"

She was silent for a moment. "What do you want, Ronan?"

To be your oxygen, Blaire, as you've become mine. Like you said—forever. And one day I'm going to get you to say yes."

There were tears in her eyes as she stared at me. "Oh, really?" she asked, her voice trembling.

"Yep." I cupped her face once more and felt a runaway tear land on my thumb. "I will never give you up, you know?"

She remained silent then because she knew it was all a lie, every word, every look, and every touch. All fucking lies. And the biggest joke was that I fell in love with her—the most beautiful lie of all. Her kisses were deceit that tasted like the sweetest venom, her laugh a lure to my demise, and her body the damn devil's playground.

But then again love is a dirty, bloody, messy game. Love doesn't give a fuck about rules or honesty. And as much as love can make one feel alive and want to change for the better, it can also kill you and, with it, your dreams. All in the blink of an eye.

"And what happened?" I hear the woman ask, bringing me back to reality, her face and blonde hair replacing that of Blaire's.

What usually happens when you forget your place in the world and dare to dream. "She broke my heart."

I take the few steps separating us until I'm standing not even a foot away from her. I raise my hand and caress the side of her face with the back of my fingers. She closes her eyes and leans in toward my touch. Then I grip her chin, tilting it up as I lower my mouth. When my lips touch hers, she closes her eyes and gives in to the kiss. I don't. I can't. And I fucking hate myself for it because even though I'm kissing this woman, it's Blaire who I taste.

With the kiss coming to an end, I say, "Undress now."

She seems unsure for the first time since we met. "I'm not young and beautiful like her."

Her words do something to me. They don't touch a chord inside me, or move me—that's impossible. Maybe if I had met her in another life, one where I was whole again. But they make me want to show her what I see. Her beauty. A beauty that becomes increasingly more obvious with every second that passes by.

I let go of her and move to stand behind her. Without touching her, I lean into her, and say, "You *are* beautiful. Let me see you. All of you."

She takes a shuddering breath and steps away. Turning to face me, I watch her slowly reach for the spaghetti straps resting on her skin, pushing them off her shoulders one by one. The sight of her undressing for me is more than erotic. It's downright intoxicating. The silk slides down her toned body as softly as running water, revealing gentle curves, small but perfect tits, and a smooth, sweet cunt. My hands itch to explore it all. I want the warmth of her skin to seep into mine, warming me even if it's only for a brief moment in time.

Nervous and hesitant, she covers herself with her arms.

"No, don't hide from me." I peel her hands away from her body. "You're magnificent."

"You're being polite. I saw her picture. I know what you're used to. And I can tell you right now that I look nothing like her."

"Yes, you're right. You look nothing like her, but I still want you."

I watch her blush, and the color is so lovely on her skin, it makes me want to put it there again. My cock hardens, agreeing with me. I bridge the space between us until my chest is touching the tip of her tits. Her nipples harden, her breathing short and fast.

"And why shouldn't I? You're beautiful, desirable, and so fucking sexy." My hand caresses her skin, starting from the curve of her shoulder to the gentle curve of her tit down to her stomach. "I want to trace my tongue along each curve and orifice of you." I grab her hair, pull it to the side, exposing her neck, and lean down to kiss it, feeling her pulse under my mouth.

"Savoring the taste of your sweat, of your desire, of the secrets your body has to offer." I straighten and place my hands on her hips, curling my fingers in her flesh, as I pull her flush against me.

Her eyes widen, showing me how dilated her pupils are. She licks her lips. "I want you, too."

I cradle the back of her neck as we begin to kiss desperately. There's no room for air. No room for thoughts. There's no room for anything other than my lips on her, my hands on her skin. I breathe her in, letting her fill my lungs with her scent, drugging me with the smell of lust and want. I seek oblivion in her warm, inviting body.

My need isn't for her.

My need is not to feel. To stifle the beating of my heart.

I break away and kiss her from her mouth to her neck, and all the way down to her tits, my tongue flicking her nipples, savoring the taste of her sweat. My teeth sink into her skin, making her cry out. Her pain is my pleasure. Her blood sates my thirst. She reaches for my hair, pulling me back up. Face to face, we kiss again but, this time, it's her teeth that search to draw my blood and her nails digging painfully into my skin. It's fucking beautiful.

I grab her hand and bring it to my erection, making her rub my cock over my jeans. "Now sit down. I'm going to fuck your mouth."

She sits down on the couch as I unbuckle my leather belt, unzip my pants, and pull out my cock, pumping it in front of her face. I step closer, watching the tip of my cock tracing her lips.

"Open."

I slide it all the way in and then grab her head with my two hands and push her closer to me, feeling her suck me greedily as I pump in and out of her, fucking that sweet mouth of hers. Fast. Mercilessly. The pace is punishing but she doesn't stop me.

Groaning, I pull out my cock that glistens with her saliva. I watch her wipe her mouth and chin. "Turn around and kneel on the couch. I'm going to fuck you now."

She follows my instructions instinctively, but before she turns, I see the hunger in her eyes, too. She wants this as much as me. Kneeling behind her, I grab a condom out of my wallet. After ripping it open and rolling it on my dick, I take her by the hips and pull her ass out toward me. With my cock in hand, I spread her cheeks, slowly caressing her asshole and cunt, coating it with her wetness. "Jesus, you're so fucking wet already."

She pushes back against my dick, wanting it, begging for it. I fist her hair and pull her head back. "I like you like this. At my mercy." I lean down and hiss in her ear, "Want me to fuck you like this, huh?"

Her head next to mine, the back of it touching my shoulder, I can see her fragile, beautiful neck and smell the aroma of her sweat mixed with perfume. I lean in and run my nose along the edge, feeling her tremble.

She nods and I push her forward aggressively, making her land on her hands, spreading her ass with my hands, admiring what I'm about to take.

"Such a pretty pussy."

I lick two of my fingers and run them over her clit, pressing them deep inside of her. She shudders as I finger fuck her from behind. The wet sound of my hand moving in and out her fills the room, and it's driving me mad. She grips the leather, her nails leaving indentations as the speed of my hand increases, as I take out my anger, my frustration, my need, my yearning on her body. I'm a selfish bastard for doing so, but I can't stop. I need this as much as I need my next breath.

I hate you, Blaire.

I fucking hate you.

I pull my fingers out of her, push myself closer, and grab her by the hip. Pumping my cock before I enter her in one swift, deep thrust. I fuck her as though I am looking for my salvation and my solace in her cunt.

It doesn't work.

I close my eyes, and it's Blaire I see, glancing back as I enter her from behind, smiling, taunting me with her smile. And the harder my cock enters this woman with the blonde hair, the louder Blaire's laughter fills my ears.

I shake my head, feeling the sweat beads crawling down my skin like the legs of a spider, trying to force her out of my mind, but it doesn't work. Nothing works. I look up and see our reflection in the window facing the street. Our eyes meet on the glass, her beauty mirrored on the flat surface, but I'm so fucking gone, so fucking numb, it makes me feel nothing. Letting go of one of her shoulders, I bring my other hand around to rub her clit with my thumb. Fast. Faster.

She's moaning, telling me not to stop, and I can feel both of our orgasms hovering within reach when my house phone begins to ring. Not caring who is calling, I let the voice message pick up.

It's her.

Haunting me. Fucking with me.

Her voice fills the small space of my apartment as I continue to bury my cock in another woman over and over again.

"Hi … It's me … I know it's late, but I couldn't sleep."

My jaw tense, I close my eyes and thrust forward again, rubbing her, pounding harder and faster each time.

"I ... I don't know why I'm calling. I'm probably the last person you want to hear from ..."

As her voice continues to surround us, our rhythm becomes more desperate. I grip her so hard I can see the indentations of my fingers on her white skin, and fuck harder into her.

"I guess ... I just wanted to tell you that you meant a lot to me."

As our bodies continue to crash as though we were the sea and rock, I rub her faster and faster, until she comes undone on my hand and on my cock.

"I miss you."

Those last words and Blaire's voice swim in my head. A scream is torn from my chest as I come inside another woman, thrusting one last time. I pull out, not bothering to remove the used condom, reach for her and wrap her in my arms, comforting her. I feel her trembling but it's not until her voice breaks through the ringing in my ears that I realize it's me who's shaking.

I'm not comforting her.

She's comforting me.

"Shhh ... it's all right," she says soothingly, caressing my hair.

I wrap my arms tighter around her. "I'm—"

"Shhh ... Don't say anything. I'm here ... I'm not going anywhere."

43

The sound of the rain against the windowpane wakes me up. I feel hazy as I look around my room, noticing the empty pillow next to me. I reach out and touch the indentations her body has left behind. I lose myself in the sensation of the cool sheet under my palm, trying to discover a hint of her warmth, looking to find a small trace that she was here. But all that remains is a mountain of ice-cold sheets tangled at my feet.

She's gone. Man, it seems like I'm on a hot streak lately. First it was Blaire, and now her, too. Well, good riddance. She saved us both from a very awkward morning after.

Looking to my left, my eyes land on the alarm clock sitting on my nightstand table. 05:13. The red neon numbers on the screen bleed their light into the bleak darkness of the room. Fuck, it's early. I get out of bed and look out the windows facing the street while I put on a pair of mesh shorts, realizing why it's so dark in here. Dense, menacing clouds hide the blue sky under a gunmetal grey blanket as it pours outside. I walk toward the window, pull the lock handle up, and push it out. Stretching my arms and back, I enjoy the smell of rain filling my nostrils.

After a few seconds pass, I head to my living room to make myself some coffee. I'm about to cross the threshold when I stop dead in my tracks. Surprised, I find the blonde woman, her hair up in a perfect ballerina bun, or whatever the fuck those are called, standing next to the coffee machine. Two coffee mugs sit on the countertop next to her.

Uncomfortable, I rub the front of my chest, taking in the familiar curves of her body clad in black silk. It's hard to imagine that this poised woman who looks as though ice runs through her veins is the same uninhibited creature from last night.

"You're still here."

She crosses her arms, leaning her hip on the edge of the counter. "You noticed." Our eyes connect, and I see a teasing gleam in hers. "I hope you don't mind, but I took the liberty of making some coffee."

"No," I clear my throat, "not at all. Thank you."

"I don't feel human until I've had my first cup of coffee," she says.

She's making small talk. "Yeah, same here."

After an awkward silence, where we stare at each other, I decide to address the big elephant in the room. "About last night—"

"You don't have to explain anything to me."

"It's not that. I just wanted to apologize for the way I treated you. I was angry and took it out on you and you didn't deserve any of that. Also," I grimace, remembering Blaire's call and what happened afterward. "Fuck, this is embarrassing, but—"

"Stop. Don't say anything more. You were very clear with me from the very beginning about what you were looking for. I understood and came willingly. I'm a big girl."

"Is this some sort of test when you say one thing but mean something completely different and I'm supposed to know it?"

She smiles. "Not at all. I promise that there's no secret meaning behind my words."

Is this woman for real? Where has she been all my life? "Fair enough." As I walk toward her, I notice her checking me out. "Like what you see?"

She doesn't look away. If anything, she slows down her perusal, taking her sweet ass time. "It's not bad."

Her words cut through an almost visible and very tangible tension, changing the chemistry of the air. Relaxing, I grin. Yeah, this woman has balls. But I shouldn't be surprised, not after her behavior last night. When I'm standing in front of her, I place my hands on the countertop on either side of her body, crowding her. And the woman doesn't budge one fucking inch.

"Careful there, beautiful."

She licks her lips, and the sight of her tongue goes straight to my cock. "What if I don't want to be?" She lowers her eyes to my naked chest and lifts a hand, the pads of her fingers gently caressing my tats—seemingly learning them. "Careful, that is." Her light touch makes me want to close my eyes and enjoy the sensations running through me, but instead, I watch her tracing the ink decorating my flesh. "The Little Prince?" she asks, finally looking up.

I nod and step away from her. Her question floods me with memories of Blaire and of an idyllic afternoon spent together, and all of a sudden I'm drowning in them, in her, and in the past.

Fuck. Fuck. Fuck. Why can't I get her out of my fucking mind?

"Did I say something wrong?" she asks, looking adorably confused.

"No, nothing wrong … " I want to say her name, but that's when I realize that I don't know it. I turn to face the living room, reclining against the countertop next to her, the length of our arms touching. "Can I ask you a question?"

"Sure."

"What's your name?"

She laughs, and I find myself wanting to smile, but I can't. "Don't you think it's a little too late for that?"

"Nope. Better late than never."

She shakes her head and extends her hand in greeting. "My name is Rachel. Nice to meet you …?"

I take her hand in mine, but don't move. "Ronan."

"It's nice to meet you, Ronan. You have a lovely apartment." She looks away, breaking the staring contest we have going on. She focuses on a replica of a famous black and white photograph of US troops running in the water heading toward the shore.

"You have good taste in art."

"Do you know Robert Capa?" I ask, pleasantly surprised.

"Yes, I do. I'm a big fan of his work." She walks toward the frame to take a better look at it. "I didn't peg you for the kind of guy to be into photography."

I chuckle and cross my arms, my hands under my armpits. "Really?" I say wryly.

"Yes, I mean, I'm well aware that I met you at an art exhibit—"

"Almost. As I recall, we never did make it inside," I interrupt, teasing her.

She blushes. "Semantics. Anyway, just because you were going to an exhibit doesn't mean that you—" Her attention is caught by something lying on the floor. My blood pumping, I watch her bend over and retrieve another framed photograph. Silently cursing Jackie and wishing her to hell for that, I watch as the blonde woman admires the object in her hands. Without looking at it, I know it's a picture of a laughing Ollie, wild hair and all, being chased by a puppy at the park. I'm proud of that one because I was able to capture in that one frame the innocence and playfulness of his personality.

"This is beautiful. Who's the artist? I don't recognize the work."

I rub the back of my neck uncomfortably, cursing Jackie once again. I remember the day I came home to find her here with a bunch of my work already framed. The walls of my apartment that had been covered in photographs from people I admired were bare.

"What's going on here?" I asked.

Hammer and screws in hand, she turned to look at me. "Hey you! Well, I hate the fact that you hide your talent, so I'm literally taking the matter into my own hands."

"By hanging photographs on my walls without my permission?"

"Your amazing photographs, and yeah, try stopping me if you dare. You might be at least eight inches taller than me and not a skinny ten-year-old boy anymore, but I'm sure I can still kick your ass," Jackie said, her brown eyes sparkling.

I groaned, wanting to pull my hair out. "Why are older sisters so fucking pesky?"

She blew me a kiss and got down to work. Not wanting to hurt her feelings, I took them down as soon as she left.

"Is this your work?" I hear Rachel ask.

I focus my attention on her once again. "Yeah, but don't sound so surprised."

She smiles, and I watch the way her smile transforms her cool beauty to one of warmth and sweetness. She puts down Ollie's photograph and reaches for another, and another until she's gone over at least five of them.

"You're very talented."

Shrugging, I walk toward her, grab the picture from her hands, placing it on the floor, and take her into my arms. "Has anyone ever told you how beautiful you look when you smile?"

She begins to trace my features, slowly, gently. I feel the pads of her fingers traveling along the lines of my jaw. "You don't like talking about your work, do you?"

"Not particularly." I lean down and kiss her on the mouth.

When we pull apart, she smiles softly. "What a lovely way to change the subject."

I grin. "That obvious?"

She nods, and I kiss her again, her arms going around my neck. Breaking apart, both of us breathing heavily, she lets me go and takes a step back, putting some space between us.

"I think I've overstayed my welcome and it's time for me to go." I'm about to tell her that she hasn't when she adds, "And don't say that I haven't. We've been honest with each other up until now, so let's not part with a lie." She's quiet for a moment, seemingly considering her next words. "Listen, I'm hosting a party next Thursday at my house, and I would love for you to come. I want to introduce you to someone who I think can do wonders for your career. And no, this isn't a ploy to see you again. I sincerely think that—"

"That what? That you can help me? You don't even know my work."

"I've seen enough to know that you're truly talented. I want to help you."

I run my hands over my face, anger and frustration stirring inside of me. "Well, what if I don't want to be helped? I don't need your pity." I'm aware that I'm being harsh, but why can't she drop the fucking subject?

Irritated, she shakes her head as an angry blush coats her high cheekbones. "It's not pity, Ronan." She walks to my kitchen, grabs a pen sitting on the countertop next to the newspaper opened at the Sudoku page, and scribbles something on it. "Here's my address, the date, and the time of the party. You don't have to come if you don't want to, but I honestly think you should."

"I'm not going to, Rachel."

"Why not?"

"Because—"

"Because you think you can do it on your own?" She scans my apartment, stopping inside my small kitchen, the old carpet underneath the coffee table, and the furniture that has seen better days.

"No offense, kid, but I think you could use some help. You have talent, and it's a crime for your work to be lying on the floor forgotten and accumulating dust. But if that's what you want, so be it. I was obviously mistaken in my first impression of you, which is odd because I'm never wrong."

"And what's that?"

"Simple. I saw a man who wanted more."

"You're wrong. I want everything."

"Then prove it, but not to me. Prove it to yourself." She grabs her clutch and walks over to the entrance of my apartment. I follow and open the door for her. As she's walking past me, she places her hand on my chest. "I'll let the people at the door know to expect you."

I remove her hand and hold it in my own. "I'm not a charity case."

"I know you aren't, you proud man." She leans forward and kisses me softly on the lips. When she steps outside my apartment, she adds, "Wear a tuxedo."

I watch her get on the elevator before I close the door. Walking to my window, I see a black limousine waiting outside my building. Smiling, but it feels more like a sneer, I don't have to guess who it's waiting for. I see a man dressed in a uniform get out of the car and open the door for Rachel as soon as she steps out onto the street.

Well, isn't life fucking funny?

chapter six.

Blaire

"WILL YOU NEED ME TONIGHT?" I ask Lawrence as I come to stand behind him, observing how he gets ready for the day. I place my arms on his wide shoulders and feel the way his muscles flex under the expensive material of his suit as he knots his tie, his Piaget watch glinting in the sunlight.

His green gaze meets mine in the mirror. I lean in and trace the outline of his ear with my lips. "Do you want me to fuck you again, Mr. Rothschild?" I ask, snaking my hand down until I reach the front of his pants and caress the outline of his cock, its heat burning my palm. What is it about Lawrence that makes me want him constantly? Whenever I'm with him, a visceral need takes over me, and nothing but his tongue on my skin and his cock moving inside of me will do.

I observe the mouth that tortured my body with anguishing pleasure and skill just a couple of hours ago curve in a way that I find both menacing and sinfully sexy. "Trying to lure me to my death with your siren song so early in the morning?"

"You know, some writers thought that Sirens were cannibals."

Lawrence turns to face me, placing his hands on my shoulders. "How fitting, my beautiful man-eater. But as tempting as your song may be, I can't. I have an important meeting this morning."

I pout sadly, making him chuckle. "Brat," he says.

"And of the worst kind, too."

His eyes shine with amusement as they travel the length of my naked body. "I won't need you tonight, but stay if you want. I'll give you a call in the next few days." He flicks the tip of my nose, smiling ruefully. "Until then, my wicked siren."

After Lawrence walks out of the bedroom, I begin getting ready to meet *the* real estate agent to the stars and start the search of an apartment. I wasn't sure that I was going to get him, and I said so to Lawrence. He laughed and told me to leave it up to him. Apparently, Lawrence's assistant placed *one* call, and this man cleared up his schedule for the entire day and fit me in. I'm not surprised, though. Who could say no to Lawrence?

Putting my earrings on, I watch my reflection in the mirror. I notice the black bags under my eyes from a sleepless night and the tiny frown on my forehead. Great. Black bags and premature wrinkles. This is *just* what I need today. Frustrated, I lean forward until my breath fogs the mirror and try smoothing the lines marring my forehead. It doesn't work. They are still there, taunting me with my imperfections, reminding me of the reason why they are there in the first place.

Why did I call him last night?

I know why. As I lay there after having sex with Lawrence, I was suddenly consumed by a drowning need to

53

hear Ronan's voice, to talk to him. I wasn't even sure what I was going to say. All I knew was that I needed to hear his voice one last time. I'd grabbed my phone and walked to the bathroom. I looked behind me, focusing on the man sleeping on the bed, and I couldn't bring myself to care. So I gave Ronan a call, half dreading he would answer, half dreading he wouldn't.

He didn't.

Enough. *Get your act together, Blaire.* Regrets are for the weak, and they have no room in my life—*he* has no room in my life. I give my head a tiny shake and finish getting ready. I leave Lawrence's room once satisfied with my outfit that comprises of ripped jeans, a Marvel Superhero fitted tee, a black blazer, and Oxfords.

As I climb down the stairs, I try to muster some kind of excitement about the fact that I'm going apartment shopping with Lawrence's money, but my chest remains as calm as the sea on a summer night. I glare at an unlucky painting and wonder what's wrong with me. I should be giddy with excitement at the prospect of finally owning an apartment without having to rely on a man to pay my rent. And, yes, I'm aware that Lawrence is still buying it for me, but it doesn't take away the fact that it will be mine after he's gone. Yet I feel nothing.

I must be more tired than I originally thought.

I walk out of Lawrence's townhouse and see Ronan reclining against the car. He's wearing a different black suit. This one fits better than the one from yesterday, molding perfectly to his lean body in a sinful way. With his Ray Bans on, a light scruff covering his jaw, he looks confident and cool and beyond untouchable. I sigh as I glance at the clear blue sky. It's time to get this over with. We better get used to the fact that we'll be stuck together for a while.

I've got this.

I won't be tempted by Ronan, the forbidden fruit in my own twisted version of the Garden of Eden.

But it hurts. So fucking much.

The moment he sees me walking toward him, our eyes lock and he peels himself away from the car to open the passenger door. My heart is beating against my chest, but I disregard my body's response to him, or the way my fingers itch to tame the familiar wild golden brown hair framing his boyishly handsome face like I've done before. *Mind over matter, Blaire. Mind over matter. He's part of the past. You can't have him.*

The cool air smells like autumn. Cold, I rub my arms chasing a shiver away, or maybe I'm just nervous of what's to come. His unwavering gaze remains trained on me, holding me captive as I close the distance between us. I lift my chin and pick up the pace. I won't cower in front of him, even when I'm quaking on the inside, even when his eyes roam my body slowly, unabashedly, making me feel exposed and dirty.

As I'm about to get in the car without acknowledging him, he drawls, "Nice to see you too, Blaire."

I stop walking, pointedly looking at him. "I wish I could say the same, but I'm not a liar." Then, I slide across the beige seat, look out the windshield as I cross my arms, and wait for him to start driving.

"Guess that makes me one then," he says bitingly before closing the door behind me. Anger gathers in my chest. His answer hurt, but I deserve everything I have coming my way.

Out of the corner of my eye, I watch him make his way toward the driver's seat as he removes his sunglasses. My thirsty eyes drink him in after going for so long without seeing him. He's even more beautiful than I remembered, but he looks different, too. Older. Harder. There's a dangerous edge in his face that wasn't there before, and it only makes him more attractive.

Once he's behind the wheel, he starts the car and pulls away from the curb. "Where to?" he asks rudely.

"The Plaza. And if I were you, I'd watch your tone. Because remember, Ronan," I pause, "I'm fucking your boss and I can get you fired."

He chuckles. "I don't give a fuck, Blaire. But I'm pretty sure that Mr. Rothschild doesn't give a shit how I treat you, or talk to you. To him, you're just another pussy amongst many. And trust me, I've driven many before you. So you better enjoy it before he gets tired of fucking you and discards you."

I laugh, crossing my legs. "*You* didn't."

We stop on a red light, our eyes connecting in the rearview mirror war wordlessly.

"That's because I was a fucking idiot, too blinded by your beauty and your lies to see that there wasn't anything worthy underneath your flawless exterior other than just a good fuck. And, yes, you hurt me, Blaire, but in the grand scheme of things you were just another pussy I had and got over."

My heart cracks, but I smile brightly. "Bravo, Ronan. Cruelty feels good, doesn't it? But, at least, you finally seem to have seen the light."

"I have, haven't I?"

"And let me guess, you're moving on to better things?" I ask sarcastically.

"That isn't hard, Blaire. Not when anything is better than you."

Our eyes lock for a moment and that moment feels like it's filled with slow passing seconds that, together, form an eternity. Too much said and not enough. When the red light turns green, he focuses on the road once more and I turn to look out the window. I notice a woman in a red dress walking her Maltese, the mundane action soothing as I try to rein in my emotions. Digging my nails into my palms, I try to numb myself with pain. But it isn't working.

I can still *feel*.

The rest of the trip is taken in an uncomfortable silence. When he pulls up to the famous curb of the Plaza, I focus on the flags hanging above the awning, the large columns, and the red carpet covering the front steps that lead to a world full of opulence and castles in the air. A world where people like Ronan and I don't belong. Yet here I am, an intruder, about to invade it in my Chanel shoes. A doorman walks toward the car and opens its door for me.

I address Ronan. "You can go. I won't need you later."

"My orders are to wait for you."

"But I'm telling you that I don't need you," I say peevishly, close to stamping my hands on the leather seat.

"You might be fucking Lawrence, Blaire, but *you* aren't *my* boss. I don't have to follow your orders."

"Whatever, Ronan. Stay or go. I don't give a shit what you do."

"I'll be here," he drawls, unbothered.

I get out of the car without looking at him, and if it weren't for the polite doorman holding the door for me who's watching us with a perplexed look on his face, I would slam the door behind me. You know ... for effect.

It isn't until I'm greeting the real estate agent helping me today that I realize that we didn't discuss my call from last night. Good. He's obviously moved on or doesn't care. I should be happy about it, but the thought makes me feel sick to my stomach.

His name is William Dowling. Attractive. Medium height. Expensively dressed. Real estate agent to the rich and famous. As we shake hands, his eyes size me up, probably wondering how I caught Lawrence Rothschild's attention. I feel exposed under his inspection. Briefly, I wonder if he knows what I am to Lawrence. I wouldn't be surprised if he did. Rich men buying love nests for their lovers is probably a big part of his business.

Unsmiling, I let go of his hand. "Shall we go look at the apartment?"

"But of course. The elevators are this way." He steps to the side, allowing me to walk ahead of him. As we near the elevator, I notice people looking at me with clear judgment in their eyes. The way they stare at me makes me recoil on the inside, but I'd rather be dead than allow them to see how affected I am. So I straighten my back, reminding myself that their opinion means nothing to me, and walk as though I own the fucking place.

My eyes land on a young woman who looks like she was born and raised in a country club, cream-colored cardigan and all. She stares at me as she grabs her boyfriend tighter by the arm, pulling him closer to her. I want to tell her, "Honey, no need to be scared of me. He's probably already screwing someone else behind your back," but I don't. Instead, I turn to look at country club girl, smile saucily at her, and wink at her boyfriend as I walk past them, leaving them both with their mouths hanging open.

It isn't until we get on the elevator and its doors close in front of us that the smile evaporates from my face.

We're now inside the empty apartment. Emotionally wrung out, I walk around the spacious area lost in thought, seeing everything and absorbing nothing. In the background, I hear William describing the different features that the place has to offer, but I'm not listening to a word he's saying. I'm looking at the view of Central Park. And as my eyes adjust to its beauty, all I can see is Ronan smiling at me, talking to me, and laughing with me once more on that fated summer day.

"I'll take it," I whisper.

"Excuse me?" William asks.

"I'll take it," I say louder, my voice firmer this time. I turn to look at him. "I want this apartment."

He smiles affably. "Exquisite taste."

I nod and go back to look at the view, searching for something—someone—who isn't there.

"Shall I send the paperwork to Mr. Rothschild's assistant?"

His question reminds me of Lawrence. I bite my lip and stare at my shoes as guilt and shame flare inside of me. "Yeah, I think that works," I say without meeting his gaze. I'm afraid that I'll see what he thinks of me reflected in his eyes.

This time, I won't be able to pretend that I don't care.

As we're getting ready to leave, he stops right in front of me, blocking the exit. "One moment."

"Yes?" I ask coolly, raising an eyebrow.

"I just wanted to give you this," he says, handing me his business card.

I frown. "Lawrence's assistant already has your information. She's handling everything with the purchase."

He smiles again, that affable smile, but this time it sends a shiver running down my spine. "For the future. When you're no longer with—"

And then it dawns on me. "Ah. I see what this is."

"Maybe we could come to some sort of arrangement. An arrangement that a woman like you wouldn't pass up."

I shouldn't be upset. I should be used to this. *Lies. Lies. And more lies.*

I scan the area around us and notice that we're standing close to the sleek grey marble kitchen island. I walk to the edge of it and sit on top of the flat surface, spreading my legs open invitingly. Wantonly. Because why not? This is what I am—who I am.

"How about now? Why wait until I'm done with Lawrence?" I reply, surprised to sound so calm. Our gazes locked, I lift a hand and deliberately bring it between my legs, rubbing my pussy through my jeans. "Is this what you want?"

His eyes leave mine briefly to follow the motion of my fingers, flaring with lust, and I realize that I've never felt this cheap before. He moves, coming to stand between my legs. This close, I grab his jaw and pull his face toward mine, fooling him into thinking that I'm going to kiss him.

When our lips almost touch, I slightly draw back and look at him in the eye. "Even if Lawrence dumped me, I would never fuck you." I smile. "I don't fuck the working class."

I push him to the side and get off the counter, my feet landing softly on the wooden floors, and leave the apartment behind me. As soon as I'm standing outside, I rush toward the elevator. Pressing the button for my floor repeatedly—urgently—I realize that it isn't coming anytime soon. Not wanting to spend another minute here, I search for the fire stairwell. I locate the door to my right and sprint in its direction, slamming it open, and running down the stairs as fast as my feet will allow me. The pace frantic, I miss a few steps and fall down on my knees at the foot of the stairs. Stunned inside out, I recline my back against the wall and raise my hands, watching them tremble uncontrollably. The emotions that have threatened to spill over from the moment Ronan dropped me off finally let loose and come crashing down on me, making the room swirl around me.

"That's because I was a fucking idiot too blinded by your beauty and your lies to see that there wasn't anything worthy underneath your flawless exterior other than just a good fuck, Blaire."

As my vision begins to blur, I whisper to myself, "You're right, Ronan. You're so right." I cover my face with my hands as a sob escapes my lips.

And I begin to cry.

chapter seven.

"BLAIRE?" I HEAR LAWRENCE ask as he opens the door.

I'm in the bathtub. The water has grown cold, but I can't bring myself to move. I've lost track of how long I've been here. Naked and with my arms wrapped around my knees, I stare at the silver faucet, its curves and grooves blurring to one grey mass. I avoid meeting his gaze, look down at my body, and notice that it's covered in tiny bumps.

"Hope you don't mind that I'm here."

"Not at all. I'm glad you came. Seeing you is the first thing that has brought me pleasure today."

"You shouldn't be, and you shouldn't say those things to me."

"Why not?"

"Because you of all people shouldn't lie to me." Finally, I turn to look at him and our gazes instantly collide. "You want to know why I'm here? I'm here because I don't want to be alone, not because I want to be with you."

His eyes never leaving mine, he watches me as though he can see all the way to my core, to every broken, sharp piece inside of me. "What happened between the time I left you this morning and right now?"

Lawrence closes the space between us and kneels next to the tub. He lifts a hand and reaches for me. I flinch when he touches me, making him withdraw. Out of the corner of my eye, I see that same hand tighten into a fist.

I lean forward, resting my chin on my knees. "I sat on a bench and watched this little girl playing by herself. She was chasing her own shadow, trying to catch it. She seemed so ... happy, you know? I saw her laughing, heard her laughter, and I thought to myself that there was a time when chasing my own shadow was exciting, too. When I was naive enough to believe that life couldn't get better than spending a day at the park. When I was good, and worthy, and innocent ..." My voice breaks.

"I wanted to run to her and wrap her in my arms. I wanted to tell her to hold on to that moment for as long as she could because the world is cruel. Because the world is unkind, and eventually, it will swallow you whole, turning your hopes into shattered dreams, and your dreams into nightmares. Until one day you wake up and no longer recognize yourself in the mirror. That the little girl who chased shadows is gone, and in her stead is someone you hate, someone who disgusts you. Someone like me. So to answer your question, nothing happened. Nothing except a daily reminder of who I am."

"Look at me," he orders in that strong voice of his.

I won't.

"Look at me, Blaire."

I won't.

He gets up from his spot next to the marble bathtub and walks away.

I close my eyes. I want to say that I'm glad that he's left, but I'm too tired, too emotionally drained to lie to myself. Suddenly, two strong arms slide under my legs and back, picking me up. I open my eyes and absorb Lawrence's beautiful profile as he straightens his back, not worrying that his suit is getting wet, before he puts me down on the floor. Wrapping a warm, fluffy white towel around my shoulders, he says, "You're cold."

I pull the towel tighter around me, thankful for the warmth. "Why are you being so kind to me?" I look him square in the eye. "Am I that fucking good in the sack that you can't see how undeserving I am of you, of all this?" I know it's illogical, but his kindness angers me.

His eyes darken. Lifting his hands and coming a little closer, Lawrence grips my towel-covered upper arms tightly. "Don't talk about yourself like that, Blaire."

I throw my head back and laugh. It's a bitter and hollow sound. *Bitter and hollow just like me.* "Oh, here comes the daddy complex."

Letting go of the towel, I push myself flush against him. I rub my tits on his chest, kiss his neck, his jaw, breathing my poisoned breath on his skin and polluting him with my touch. "Nice old men like you *love* saving girls like me, don't you? You think you can protect us, change us. Well, newsflash: I don't need saving. I don't need your protection. I just want your money. Nothing more, nothing less."

His grip grows painful, and I love it. *Punish me, Lawrence. Go ahead and be disgusted like everyone else.*

I sneer, a scornful smile on my lips. "So come on, fuck me and stop pretending that you care. Show me how much you want me." I grab his face with both of my hands, my nails digging into his skin as I grind my pussy on his growing erection. "You bastard. The thought makes you hot as fuck, doesn't it?" I close the space between our mouths and kiss him. I kiss him as though I want to tear him apart, wound him, and destroy him with my teeth, with my tongue, with every soiled part of me.

Letting go of his face, I lower my gaze and unbuckle his belt.

"Stop it, Blaire." He places his hands on top of mine, halting my every move.

"Shut up, and fuck me like a whore. After all, you're paying for this and dearly." My voice cracks as I push his hands away. I unzip his pants, and pull out his dick, wrapping it with my fingers and rubbing the head of his cock on my clit.

"Look at me," he orders, his voice thick and soft. When I don't, he lifts my chin with one finger and makes me look up at him. I hate myself for what he sees.

Lawrence cups my face gently in his hands, leans down, and begins to kiss each of my tears away. His lips, soft like feathers, land gently on my skin, warming me from the inside out over and over again. "When I first saw you at The Met"—*kiss*— "I watched you from across the room." *Kiss*. "I could see that you were alone and uncomfortable. That selfish piece of shit that you arrived with had left you on your own while he went in search of his friends." *Kiss*. "Yet, you stood there in a room full of strangers ready to condemn you, looking like a Queen. Proud. Brilliant. Then you were making your way to the other side, and as you crossed the room, I had never seen anything more beautiful than the young, brave woman with the eyes full of fire and pride. That girl took my breath away." He stops kissing me to gaze into my eyes. "Bring her back to me, Blaire."

"She doesn't exist. That girl was just an illusion."

"No, she isn't. She's here, in my arms, pretending to be someone else, letting bullshit get to her." He tightens his hold on me. "My beautiful, wild thing. They are dust at your feet. They can't touch you. Don't let them." Drawing back slightly, he smiles. "I won't let them."

Oh, Lawrence. "What are you going to do, sweet man?"

At that moment, as we stare at each other, understanding reflected in his green, green eyes, I know that I've found a friend—that I'm not alone. It's a simple thing, but how it unravels one so.

"Don't worry your pretty head about it. Just know that as long as you're under my protection, I won't let anyone hurt you."

My lips quiver. Who would have known that underneath that hard exterior, Lawrence Rothschild was such a good man? Usually, compassion would drive me away—I don't want people's pity—but I'm just too tired to fight it. All I want is some peace from my inner turmoil and the comfort that Lawrence's arms bring to me.

"Come, let me take you to bed. It's been a long day."

I nod. He shrugs out of his suit jacket and drapes it over my naked shoulders. He leans down, places an arm under my legs and the other behind my back, picking me up once again, and carries me to his bedroom. I recline my head on his chest and listen to the beating of his heart. "I'm sorry for the way I spoke to you. You didn't deserve that." I look up as he looks down.

"Don't apologize. There's no need. Now tell me, darling. What happened with the apartment? Gina mentioned to me that you went to look at some today. Find anything to bankrupt me with?" he teases.

I break his gaze. "Nothing. I didn't like anything."

"You're lying to me. I can see it in your eyes. Tell me the truth, Blaire."

I smile ruefully. "I can't hide anything from you, can I?"

"I'm afraid you can't."

I rub my cheek on his shirt, the silk tie soft against my skin. "And must you always get your way?"

"Yes. I don't know any other way. And now I want you to stop avoiding the subject and tell me what happened."

I sigh, suddenly feeling much older than twenty-three years old. "It was everything. I clearly don't belong in The Plaza, and then the"—I pause, taking a deep breath—"and then the real estate agent, William Dowling … He, ah, he—"

His hold on me grows tighter, firmer, and stronger. "He what, Blaire?"

I shake my head and drop my gaze. "Never mind. It isn't worth it. I really would like to just forget the whole thing."

"Blaire, I'm going to ask you one last time to tell me what happened, and you better tell me. The next time, I won't ask so nicely," he warns, danger carrying in the low notes of his voice.

I bite the inside of my lip, shamefully blushing. "In not so many words, he told me when I'm no longer with you, he wants what you have. 'Some sort of arrangement that a woman like me wouldn't pass up' he said."

He's quiet then. And as his silence grows, I can't take it anymore. I must look at his face to gauge what he's thinking.

When I do, I'm surprised by what I see. He looks pissed. Angry. The angriest I've ever seen him. And suddenly, I'm afraid. *But not for me.* I'm afraid for William asshat Dowling.

I place a hand on his chest, feeling his heart beating so fast. "Lawrence?"

"Don't say another word, Blaire. I will deal with that man tomorrow," he hisses, his jaw set in a hard line.

"Don't be angry," I say softly. "I'm not worth it."

"Angry? I'm not angry, Blaire. I'm fucking furious. I want to find out where that pathetic fuck lives and break every single bone in his body. No one should speak to a woman like that. Especially you."

I grip his suit jacket in my hands as though I would never let him go. His kind words, words that I didn't expect from him, are a soothing balm for my heart. "Lawrence." *Thank you. Thank you for not judging me, and accepting every messed up part of me.*

He lowers his mouth and places a soft kiss on my hair. "Blaire."

When we reach his bedroom, he deposits me carefully on the floor as he reaches behind me, opening the door for me. "Go to sleep, darling. You need rest," he says, tucking a stray lock of hair behind my ear. "Good night."

I grab his forearm, halting him as his jacket slides off my shoulders. "Aren't you coming in?"

In the silence that follows, he stares at me, his gaze swallowing me whole. Then when I think he's about to leave, he leans forward and kisses the corner of my mouth, the crest of my cheek, the tip of my nose. Trembling, I gather his shirt in my fists. He places his hands on top of mine. "If I come in, I won't be able to leave you alone."

"I don't want you to. Stay."

Nodding, he follows me inside. I lie in the middle of the bed but he drags me to the edge of it as he sits on his haunches in front of me. The moon, the only source of light cutting through the darkness of the suite, illuminates his harsh yet breathtakingly beautiful features. Mesmerized, I imagine that's what it would be like to stare into the eye of a tornado.

As our gazes lock, he spreads my legs apart and reaches for one of them, placing the heel on his knee. He bends down, lowering his head and placing kisses as decadent as sin along my calves, my knee, the inside of my thigh. He absorbs me, his gaze burning me, swallowing me.

Grabbing me by the ass, he pulls me forward, closer to the edge of the bed and to his mouth. Kneeling now, Lawrence lets the back of his hand trace my skin until it reaches the center of my body, teasing me, taunting me, before it continues its lovely exploration. He turns his mouth to the other leg, repeating the same torturous steps. Lawrence casts a spell on me, bewitching me, stealing my breath and making it his. His tongue absorbs my every thought until his name is all I can think of.

Lawrence …

Lawrence …

Lawrence …

Lawrence …

When he reaches my right knee, I flinch in pain. Sitting back on his haunches once again, he looks at the red, angry gash on my skin. "What happened here?" he asks, his fingers grazing the cut reverently.

"I fell," I manage to say.

He lowers his lips, kissing the cut and the pain away. Standing, Lawrence undresses in front of me, revealing his gorgeous, hard body. How can a man be so perfect? It's as though in the beginning when God created life, he said, "And I create this man so you can see what I'm capable of—the magic in my hands."

"Stay right there. Don't move," I whisper and get off the bed, closing the space between us. I kneel in front of him, place my hands on the sides of his legs and lean forward, rubbing my lips back and forth on his hardness. Lust floating in my veins, I don't feel the pain on my knee anymore, and even if I did, I wouldn't care.

He wraps my loose hair in his fist and forcefully pulls my head back, making me look at him. "What am I going to do with you?"

I lick my lips, that never-ending hunger for him, for his body, for what he makes me feel flaring again. I grab his rock hard erection in my hand and stroke it, raising my eyes to meet his. "Want me." I lick the head. "Need me."

"You're blind, Blaire. So blind." He bends forward and kisses me. Deeply. Senselessly. Ravenously. It isn't a kiss. It's a man brandishing himself on my lips and claiming them as his own.

After he pulls away, both of us breathing heavily as though we've run a marathon, Lawrence bites my lower lip. "Now put my cock in your mouth."

"With pleasure."

I'm lying on top of him, chest to chest, heart to heart. And with him still inside me, I feel him under me, inside me—

everywhere. Trying to catch my breath, I push some of the long dark hair that covers his eyes to the side to better see him.

I smile. "You're mad for wanting me. I'm a fucking basket case." I lean in and press my lips on his Adam's apple, leaving a trail of kisses up his jaw.

He palms my ass, kneading the soft skin there, pressing us closer together. "Perfection bores me."

After a few moments pass in silence, I say, "Lawrence?"

His fingers caress my naked back, the movement soothing and erotic. "Yes, Blaire?"

"Did you really notice me from across the room at The Met?"

"Yes, darling. I saw you the moment you walked into the room. I couldn't take my eyes off of you."

"And?"

"Are you fishing for a compliment?"

I grin. "Maybe."

He chuckles deep and low. "I saw you and thought to myself, 'If there's a God, please let me make love to her at least once before I die.'"

I blush. "Oh."

"Happy now?"

"Yes."

"And Blaire?"

"Yes?"

"Don't ever repeat that you're unworthy in my presence again," he orders, leaving no room for a rebuttal.

I snuggle deeper into his chest, hiding a delighted smile from him. "Yes, Lawrence."

chapter eight.

I WAKE UP ENVELOPED in an invisible blanket of calm. The usual turmoil inside of me is missing, and in its place, there's a quiet contentment—a peace. And I'm pretty sure it has to do with Lawrence and the acceptance that I found in his arms last night. It leaves me wanting more of him, but I don't think it's supposed to be this way—I don't think I'm supposed to feel this way. Yet I can't help but smile as the golden memory fleets across my mind.

My friend.

As I stare at the window, watching the sunlight come in, an idea takes root inside of me. Without giving myself a chance to second-guess myself, I get off the bed, dress quickly, and step out of the house. Relief washes over me when I find Tony waiting for me today. Lawrence's Rolls Royce sparkles in the background.

"Good morning, Tony," I say brightly, stepping down the stairs.

He moves to open the door. "Good morning, Miss Blaire."

Upon reaching the car, I place a hand on the hood and turn to look at him conspiratorially. "Let me ask you something. Do you think Lawrence would mind terribly if I were to surprise him at work?"

His old, kind eyes sparkle with mischief. "He'd be delighted."

Many thoughts run through my head like a train chugging along with no stop in sight as we drive across town, but I won't allow myself to analyze their meanings—at least not right now.

Tony drops me off outside Lawrence's headquarters. Awestruck, I stand on the pavement and stare at the massive building that houses Lawrence's offices. *Jesus Christ. Will this man ever cease to amaze me?*

Uncertain, I look back and meet Tony's encouraging smile as he mouths to go ahead and keep walking. Belatedly, it occurs to me to head back to the car and tell Tony that I've changed my mind, but I stay put. Wiping my hands on my jeans nervously, I begin to walk in the direction of the revolving glass doors.

Once I'm through security, I take the elevator to his floor. A pretty, vibrant receptionist greets me warmly as soon as I stand in front of the granite counter. I place my hands on the cold stone, trying to absorb my surroundings all at once. The floor to ceiling fountain wall behind her is both mesmerizing and soothing.

"Good morning. I'd like to speak with Lawren—I mean, Mr. Rothschild, please."

"Sure." As her open and kind gaze studies me, I want to fidget and straighten my clothes, but I don't. "Do you have an appointment with Mr. Rothschild?"

"Uh—no. I don't think he's expecting me, actually. But I'm a … uh … a friend of his."

"Not a problem, Miss …"

"Blaire. My name is Blaire."

She smiles. "Would you please have a seat, Miss Blaire? Mr. Rothschild is currently tied up in a meeting but I'll see what I can do."

"Sure. Thank you so much."

I move to sit on a comfy-looking leather chair. Tapping my foot nervously on the floor, I watch people dressed in expensive suits move around the office, the buzz of conversations interrupted every few seconds by the sound of ringing phones. My eyes land on the elevator as its doors open, drawing my attention to a pair of sleek businessmen stepping out of it. I see the instant they notice me, their eyes roaming my clothes, body, and face. Their perusal makes me uncomfortable. However, I won't allow them to see it. I sit up straighter and arch an eyebrow. They immediately look away and continue on their way.

As minutes pass, I grow uneasy that I did the wrong thing by coming here. *God, you're stupid, Blaire. What did you think? That Lawrence would be just sitting around doing nothing?*

I walk up to the reception area. "Excuse me, I think I'm going to go."

"But Mr. Rothschild should—"

"No, it's okay," I say, getting ready to escape. "I don't know what I was thinking."

"Blaire? Is that you?"

Shit. I close my eyes and open them as I turn in the direction of his voice. "Hi, Lawrence." I watch an

75

immaculately dressed Lawrence hand a file to someone next to him before coming to stand in front of me.

"What are you doing here?"

"Surprise!" *Is he mad that I came? Shit. Shit. Shit.* I school my features trying to appear blasé and flirtatious when I'm anything but. "I hope you're not mad."

He frowns. "No, not at all. Why would you say that?"

"I don't know... You're obviously busy and the last thing you need is someone bothering you. I didn't think this through."

"You would never bother me, Blaire—you know that." Lawrence takes my hands in his. "But tell me, darling, why are you here?"

"I wanted to see you." And that's the God's honest truth.

"Yeah?" He lets go of my hands to cup my cheeks. "My God, you're a sight for sore eyes."

My cheeks burn like fireballs. I blink a couple of times dazedly. Hypnotized by him, I gaze into his eyes. There's a teasing glimmer making them shine so brightly that it's impossible to look away. I nod. "Yeah, very much so." Suddenly feeling ridiculously exuberant and daring, I close the space between us and place my hands on his chest. "Don't go back to work. Spend it with me."

"And what would you like to do?"

"I don't know. Nothing. Everything! Let's do something crazy. Oh, I know! I know!" I say excitedly. "Let's go to Coney Island. I've never been. Have you?"

A lazy smile appears on his face, and the sight of it does crazy, wild things to me. "What do you say, my dear friend?" I ask.

"Has anyone ever told you that you're out of your mind?"

I grin devilishly. "A couple of times."

"I have a feeling that I might regret this decision but yes, why not?"

"It's good to regret, Lawrence. It shows that you have lived."

Lawrence and I get out of the car and stand staring straight ahead of us. In the silence that follows, I'm not sure whether I should laugh or cry. I avoid looking at Lawrence because I'm embarrassed to have made such a mistake in front of him, and the last thing I want to find in his eyes is the same disappointment I see everywhere else.

"Well, I guess this is where you regret listening to me," I say, trying my damn best to sound amused. I fail miserably. After a pause, I add, "This sucks. I suck. I can't seem to do anything right."

"Oh yes. What a waste of my fucking time." He surprises me by taking my hand in his and intertwining our fingers. "Come on, Blaire. Give yourself a break. So what if the park is closed? I'm sure there are plenty of things to do."

I let go of him and hug myself with both arms, feeling deflated like a day old balloon. "You don't get it. This was supposed to be special and, obviously, it isn't."

"Of course I get it, but go ahead and sulk. I won't stop you."

"Are you trying to pick a fight with me?" I ask incredulously.

"No. It's called trying to reason with you."

Tou-fucking-ché.

I steal a sideways glance at him. He's watching me with what I could describe as an amused smile. Really, the whole thing is ridiculous. I bump his shoulder while I fight a smile from escaping, but it's no use. I smile anyway.

"Wise-ass."

"You better believe it, darling."

"Sorry. I can be such a baby when I don't get my way, but I wanted to do something nice for you for a change. You've done so much for me. And the one day ..." I sigh. "I should've known that the rides are closed during the off-season."

"But you didn't, so what are you going to do about it?"

"I don't know. I'm not sure if you've noticed but spontaneity and I don't usually go together."

"I can think of two scenarios. Would you like to know what they are?"

I nod, staring at him.

"We could get back in the car. I could drop you off wherever you want and I'll go back to the office. The day will go on as if this little adventure hadn't happened at all."

"What's the second one?" I ask, not liking the first option at all.

"The second one is," he extends his hand, pointing in the direction of the park, "the unknown—with me."

I take one last glimpse at the outlines of the aging rides embedded on the autumn sky of Coney Island before focusing on Lawrence once more. *Oh, what the hell. Why not?* I reach for his hand and begin to walk in the direction of the park. "You make the unknown sound very inviting, Mr. Rothschild."

He tightens his grasp. "Likewise, Miss White."

We stop at Nathan's on the boardwalk for an early lunch. While I wait for Lawrence to bring back our order, I find it extremely hard to focus on anything other than him. He sticks out like a sore thumb wearing his thousand-dollar suit in a sea of casually dressed locals and tourists. I giggle when I notice the dazed expression of the cashier who's serving Lawrence. It's the Lawrence Effect—complete immobility and the loss of all coherent thought and speech. Code word for making an ass of yourself.

Still smiling, I shake my head and look away when the famous Ferris wheel sticking out behind the building comes into focus. A memory long forgotten becomes so clear I can almost taste the funnel cake I ate on that occasion. It's one of the few happy memories I have of my parents and my childhood. Maybe even the last. I'm not exactly sure how old I was, but I remember that a traveling carnival stopped at our town. It was during one of my father's dry spells. He had been sober for a while and hadn't missed any of his AA meetings. Mom seemed to be home more often, too. They were kind to each other. For once, laughter and the music of The Beatles and The Eagles filled our home instead of yelling and the usual fighting words.

In my innocence, I thought that we were finally going to be a family, that they would finally love me as I loved them.

In retrospect, it seems like we all knew that it was a borrowed moment, a temporary delight—a daydream that would eventually come to an end. I think that's when I learned that good things never last. So, in silent agreement, we laughed harder, we held each other closer, and we pretended to be the perfect family for a little longer. However, we never spoke of the future. We just enjoyed the present as it came.

But the most perfect moment of the night came when my dad took me on the Ferris wheel.

We were up high, my small town a collection of faraway twinkling lights, when my dad put his arm around me and pulled me close to him. He placed a kiss on my head, and said, his voice shaky, "Beautiful, isn't it?"

"Yes, Daddy. I will never ever forget this day."

"I won't either."

But I knew by the sorrow in his voice that my dream was coming to an end, and it was breaking my young heart, fear choking me and making it hard to breathe.

"My beautiful girl. I'm sorry for not being able to be the dad you deserve."

"But you are, Daddy. You're the best daddy in the world," I said and hugged him. I didn't realize that I was crying until I saw a wet mark on his shirt.

"You're the light that stops me from drowning in the darkness that I live in." He paused. "Whatever happens, know that I love you, my little Blaire. And that if I'm proud of one thing in my life, it is of calling you my daughter. Don't ever forget that."

But eventually things went back to the same old, and his little Blaire did forget.

"Here you go," I hear Lawrence say, bringing me back to the present. As he places the tray full of steaming and heaven-smelling food on the table, he must notice that something is bothering me because he asks, "What's the matter?"

I paste a fake smile on my face and reach for a hot dog. "Oh, you know—the same old. Don't want to talk about it. Let's eat. You're probably starving and so am I." The words spill out one right after the other, without giving him a chance for a rebuttal. And he knows it, but Lawrence chooses to give me the space that I need by not probing any further.

Once we're done eating, I get up and walk to the closest garbage can, disposing of the napkins and leftover food. I stand still, close my eyes, and lift my face toward the sky, absorbing the heat from a fleeting ray of sunlight. The air has turned bitterly cold, but I don't want to leave just yet. Breathing deeply, I enjoy the salty smell of the water and the call of the seagulls nearby. As the chilly wind picks up speed, blowing my hair in all directions, my senses come alive. I sense Lawrence standing behind me before the warmth of his suit jacket enfolds me. His hands rub the length of my arms, warming me as he pulls me toward him. I lean my back on his chest and slowly open my eyes. Each blink brings the cloudy sky, the stormy ocean, and the seemingly endless horizon into focus.

And it's peaceful.

And it's magical.

And maybe it's the security of Lawrence's arms around me, or maybe it's Lawrence's quiet strength seeping into my bloodstream, but somehow I find myself opening and sharing my deepest secrets with him. I tell him about my childhood, the Ferris wheel ride with my dad, of my mom packing her shit and leaving me behind. I tell him of Paige Callahan and her father, Matthew. I tell Lawrence how Matthew used to fuck me in a dirty motel in exchange for pretty gifts and money, and how after he was done with me, he'd go back to his big house on the fancy side of town and pretend to be the exemplary father and the pillar of the community.

When I'm done, I feel unburdened and, oddly enough, unashamed. This is the difference between Ronan and Lawrence. Ronan held me on a pedestal. He saw in me the person he desired me to be—someone worthy of him. And I was too afraid to shatter that illusion. I wanted to believe it myself for however long we were together so I would be worthy of him. If I had told him about my past—of who I really am—he would have run for the hills, and I was too selfish to do so. I wanted him too much. But you can only live a lie for so long before it smothers you, poisoning every word, every touch, and every kiss. Lawrence, on the other hand, holds no illusions of me. He knows me for who I am, and it's freeing. So freeing.

"Before you say anything, I just want you to know that it's all in the past. It doesn't bother me anymore."

Lawrence rests his chin on top of my head, hugging me harder. "Is it?"

I remain silent, trying to find the answer within me.

"I'm not going to pretend to know what's in your heart, Blaire. Only you're privy to that. But what I can tell you is that I hope one day you wake up and realize that all those people and memories don't determine who you are. *You* get to do that."

"You make it sound so easy. Tell me, what have you done with my cynical friend? You look the same, but you don't sound anything like him."

I look up as he looks down, our gazes locking. "He's currently unavailable. So, in the meantime, you're stuck with me." He grins.

"Oh, yeah? And who are you?"

"Just a regular guy enjoying the company of a beautiful woman."

Blushing, I feel butterflies doing their usual chaotic dance in my stomach. I push myself away and turn to face him as I start to walk backward, giving my best come-hither look. "Come on, Casanova. You promised me the unknown and I'm still waiting for it."

The thing about happiness—beautiful chaos that it is—no matter how short or lasting the moment is, is that it makes you soar, makes you want to dance and laugh. Happiness makes everything seem possible, and there's no better feeling than to share it with someone special.

I run toward the steps that lead down to the beach. Once I reach the sand, I take my leather booties and socks off, place Lawrence's coat on the steps, and sprint in the direction of the ocean. The water is freezing, but it's invigorating. I spread my arms, tilt my head back, and begin to spin, faster and faster until I lose my balance and fall in the water. Laughing, I try to stand up on shaky feet and fail miserably, landing on my ass once again.

I spot Lawrence coming down the stairs. He puts his cell away and buries both of his hands inside the front pockets of his pants. Windblown hair. Crooked grin. I'm drowning in his manly beauty. "How's the water?"

"Toasty," I say, my teeth chattering.

"Liar."

I push a wet strand of hair off of my face. "Why don't you come and try it?"

"I think I'm going to pass. I don't want to spoil your fun. Besides, I can admire you better from afar."

"Aww, what's the matter?" I pout, taunting him. "Afraid to get a little wet?"

"Is that a dare?"

I raise an eyebrow. "It's whatever you want it to be, baby."

"Minx."

He removes his shoes and socks and rolls up his pants, the muscles of his chest and arms stretching the white fabric of his dress shirt. With his tie long gone and the top two buttons undone, he looks like pure sex, and I find it hard to breathe. I lick my lips, feeling a different kind of warmth spreading through me.

He steps into the water, walking my direction. "Jesus Christ, this water is cold."

"Help, please. I can't get up," I ask, extending my arm out.

Lawrence takes my hand in his. "You're cr—" I tug his hand with all my strength, pulling him toward me, and make him fall in the water too. After the initial shock, he wipes his face clean as I'm rolling in the sand unable to stop laughing. The poor man looks like he wants to kill me.

He runs his fingers through his wet hair, pulling it back. His deadly gaze focused on me. *Oh boy.* "You're going to pay for that, my dear Blaire."

"Is that so?" I mock, appearing to be unafraid as I get ready to make a run for it.

A challenge, or mischief, lights up his eyes as a wolfish grin darkens his face in a dangerous but delicious way. And before I know it, he lunges forward, catching me by the ankles and pulling me toward him until his body cages mine. I scream and laugh at the same time.

Nervous, I lick my lips that suddenly feel so dry. He kneels over me as he captures both of my hands in his and raises them above my head, holding me his prisoner. "Gotcha, little girl." He leans forward, and I think he's going to kiss me but instead he bites my neck. "Should I fuck you right here as part of my payback?" He grinds his cock against my sex. Hard. Making me moan.

"Lawrence," I breathe throatily and tilt my hips up to welcome him as I wrap my legs around his waist.

"Men don't fall in love with women like you, Blaire." He burns me with his gaze. "They lose their fucking minds."

He closes the space between our mouths with a smoldering, soul-reaching, logic-defying kiss. The cold sand, the freezing water, and the howling wind disappear around us. All that matters is the man on top of me, his body touching mine, his lips breathing fire into me.

We pull apart, and I'm trying to get my wits together when I feel a lump of sand land on my face. Opening my eyes, I find him above me staring at me with a lopsided smirk.

"Oh, you ass. That was so not fair."

"Quid pro quo, quid pro quo, my friend."

I wipe my cheeks broodingly. "That's easy for you to say. You're not the one left with a lady boner and sand on her face."

And then the most beautiful thing happens in front of me. Lawrence throws his head back and barks with laughter. Freely. Easily. Spontaneously. Could he be the same man I met at the Met in what seems a lifetime ago? Gone are the rock hard eyes and the mocking smile. He's been replaced by this carefree stranger with bright evergreen eyes.

Yes, the unknown with Lawrence is definitely inviting.

We're walking back to the car when Lawrence changes trajectories and walks back to the park. "Forgot something."

I nod drowsily. With my arm wrapped around his waist and his around my shoulders, I lean my head on his side. Glancing up, I see that the Ferris wheel is lit up and functioning. "Look, Lawrence! The Ferris wheel is open." I take a moment to admire its lights against the purple, pink and orange twilight. "I wonder if they only open it at night?"

A moment or two later, Lawrence says, "No idea."

I'm so tired that I don't even notice where he's taking me until we're standing in front of the large, colorful wheel and there's a man dressed in uniform, waiting for us. Puzzled, I let go of Lawrence and turn to look at him.

"What's this?" Frowning, my gaze ping pongs between the ride, Lawrence, and the man. "You didn't?" But even as the words leave my mouth, I remember seeing Lawrence putting his cell away out on the beach. Breathless, my heart beats as though it were a stampede crushing my chest.

He caresses my cheek before tenderly tucking a piece of hair behind my ear. "I did."

"Why?" I ask with a trembling voice.

He grabs my chin, making me look at him. "I think it's about time to make new memories, and what better time than right now?"

He begins to look very blurry. *Fucking tears.* I close the space between us and hug him, really, it's more like I'm trying to crush him. I shake my head, unable to speak as I bury my face in his chest. When I'm able to stare at him without making a fool of myself, I tilt my head back and meet his gaze. "How can I ever thank you?"

"You could start with a kiss," he counters smoothly.

"Is that all?"

He raises an amused eyebrow.

I giggle before kissing him hard on the mouth. "How's that?"

"You could try harder," he drawls, looking lethally attractive.

"You wicked man," I say as my lips land gladly on his once again.

chapter **nine.**

Lawrence

ON OUR WAY BACK TO THE CITY, Blaire kept falling asleep on my shoulder, so I suggested that she spend the night at her own place and get some rest. I look out the window as we leave Blaire's apartment behind.

"I like her," Tony says after driving silently for a couple of minutes.

I chuckle wryly. "I see that she's bewitched you, too."

"Why not? She's a breath of fresh air." Tony pauses for a moment, weighing his next words. "You're changing, Laurie."

"Am I?" I drawl, pretending to be bored.

"I don't think I've ever seen you take a day off since you started running the company. I'm glad." His eyes meet mine in the rearview mirror. "She makes you happy."

Leaning my head back on the leather seat, I close my eyes momentarily and imagine Blaire's pale face when I first saw her. A raven haired sorceress with hollow eyes and an empty smile. So different from the girl with the wild hair and wild heart who spun and laughed on the beach a couple of hours ago. And as I stood there, watching her, transfixed and in awe of her tempestuous beauty, I realized that I wanted to be the one to protect her from everything and everyone who had ever hurt her just so she could look at me like that again— without a shadow of another man in her eyes.

Today as I watched her on the beach, the oddest sensation came over me. I felt as though I was staring at the beginning and end of my life. My salvation and downfall. Call me stupid, but I thought that every action and every path taken and not taken had conspired to bring me to that place. To that moment. To her. "She does."

"It's a beautiful feeling, isn't it?" Tony says, and I can almost hear the smile on his face.

"No, it's fucking terrifying."

I open my eyes and stare at the dark ceiling of the car, shadows morphing into living creatures. It's so damn easy to fall in love, to lose one's head in a woman's body and her aphrodisiac taste. That is until the idyll comes to an end and it takes you a lifetime to forget her and the man you used to be. And I would know ...

"I'm in trouble, Tony." The debilitating admission is torn from my chest.

"I know you are, my boy."

"I thought I was safe."

"From a woman?" He laughs. "No man is ever safe."

But it didn't start like that, did it?

No. She started as an obsession—one that I couldn't seem to shake. I thought if I got close to her, I would find just another pretty face sleeping her way up to the top with nothing inside. I thought that once I fucked her, I'd be able to flush her out of my system and obliterate her from my body and mind.

I was wrong and a fool.

If anything, every minute and every second that I spend with her, I'm more and more consumed by this violent need. A need that won't leave me alone and constantly calls for her.

"You know what I think?" Tony says.

"Go ahead." I run my hands frustratingly through my hair.

Tony's opinion is one of the few that I trust and respect without question. When my father and mother were too busy with their lives to pay attention to their son, it was Tony who was there for me. He taught me how to drive, how to throw a punch, and he made me feel loved.

"I think you're in grave danger of falling in love ... if you haven't already."

I'm about to reply when my cell phone begins to ring. I pull it out of my pocket, read the name on the screen, and take the call.

"Is everything all right, Laurie? I thought we were supposed to meet for dinner at our restaurant. I've been waiting for you for over an hour."

I look at my watch and curse under my breath. "I'm terribly sorry. I—"

"It's fine, I get it. Things happen. I was just worried because it isn't like you not to show up. Actually, I don't think this has ever happened before."

As I listen to her voice on the other line, I become aware of one simple fact. For the first time since I met her all those years ago, I can't quite recall what the woman on the other line looks like. The usual yearning for her that fills my chest like a burning fire has gone out, leaving memories slowly crumbling like ashes in its wake. Instead, it's Blaire who inhabits my every thought. I feel a smile tugging at my lips as I think of our day together at the beach. Her contagious laughter echoes in my ears. The realization that I can't wait to see her and hold her in my arms again takes hold of me.

"Laurie? Are you there?"

"Sorry. What were you saying?"

"Are you sure you're okay? You sound ... I don't know—funny."

I look out the window trying to focus on the passing cars, but it's no use. All I see is Blaire. My fingertips tingle with the memory of my hands gliding across her skin as I kissed her. "I don't know."

"What's the matter?" she presses, her voice soft.

The matter is that nothing is as it should be.

"I think I've lost my Goddamn mind."

chapter ten.

Blaire

THE NEXT MORNING, I'm toweling my hair dry when I hear the doorbell ring. After placing the towel on a nearby chair, I tighten the belt securing my silk robe before I go check out who's at the door. I look through the peephole, my eyes widening, and smile a slow smile when I see him standing outside my apartment.

My blood rushing, I unlock and open the door as fast as I can. "What are you doing he—"

Before I can react, Lawrence steps inside my apartment, buries his fingers in my hair and pulls me close to him, pressing his body against me. His mouth seizes mine as I slide my arms instinctively around his neck and surrender myself to the onslaught of his savage kiss.

And what a kiss it is.

Weak-kneed, I'm barely able to stand straight by the time he pulls away. "Good morning, darling," he says huskily.

"Whoa," I manage to say in a daze, slightly shaking my head.

He tightens his arms around me, infusing my body with warmth. "Damn fucking right."

"Modest much?"

"I wouldn't know." He grins crookedly. "What's that?"

"Impossible man." Standing on my tiptoes, I grin and place a soft kiss on his chin. "Good morning ... Wait, aren't you supposed to be at work already?"

His gaze unwavering, he raises a hand, letting the back of his fingers trace the curve of my jaw. "Fuck work. Spend the day with me."

"Again? So soon?"

He shrugs carelessly. "Why not?"

Oh, Lawrence, my friend, if you only knew how happy you make me. "And what would you like to do?"

He surprises me by scooping me up in his arms. As he nears my bedroom, Lawrence leans down so his mouth is close to my ear and whispers huskily, "You. All—day—long," scattering shivers down my spine.

By the time he steps inside my bedroom, I notice that Dust to Dust by The Civil Wars is playing in the background. I step away from him once he places me gently on the floor. Suddenly feeling shy, I walk toward the windows to pull the curtains closed.

"Don't," Lawrence commands. As my hands grip the fabric, Lawrence steps behind me and wraps his arms around my waist. "I don't want to miss a thing. Dance with me."

I let out a shuddering breath. I nod and wrap a hand behind his neck as the other falls naturally on top of his, bringing our bodies much closer than before. And in this fashion, we begin to sway slowly to the melody. My room and everything inside of it disappears. Nothing remains but Lawrence and the feel of his arms around me.

93

Slowly he unties the belt securing my silk robe and spreads it open until my naked body is exposed to him. One of his hands begins to travel a leisurely path across my body, caressing my hips, his fingers sliding across my stomach, grazing the edges of my hot core, driving me wild purposefully. He cups my breasts, pinching my nipple as he bites into my neck hungrily, making me cry out in pain. His touch is teasing—taunting—divine—revering. Our breathing becomes labored, shallow.

"Here, Lawrence," I reach for his hand and guide him to where I need his touch the most. Want and lust emanate from our bodies as we get lost in the heat of the moment and the erotic rhythm of our hips. "I need you here."

Lawrence lets go of me and pushes me against the window. Belatedly it occurs to me that someone could be getting an eyeful but I can't bring myself to care. With my back pressed against his front, I close my eyes when I feel Lawrence's magic hands spreading my ass, rubbing me in that forbidden place, setting me on fucking fire.

"Do you like this?" he asks, his voice husky with desire. I turn my head to stare at him as he slides down my body, kneeling behind me. I watch him bring a finger to his mouth, lubricating it with his saliva, and then he rubs me, massaging in small circles until he slowly enters me, stretching me. It's painful. Beautiful. Forbidden. He adds another digit, increasing the pain, increasing the pleasure.

"Do you like my fingers fucking your sweet and tight ass?"

I nod desperately. "Yes, God. I need your mouth there."

MIA ASHER

Lawrence chuckles and withdraws his fingers, replacing it with his mouth over my tight hole, kissing, probing, and lapping with each relentless flick of his tongue. Lust flows through my veins.

Fuck.

Fuck.

Fuck.

Fuck.

He eats me as though he is starved and I'm his last meal. Spreading my ass wider, I feel his tongue getting lost inside me, pumping in and out of me, the pace ruthless. And when he adds his fingers once more, the earth shakes underneath me and I see stars. Without saying a word, I push myself away and turn to face him. My breath is uneven and my body hurts from the lack of an orgasm, but I feel like flying.

Placing my hands on the lapels of his suit jacket, I say throatily, "Lie on the bed. I want to make love to you."

Once Lawrence is undressed, he lies on the bed and watches me closely. His green gaze, sparking with lust, roves over my figure. I stand in front of him and deliberately allow the robe to slip down my body, leaving me completely naked. There's nothing between us but the invisible walls protecting my hardened heart. But even those are slowly being chipped away by him.

His eyes on me, I make my way toward him, each step bringing me closer as something inside me that I don't understand desperately calls for him. It's not the way he touches me or the way he makes me feel when he takes me that makes me tremble with fear or with exhilaration—it's him.

95

Calling for me.

And today, I go. I want to be consumed.

He reaches for me or I reach for him. It doesn't matter. Everything becomes a swirl of emotions where my hands, my mouth, my lungs are full of him and what he makes me feel. His taste, the feel of him, his voice caressing me as his touch corrupts me. That's all that matters. I swallow his kisses as he swallows my moans. He tortures me with his fingers and brings me rapture with his wicked tongue. And when my body aches with unfulfilled passion and I'm begging him to bring it to an end, he enters me in one deep thrust, fucking me until fucking ceases to be fucking and becomes the union of two bodies seeking to be one. He fucks me until all I see is a blinding light as I climax and heat rushes through my entire body. And when he's buried so deep inside me, filling me with his cum, I know that, for one exquisite moment, I'm not alone.

And, maybe, that's enough.

In bed, we're lying on our sides and looking at one another. Lawrence looks adorable with the color high on his cheeks, his lips swollen from my kisses and his hair rumpled because of my hands. It's hard to imagine that this man runs a multi-million dollar empire. Leaning forward, I place a peck on the tip of his nose.

He smiles a satisfied and relaxed smile. "What was that about?"

I grin happily. "I just felt like it, Mr. Rothschild."

We continue to gaze into each other's eyes silently while our smiles fade like the light coming from outside. In the peace that follows, I sense a stirring in my chest of something that I don't quite understand or want to admit to myself. The truth always complicates things, and my life is already complicated enough.

So I ignore it all, bury it deep down where things are always easy to forget, and let myself enjoy the moment. "You know, after I met you, I went home and googled you," I say.

He quirks an amused eyebrow at me. "And what did you find, my little detective?"

"Besides how much you're worth and your penchant for models and actresses?" I slant him a wry look and then roll my eyes when he has the decency to chuckle and *not* deny it. "Not much. But there was an article that caught my attention. There's this blogger who thinks that you suffered a grand disillusionment when you were young and that's why you can't seem to settle down with anyone. So romantically cliché, no? But I wonder, is it true?"

Staring at his own hand, Lawrence begins to trace a path on the curve of my waist, drawing small circles. The gentle stroke raises goosebumps over my skin. A shadow crosses his eyes momentarily, darkening them. "Don't you know that curiosity killed the cat?"

I close my eyes and turn flat on my back, surrendering myself to Lawrence and his wandering fingers. My breathing becomes uneven as his hand searches every nook and cranny of my body, learning it, memorizing it, and setting it ablaze.

He hesitates momentarily, seemingly waging how much to tell me. "She was seventeen years old when I met her, and completely out of my reach. I was a serious, stoic and humorless twenty-eight year old man going on forty, or so my friends used to joke. Pursuing her was out of the question. In my defense, I didn't know how old she was when I first saw her. All I knew was that I had never met a more beautiful woman than her.

"I'd got caught in the rain without an umbrella on my way to the office, and sought refuge at an Irish pub. I walked in and headed toward the counter where an older man was polishing some glasses. After I sat down and ordered a drink, I looked around the place and immediately saw her. She was writing on a notepad at one of the tables to the side. I assumed she was a college student working on a paper. She had this tiny frown between her eyebrows and I found myself wanting to smooth it.

"She looked up and our eyes met as she smiled. I was embarrassed and wanted to look away but her smile made it impossible. It was guileless, artless, and inviting. So different from what I was used to."

"She sounds nice." I place my hand on his. "Go on … What happened after? Did you talk to her?"

"Not that day, but eventually I did. You could say that I became a regular and one of the more esteemed customers of the pub."

I laugh. "How regular?"

"Didn't miss a day."

"What about her? Was she always there, too?"

"She was. She was actually the one who approached me first. I went there every day with the sole purpose of finally talking to her, but as soon as I saw her chatting with other customers, filling the entire place with her inner light, I felt unworthy and changed my mind. One day when I was getting ready to leave, she came up to me and introduced herself. She said that she was tired of waiting for me to make the first move, so she was taking matters into her own hands."

I try to picture Lawrence's expression when the girl said that to him, and laugh softly. "She sounds awesome. I like her."

"Once I found out her age, I decided to forget about her and stopped going to the pub. But the longer I stayed away, the more I missed her and wanted her. I fought myself but my heart won. The heart is a capricious thing, you know? It wants what it wants, logic be damned. Eventually, I went back. With time, we became close friends, and I accepted it because I was biding my time until the day she came of age and I could properly ask her out." He pauses, appearing to be lost in the past.

"For the first time in a very long time, I felt like someone saw me as me, not Lawrence, son of Alexander and Barbara Rothschild and heir to Rothschild Media." He shakes his head, a soft smile on his handsome face. "She was young but there was something about the way she moved and looked at me that drove me wild. As the days passed, I fell madly in love with her and was happy to love her from afar. I knew she had feelings for me, too. But I wasn't sure how deep they ran.

"One time, on our way home from watching a movie, she asked me why I hadn't kissed her yet. I was dumbfounded, but she laughed and kissed me anyway. On the day she turned eighteen, I spoke to her grandfather and told him that I loved his granddaughter to distraction and wanted his permission to ask her on a date."

"Why not her father?"

"Her parents died when she was very young, leaving her and her little brother in the sole care of their grandparents."

I frown, thinking that her story is very similar to Ronan's. But I push the thought to the back of my mind, not wanting to think of him.

"Her grandfather gave me his blessing. My plan was to invite her to my grandmother's eightieth birthday weekend bash as my date and once we were there, finally make a move. When we arrived, I introduced her to family members, close friends, and my best friend—Bradley Stanhope."

My eyes widen in surprise. "Of Stanhope Steel?"

His jaw clenches. "You know him?"

"Of course. I don't know him personally, but he used to date my favorite actress, Penelope Pitt."

He laughs bitterly. "Yes, that's Bradley. He was the golden boy. Always a beautiful woman by his side, liked by everyone, while I was withdrawn, extremely shy around girls, and always had my nose stuck in a book."

"If you were so different from each other, how come you were best friends?"

"Our families were very close. We grew up and went to school together. I saw in him what I wasn't, and admired him for it. He was free to do whatever the hell he wanted while I drowned in responsibilities set by my parents. I guess a part of me wanted to be like him, to know how it would feel to be liked by everyone."

"What happened after you got there?"

He shrugs nonchalantly, but he can't hide the way his eyes harden at the mention of his name. "Bradley saw her and wanted her. He dazzled her with his looks, family name, and the attention he gave her."

"What! Oh my God ... no." I shake my head, my heart breaking for Lawrence. "But didn't she—"

"Love me?" he mocks, his voice cold. "No, Blaire, I don't think she did. They began to date soon after, and I moved on."

"But you never forgot her, did you?"

He holds my gaze, and I know the answer to that. "One day I ran into her. As soon as I saw her, I knew that something was wrong. The usual light that illuminated her eyes was gone. I was going to keep walking and pretend that I hadn't seen her."

"But?"

"She sobbed, begging me to forgive her for being weak. Once she calmed down, she confessed that she was pregnant with Bradley's baby but that he didn't want her anymore. Bradley told her to get rid of it. Offered her money so she'd disappear from his life," he utters with disgust.

"Bastard. What did you do?"

He pauses. "I asked her to marry me and let me raise the baby with her as my own. But she declined my offer. She said that she had been too blinded by Bradley to realize that it was me who she loved, but because of that she wouldn't take advantage of me."

"You sweet man." My heart aches for the woman who was too late and the man lying next to me. Love played him cruelly. "And after that?"

"I went to see her grandparents. At first, they wouldn't take my money, but when they saw that nothing would change my mind, they accepted my help, and I'm glad of it."

A wave of jealousy hits me straight in the chest. "Do you still love her?"

His eyes burn into mine. "No, Blaire. I don't."

A sudden surge of tenderness for the man in front of me sweeps through me, leaving me lightheaded. I crawl on top of him and rain kisses all over him, wanting to erase the bleak look in his eyes. "You know what I think?"

"What's that, my darling?"

I trace my tongue on his nipple, a deviant smile adorning my face. "I think we should get completely wasted on champagne." I snake my arm behind me and wrap his cock in my hand, pumping it slowly, feeling it grow hard between my fingers. "Maybe order fattening, greasy takeout …"

"Yeah?" he breathes, closing his eyes.

Gotcha, baby. With his defenses down, I let him go swiftly and attack. I tickle him under his armpits and on his sides, making him laugh. I think I'm winning when Lawrence shocks me by flipping me over, caging me under his body, and begins an unforgiving assault on my body with his tickling fingers. And we laugh, and laugh, and laugh until our stomachs hurt and both of us have tears in our eyes.

"Oh God, stop, Lawrence," I croak. "I beg you."

"Say the words."

"You win! You win!"

Lawrence stops and begins to kiss every inch of my body, soothing me with his tongue. By the time he reaches my mouth, I open it and welcome his assault, hungry for him. .

"Goddamn, Blaire," he says huskily, breaking away. Lawrence wraps my hair in his hands, his gaze roaming my face. "Do you have any idea what you do to me?"

I shake my head, but what takes me by surprise and leaves me momentarily speechless is the glimpse of emotion that I see peek through his eyes.

"You make me remember what it feels like to live again, Blaire. You make me—"

As his words fill my ears, it's another voice that I hear and another face that I see …

He grins. "—go out with me, Blaire."

I shake my head, fighting a smile. "I know I'm going to regret this."

"Maybe … but live a little."

"I like my life to be planned and uncomplicated."

"It's better to live a life full of regrets than not live at all." He lowers his voice and adds huskily, "Let me show you how it's done."

No, no, no, no, NO! Ronan can't disrupt this moment. He can't. He can't. Not now, please, please, *please*. Cupping Lawrence's cheeks, I hope he doesn't hear the ache in my heart as I pull him closer to me. "Hush … kiss me, Lawrence."

When our mouths become one, I find myself kissing him with everything that I have, fooling myself into believing that this man is who I want. And as the war between our lips becomes more urgent, harder, I find myself believing my own lie.

He pulls away. "Let's go back to my place."

"Why?" I blink drowsily. "What's wrong with my apartment?"

"Nothing's wrong." He tightens his arms around me. "I want to wake up with you in my bed."

Back in the safety of his room, warm and content, I begin to fall asleep in Lawrence's arms. And it's in that semi-conscious state, where my lies peel off their deceitful layers, revealing the truths within, that I wish for a different set of arms.

chapter eleven.

Lawrence

WITH MY ARMS WRAPPED AROUND HER, I pull her closer to me and watch her sleep. I bury my nose in her hair, breathing her in, and wish I could tell her what she does to me, what she makes me feel, what she makes me yearn for. I wasn't planning on telling her about my past. I've never told anyone before. Yet I found myself opening to her, and for once, revisiting the past didn't hurt. It's as though it is truly in the past now.

I chuckle ruefully and ponder how she can drive me to such madness, such want and need?

Sometimes, I wonder if karma enjoys laughing at our expense. You tell life that you want to go left, only to find a rock blocking that road so you must go right. You tell life that you found the woman you want to marry only to discover that she loves your best friend. You tell life that your dormant heart doesn't beat anymore at the sight of anyone or anything, and what does it do? It sends you a slip of a woman with a quick tongue and fire in her eyes who not only makes your heart beat at the sight of her, but she makes it throb with such intensity, so much passion, you're surprised it hasn't shattered yet. You tell life that work and success are all you need to be complete, and they are … until you make her smile. And then you know it was all a lie because you would sacrifice everything you own and even the clothes on your back just for one more smile from her.

So I shouldn't be surprised by the fact that owning her body isn't enough for me anymore. I want it all. I want everything from her.

Watching her come undone in my hands, my cock pulsing inside her, her nails clawing my back. Watching her lose herself with me, in the pleasure I bring her …

Christ, it's a sight to behold.

I live for those moments because it's when I see my wild beauty. The one without fears, without mind games. And she's beautiful. And she's devastation. Just thinking of anyone who's owned part of her, who may still own her, drives me mad with raging jealousy, because she belongs to me, even if she doesn't know it yet.

I've always believed that it's too late for me. When love disappointed me for the first time, I vowed to myself that I wouldn't be fooled into believing in it again. But as I stare at the woman sleeping in my arms, I feel my resolution crumbling. Hope rekindles like a flame that never quite went out. And maybe I'm wrong—maybe there's another chance for me, after all.

I caress her cheek, my fingers lingering on the softness of her warm skin. It may be foolish to hold on to hope, but sometimes hope is all we have left. And this woman makes me want it all. Every laugh. Every kiss. Every moan. Every thought. I want them all to be mine, even if I have to pay for each one with my own blood. But that's the thing, isn't it? I want her to be mine.

And only mine.

Blaire stirs in my arms, mumbling something unintelligible. I lower my head and kiss her forehead, saying, "Shh, my love. Sleep."

After a few minutes pass, she's lying still, her breathing slowing down, when I hear her say in her sleep, "Ronan … come back. Come back to me."

chapter twelve.

Blaire

I WAKE UP, SMILING. Spreading my arms on the bed, I reach for Lawrence only to find an empty, cold pillow next to me. I sit up quickly as the sheets fall down to my waist. Looking to my left and to my right, I see no trace of him. Not in the bathroom and not in his walk-in closet.

"Lawrence?" There's no answer. "Are you there?" Still no answer.

Frowning, I wonder why he left without saying good-bye. It's not like him at all. He always wakes me up before heading to work.

I lift a hand to touch my lips, swollen and hot, and try to figure out why I feel so disappointed and … hurt? I woke feeling happy and content for the first time in a very long time. All I wanted to do was kiss him and talk to him. Instead, there's an empty bed and no Lawrence in sight.

I'm about to recline my back on the headboard when I think of my cell phone. Maybe he sent me a text explaining why he left without saying good-bye. As I'm reaching for it, I ignore the voice inside my head telling me that he's paying to fuck me, that he has no obligation toward me and that whatever we shared these past few days was just Lawrence being nice. When I have my phone in my hands, I slide the screen open, ignoring the fact that there are no new notifications, and look at my messages anyway. There's nothing from him.

My hand with the phone falls listlessly to the bed as I stare at the wall in front of me when I hear a knock at the door.

"One moment, please." I grab the white sheet and pull it up quickly, covering the front of my body. My heart begins to beat faster, thinking that maybe it's Lawrence who didn't leave after all. "Come in," I say, glancing down to make sure that nothing's showing before focusing in the direction of the door and smile.

My smile falls.

I watch the housekeeper carrying a tray filled with food step into the room. The aroma of butter and fresh fruit make my stomach grumble with hunger.

Mrs. Woods, a woman in her early sixties who seemed to dislike me at first glance, regards me with eyes that remind me of a hawk. I see so much disapproval in them. Under her gaze, I feel as though I am a little girl about to be punished for spilling grape juice on a rug.

"Laur—Mr. Rothschild mentioned that you would need breakfast. Where would you like this to be placed, Miss White?"

I sit up straighter as I try to fight a smile. "He did?" *Oh my God, Blaire. You're acting like a child. Get your act together.* I clear my throat, and nod toward the nightstand next to me. "Here's fine, thank you."

109

I'm watching her arrange the items on the tray when I notice a bouquet of white orchids lying next to the China coffee pot. I reach out to touch the petal of one.

"They're a gift from Mr. Rothschild."

I raise my eyes to meet hers. "How in the world did Lawrence get them so early in the morning?"

"Special delivery," she says dryly.

"Of course." Whatever Lawrence wants, Lawrence gets. I shake my head, grinning. "Thank you for letting me know."

She nods, pursing her lips. "Will that be all, Miss White?"

"Please, call me Blaire. I hate formalities." There's something about her that makes me want her to like me. Maybe it has to do with the fact that Lawrence said that she's been under his family's employment since he was a baby. I grin at her but she remains aloof.

"Enjoy your breakfast, Miss White." She lowers her head ever so slightly as if the gesture caused her bodily pain before she turns on her feet and leaves me alone in the room.

Well now, that went well, didn't it?

I'm about to reach for the food when I hear my phone ring. Grabbing it quickly, I see that it's Lawrence's work number. Excited and nervous, I answer immediately. "Lawrence?" I breathe, thinking of the smiling man from last night.

"Hello, Blaire. It's Gina, Mr. Rothschild's personal assistant."

"Oh hi, Gina," I say half-heartedly, unable to hide the disappointment in my voice.

"Mr. Rothschild wished me to let you know that he's going out of town today and won't be back for a week. He said that, in the meantime, you're more than welcome to stay in the townhouse and use the estate on Long Island if you'd like to get out of the city for a change."

The news is like a punch in the face. "I didn't know he was traveling today. He didn't mention it at all."

"It's a very last minute trip."

"I see." He didn't even call to say good-bye. I guess I'm just a business deal for him after all. I knew this. I *know* this. It's what I want. So why do I feel so shitty about this? Why does it hurt so much?

"Also, I've contacted a different real estate agent. Her name is Claire Michaels. She will be helping you from now on."

I groan, remembering Lawrence's anger from other night. "Gina ... what happened to William? Please tell me the truth."

"Don't worry about it, Miss White. It's all taken care of."

"Oh."

"Anyway, I must get back to work, but do call me if you need anything. Have a good day."

"Wait! Just one more thing."

"Yes?"

I close my eyes, hating myself for asking the next question. "Did, um, did Lawrence happen to have another message for me?"

"I'm afraid not. But would you like to leave one for him?"

Yes. *Why did you leave me without saying good-bye? Was everything we shared a lie?* "No, that's okay. Thank you."

After we hang up, I turn to look at the food and push the tray to the side, not hungry anymore. As an inexplicable sorrow fills my chest, I have the odd sensation that it's the beginning of the end of something beautiful that never fully developed.

Or maybe it already has.

I call Elly to invite her to come over and spend the day with me. At first, she doesn't want to come, giving me some bullshit about principles or something like that, but curiosity wins, and she ends up accepting my invite. She's also bringing her boyfriend—the musician she talked about a while back.

After running on the treadmill for an hour, I take a shower and get dressed, putting on my favorite pair of boyfriend jeans and an off the shoulder slouchy gray sweater. Looking down, I recall my short conversation with Elly. Apparently, things are getting serious between her and her musician. I'm so happy for her, but part of me feels both guilty and sad because I haven't been there for her in the last couple of months. I know that I've been avoiding her, but I'm not ready to tell her what a mess of things I've made. And knowing Elly, she wouldn't shy away from pointing out that I only have myself to blame.

I bury my hands inside my front pockets and reflect on how two girls as different as we are became the best of friends. And let's be honest here, she's a saint for not judging me and for putting up with my manic moods.

I had been living in the city for about two years when I met Elly. The moment she started to work at Homme, everyone in the staff fell in love with her outgoing personality. That is, everyone but me. I didn't trust her friendly demeanor and ready smiles even though I *knew* that the girl didn't have a bad bone in her entire body. She radiated positive energy.

After working together for three months, a waiter slash struggling actor slash really hot French model named Pierre threw a party at his loft in Astoria, Queens, and invited everyone.

She was there with her boyfriend at the time—a total douchebag if you ask me. As soon as I saw him, I knew that I couldn't like him. Maybe it was the way that he flirted with everything in a skirt, or how he kept going on and on about his job and how much money he made. Really, the more he bragged, the smaller I imagined his dick to be. I couldn't understand what Elly was doing with him, but love works in mysterious ways.

It had all started to go downhill when Pierre asked douchebag how he met Elly. I remember it so clearly. She looked up at him as she placed her palm on his chest.

"She had the best tits in the room," he said, smug as shit. He wrapped an arm around her shoulders and pulled her closer to him. She froze. And for the first time, I noticed how much pain and insecurity she hid behind her ready smiles. I also had an inkling that it wasn't the first time he'd put her down in front of people.

As our group grew quiet, Elly gently disengaged herself from his hold and said that she needed to use the bathroom. After we'd watched her figure disappear into the crowd, I turned to address him. "*Wow*, I feel so bad for you." I let my gaze run over his figure, and I hoped he could see all the contempt and disgust I felt for him. "You must have *such* a small dick if you need to talk about her like that." I smiled sweetly before I walked away without giving him a chance to reply.

Needless to say, the coward avoided me for the rest of the night.

Later on, after bidding everyone good-bye, I was making my way to the elevator when I heard the familiar voice of a man yelling at someone. I paused on my spot, the fluorescent light above me casting a yellow tint on my skin, as I contemplated whether to keep walking or to go back and find out if someone needed my help. Common sense told me to disregard it, not get involved.

In the end, my instincts won. I walked in the direction of the yelling. It was coming from behind the door of the exit staircase. As I held the doorknob, I could hear the man shouting, his words carrying so much hate and anger. I really should have walked back to the apartment and gotten Pierre, but all I could think of was that someone needed help. I grabbed the pepper spray I always carried with me from my bag and opened the door. My gaze immediately zoomed in on Elly being slammed against the wall by her boyfriend before focusing on her face, blood oozing from a cut on her lip.

They both turned to look at me at the same time. I don't think I will ever forget the sheer terror I saw in her eyes as our gazes met. And the hate I saw in his. He looked gone, lost in anger—soulless.

"Leave us, you fucking bitch. Don't you see that we're busy?"

Right away I realized that the pepper spray wouldn't be as effective from my position. I thought about approaching them but I dismissed that notion as quickly as it came. I didn't want to put Elly in more danger by making him angrier. I needed him to get closer to me.

Think, Blaire, think.

Oh God.

Fuck. Fuck. Fuck.

"No. Let her go."

He smiled, chilling me to the bone as he gripped her shoulders harder and made Elly whimper in pain. "And what if I don't? What are you going to do, huh? I can probably break your pretty little neck in two with one hand."

Appear at ease. Don't let him see how scared you are, Blaire. "I'm not scared of you. Pierre's apartment is just past this door. I could go get him, giving him and the boys the excuse they've been waiting for to kick the shit out of you." And I did think about calling for help, but I was terrified that he would push Elly down the stairs in an attempt to escape and get rid of her.

I saw him loosening his hold on Elly, my words sinking in. "Fuck off. I'm not fucking scared of a bunch of pussies."

I leaned my shoulder on the wall and crossed my arms over my chest, making sure I kept the little bottle hidden as I flipped its safety cap open. "That might be so, but it would be you against at least ten guys. And ten guys who happen to be really good friends with Elly. *Ten* guys who will be extremely pissed off when they see what you've done to her." I wasn't even sure that they were friends with Elly, but he didn't need to know that. "If you let Elly go now, I won't go get them. I'll let you leave before they hurt you." Smiling at him, taunting him with my words, I got ready to spray. "I'll take pity on you."

And that did it. He shoved Elly to the side and started to stalk toward me. But Elly surprised us both when she kneed him in the groin, making him fall to the ground as he cried out in pain. She grabbed the pepper spray from my hand and walked over to him. With tears running down her face, she said, "We're over, you asshole. That's the last time you put a hand on me." And then she proceeded to use my pepper spray on him. We left him howling in pain as we walked back to Pierre's apartment.

Pierre called the cops as soon as we explained what had happened. Holding a bag of frozen peas on her eyebrow, Elly turned to look at me and nudged me on the shoulder. "Thank you. I—"

"You don't have to explain yourself. And don't even think about it."

She was quiet for a moment, staring at the floor, when she broke the silence. "That was *really* dumb, you know?" she said warmly.

My eyes zoomed in on her split lip before meeting her gaze. "I know, but it's the least I could do."

"I don't want to sound ungrateful because I'm so lucky that you were there …" She closed her eyes momentarily and sighed. "I-I don't know what would've happened if you hadn't, but why didn't you just go get Pierre? I didn't take you for the kind of person to—"

"To go out of my way to help others?"

Blushing shamefully, I saw color return to her pale face, accentuating the red of her lips. "Yeah ..."

"I'm not," I said, shrugging carelessly, uncomfortable by the heart to heart that I felt coming.

She stared at me for a moment too long, almost as if she were seeing me for the first time. I fidgeted under her penetrating gaze because maybe she was seeing through me after all. "Actually, I was wrong. You *are* the kind of person to go out of your way to help others, you just like to pretend you're a—"

"Cold-hearted, self-serving bitch?"

"I wasn't going to put it so bluntly, but yeah ... *that*."

"I *am* all those things, Elly, and much more. Don't be fooled by what I did. Anyone would've done it."

She shook her head as her smile widened. "Keep telling yourself that, but you won't make me change my mind. You're a good person, Blaire, even if it pains you to admit it."

"Listen, what happened doesn't make us friends."

"Yes, it does."

"No, it doesn't. I like to be alone. I don't do girlfriends and shit like that."

"Thank you, Blaire."

"Don't think about it. I did what anyone in my position would have."

"That's a lie and you know it."

And thus, our friendship was born.

I find Elly and her date admiring a very famous painting of a landscape hung above the fireplace in the formal living room. I'm not surprised because I did the same thing when I first saw it and immediately recognized the artist's timeless work.

I stop and admire the bold colors jumping out of the canvas once again. "Insane, huh?"

Elly turns to look at me, and the expression on her face makes me want to laugh. It's hard to impress my best friend, and I think Lawrence just managed to do so. Really, it's so typical of him and so unfair.

"Please tell me that it isn't real, Blaire," Elly says, awe and disbelief warring in her voice. But she interrupts me before I have a chance to reply. "Seriously? The dude owns a fucking Monet?" She pauses, shaking her head. "I can't believe it."

My gaze lands momentarily on the beautiful man standing next to her, before bouncing back to a flabbergasted Elly. He seems bemused by her reaction as well. "Believe it, my friend, because he does. He's what you'd call a collector."

"How billionaire and cliché of him."

"Isn't it?" I walk up to her and give her a big hug. Gosh, I've missed this woman. "And you haven't seen the half of it."

I let her go and watch her scan the room as she absorbs the grandeur of Lawrence's house. The rich silks parading as curtains, the mandatory Persian rug, the brilliant finish on the wood furniture, the Tiffany lamp adorning one coffee table, and the list goes on. It should be vulgar, but it isn't— it's elegant and timeless. Truly, it's the kind of elegance that you can't buy—one must be born into it. And really, there's no money like family money. "So this is how the one percent lives, huh? It's obscene."

"Ridiculous, but you're impressed."

She sighs and rolls her eyes at the same time. "I hate to admit it, but yeah, it's hard not to be. Honestly. I was impressed the moment you sent Ronan to pick us up in a Rolls Royce." The mention and familiarity of Ronan's name on her lips takes me by surprise, but Elly doesn't seem to notice.

"And I'm being very rude." She grabs my hands and guides me toward her handsome companion who remained standing by the fireplace. "Blaire meet Alessandro and Alessandro meet Blaire."

I take him in as we shake hands. Elly sure knows how to pick them. The man looks like the mistake I wish I'd made but never did. Piercing dark eyes that look like bottomless pits of sin, hair as black as my soul, and a body made for pleasure. Forget about sex on legs, he's an orgasm waiting to happen.

"It's great to finally meet you," I say.

He smiles a slow smile that is half smirk and half seduction. Jesus. "Same here. Elly has told me a lot about you."

"Oh God. That doesn't sound too promising."

Elly laughs as she takes hold of his hand, intertwining their fingers. "Alessandro, babe, would you mind getting the gift we brought for Blaire? I left it outside by the door."

Beautiful Alessandro grabs her by the back of her neck, pulling her forward and kissing her deeply and intensely. As their tongues tangle, I find myself blushing. I'm no prude, far from it actually, but the sheer level of intimacy and passion shared in that one kiss easily conjures images of them fucking, and even *I* have my limits.

Uncomfortable, I clear my throat. Alessandro pulls away from her. "Don't get into too much trouble."

Elly grins. "Us? *Never.*"

He places a hand on the curve of her hip, pressing his fingers there, and walks away. As she's watching him leave the room, I hear my best friend—steadfast, no bullshit Elly—sigh and flutter her eyelashes like a cartoon. What the fuck?

"Who is this woman and what happened to my best friend?"

"He happened." She nods toward the door.

"Dude, if he kisses like that I can only imagine how he eats your pussy," I tease.

"Ewww, Blaire!" she exclaims, laughing.

I wink at her and chuckle. "Well?"

She smiles big before covering her face with her hands. "Oh God, you have no idea … I get all twitchy just thinking about it."

"You slut."

"It's his tongue … What can I say? It should be a national treasure."

We laugh and fall onto the couch. She pulls my hair to the side and begins to braid it. "All joking aside …"

"Yeah?"

"How are you? Are you happy? Is this what you want?"

I look up at the ceiling before focusing on her face once more. "What is happiness? To me, it's a sporadic feeling that never lasts." I think of Lawrence and our time together and how he left this morning to go away without even bothering to say one word to my face, showing me exactly what I am to him. I think of my magical summer with Ronan and how he looked at me the last time I saw him.

"No, Elly, I don't want happiness. I want safety, so yes … this is what I want."

"Oh, Blaire."

"Don't oh, Blaire me, Elly. I'm fine. Truly, I am." Her eyes, so full of doubt and sadness, tell me that she doesn't believe a word I just said.

I smile brighter. "Anyway, how about some champagne?"

"Blaire, champagne won't make your problems go away."

"You're right. However, champagne makes *everything* better."

chapter thirteen.

Ronan

"DO YOU HAVE AN INVITATION, SIR?" the uniformed man standing by the iron gate asks, doubtfully looking at my beat-up truck.

"I don't, but I'm expected." *I hope.*

"What's your name?" he asks less politely than before, probably thinking I'm full of shit.

"Ronan Geraghty."

I observe the man search for my name on the guest list he's holding. After flipping a page or two as slowly and leisurely as he possibly can, he looks up, and grudgingly says, "Have a good evening."

I start the engine again. Rachel wasn't kidding.

He moves to the side and presses a button on the brick wall. I watch as the grand iron bars open for me, luring me—welcoming me into the unknown. They faintly whisper to enter the exuberant world that they zealously protect, where everything is possible and easy and only champagne problems exist. As I begin to drive up the long winding path that will take me to the main house, a house that I can see rising as high as a brightly lit mountain up the hill, I think I'm about to *willingly* swim with sharks in uncharted waters.

I'm so fucked.

I hand my keys to the horrified valet and watch him drive away in my second-hand truck. And like my car, I don't belong here. Tugging at my tie that suddenly feels as though it were a noose around my neck, I turn to face the front doors of one of the biggest houses I've ever seen.

I hesitate as I consider leaving none the wiser. But in that short moment, my past, present, and future flash before me. My mom reading The Little Prince to me in bed. My parents slow-dancing in our kitchen while Jackie and I secretly watched them behind the couch. My parents happily waving good-bye to me as I rushed to class, my head full of comic books and sports. Grandma and Grandpa telling us that Mom and Dad were in heaven. Growing up in the blink of an eye, weeping my childhood away on a tear-soaked pillow—a shattered childhood. Learning how to live, how to laugh again. Finding solace in photography and eventually Ollie. Standing outside the Met, waiting for my boss to come out, waiting for my life to begin. My life beginning the moment my eyes landed on her, a blue-eyed enchantress hiding a deceiving soul behind her poisoning beauty. Her laughter filling my once empty bedroom walls and empty heart. Her kisses, her mouth, her body, her moans, her taste on my tongue bringing me down to my knees, fooling me into thinking that she was mine. Her words telling me that I wasn't enough, that it was all a dream and that it was time for me to wake the fuck up. Watching her disappear inside her apartment, taking with her whatever was left of me.

Long days and even longer nights ahead. My friend Edgar having everything. Resenting Edgar. Hating myself for resenting him. Meeting Rachel. Her welcoming body moving underneath me. Her seducing words. Looking around my shitty apartment after she left, wondering why not—why not me. Coming here, chasing pipe dreams.

If I leave now, I'll go back to nothing—back to being no one—but if I stay …

Maybe.

I imagine myself surrounded by opulence and success. And what a seductive picture it paints. I run a hand through my hair and walk inside the gilded world shining in front of me.

She's standing at the foot of the grand staircase. Rachel. Her ivory white body covered in form fitting cream-colored silk shines like a lone star in a sea of black gowns and tuxedos.

I should go to her, but I want to admire her for a moment longer. She's breathtaking. I watch a man standing too close to her place his hand on her lower back as he leans in and whispers something in her ear. She turns to look at him and smiles politely, but the smile doesn't reach her eyes. It's the smile I first saw outside the gallery. Ice cold. Untouchable. And somehow, I find myself pleased that there are no traces of the Rachel who spent one uninhibited, wild night in my bed. The Rachel who I know exists under that finely manicured and expensive exterior hidden from him.

I take a swig of the beer I'd grabbed from a passing waiter. I'm about to walk toward her when I sense someone coming to stand next to me. "Ronan? Is that you?"

I turn to look at the woman on my left, taking in her familiar features. Chin-length brown hair. Very pretty. "Elly, right?" She's the girl I brought to Lawrence's townhouse the other day. Blaire's best friend.

"Yep. What are you doing here? Are you work—" She catches herself, and blushes. "I'm so sorry. I can be such a dickhead at times."

"Don't apologize. To be honest, I'm wondering the same thing."

She laughs, her brown eyes sparkling warmly. "Same here. This party's insane, isn't it?"

"You could say that." She scans the room, taking everything in. I clear my throat and try to appear indifferent as I ask, "is Blaire here with you?"

"No, I'm here with Alessandro. His parents know the woman who's throwing the party. Rachel, I think?"

"I see," I say, burying a hand in the pocket of my rented tuxedo.

Elly watches me for a second too long as a small frown forms on her forehead. She's quiet for a minute or two. "I feel like a heroine in one of those Regency books that Blaire loves so much. You know? Where the girl goes to a ball dressed in a beautiful gown and steals the duke's heart with one dance or some shit like that."

I stare straight ahead of me, picturing a blushing Blaire on my bed with an old paperback in her hands as she reads out loud to me. The memory makes me smile. "I always joked that I couldn't compete against a duke."

As soon as I utter those words, I realize the mistake I've just made. I steal a glance at the girl who just baited the truth out of me and see understanding dawning in her deceptively innocent face. "It's you, isn't it? You're the guy Blaire was seeing over the summer. The one she was crazy about."

I look away, flinching.

"I *knew* it. She stared at me funny when I mentioned your name. At the time, I thought it was my imagination, but now I see it all so clearly."

"So what if I am? It's over."

"No, I don't think so. Like Blaire, you carry your heart in your eyes," she says quietly.

I clench my fists. Even when she's not here, she manages to fuck with my peace of mind. There's no reprieve from her. She once was heaven and now she's the hell I'm burning in. "She's part of the past. Now if you'll excuse me," I say, beginning to move away.

She grabs my forearm and stops me, her small hand gripping it with strength I didn't know she possessed. "Don't give up on her," she pleads.

"I'm done. She made her choice, and I wasn't it."

"You love her. Still. I can see it in your eyes."

"No, Elly. You're wrong. I never loved Blaire." I smile wryly. "I loved a lie." I walk away then, leaving Elly behind.

"She loves you. She's just too afraid to admit it!"

Closing my eyes, I stop momentarily. Part of me wants to go back and ask her what she means. I want her words to give me hope, illuminate the darkness I'm drowning in, but I don't. Instead, I continue walking. I turn my back on Elly and the man I used to be; anger, resentment, jealousy propelling my each step.

I move to stand behind Rachel, who's now talking to a man. Pushing myself flush against her back, her sweet ass cradling my cock, I pull her long hair to the side and kiss the curve of her neck once, not giving a fuck about the stranger watching us. She trembles under my mouth.

"Hello, Rachel. Miss me?"

She turns to face me, blushing. "You came."

I raise an eyebrow. "You don't seem surprised."

"No, I'm not. I knew you would come."

"Really?"

"Yes."

I caress her blushing cheek with the back of my fingers. "I forgot how lovely you look when you blush like that for me."

Someone clears his throat, reminding us that we aren't alone. She licks her lips as though she could taste me there.

"Behave," she mouths.

"I don't want to." I lean in, whispering in her ear, "What I want is to fuck you again."

"You're impossible."

I grin as she shakes her head, hiding a pleased smile. She grabs my hand and spins on her feet until we're facing her guest, an older man wearing a funky bow tie and bright green glasses. "Carl, I'd like to introduce you to Ronan. He's the photographer I was telling you about. And Ronan, this is Carl Brunswick, my closest friend and owner of The Jackson."

Fucking hell. My eyes widen. *The Jackson?* The Jackson is the most exclusive art gallery in New York, Los Angeles, Paris, Honk Kong, Dubai, Tokyo, and Milan. Hell, if *the* Carl Brunswick takes an interest in you it means that you've made it. Not even Edgar with his million dollar paintings has been able to get in The Jackson.

"A pleasure, sir," I say.

He shakes my hand. "Oh yes, I remember now. Our diamond in the rough." He pauses, studying my clothes, my hair, my face, and my hands. "He's beautiful, Rachel. Where did you find him?"

She hesitates. "I met him at Edgar Juarez's exhibit."

A sly smile appears on his face. "Really? If my memory doesn't fail me, which it never does, by the way, I seem to recollect that I waited for you *inside* the gallery for hours and you never showed up."

I sense Rachel's discomfort, so I interrupt them, saying, "It's my fault. I asked her for a drink before going in."

"Drinks, eh? Is that what you young people call it nowadays?" He chuckles. "But never mind that. If Rachel says you're talented, you must be. She has one of the most discerning eyes in the business." He addresses Rachel, but his sight remains trained on me. "Rachel, honey, if his work is half as good as his face, I have a feeling that your *protégé* will go far ... very far. With a little help from my good old self, of course."

The rest of the evening passes in a blur. Champagne toasts. People treating me like a person rather than an afterthought. Women standing too close to me, their hands caressing my arm invitingly, whispering seductive words. I'm not invisible anymore.

I hear you're a photographer. I would love to see your work.

Rachel introducing me to more important and powerful people. More champagne. More caviar. Cuban cigars. Vintage wines.

Who is he? He's Rachel's new boy toy. He's sumptuous. Some people have all the luck. I hear Carl took an interest in him. I wonder if I could introduce him to my Laura—she loves the artsy type. We should invite him to a dinner party.

Whispers and conversations about me. Eyes on me.

My goodness, but he's breathtaking. Have you ever seen a mouth like his before? No man should be allowed to be that beautiful. I wonder if he's sleeping with Rachel because of her money? But of course, why else? He probably wants to get ahead. He could use me to get ahead anytime. Elizabeth! He could be your son. Wouldn't be my first, you know?

For once, I know what it feels like to be standing on the other side—the side where you don't open doors for people but people open them for you—and I would be lying if I said that I didn't enjoy it. I would be lying if I said that I didn't like how it felt to be someone in a room full of someones when all my life I've been invisible to them. Yet there's something stopping me from losing myself completely in this very vivid dream.

We're standing on the veranda, watching the stars and getting some fresh air.

"I think you've made a good impression."

"Yeah?"

"Yes, especially on Carl. He wants to see some of your work as soon as possible. He's very interested."

I take a sip of champagne, shrugging. Rachel removes the crystal flute from my hand and places it on the balustrade. Then, she turns to face me, taking my hand in hers.

"What's the matter? I thought this was—"

"You thought this was what I wanted?" I stare at the rolling gardens in front of us. "I don't know, Rachel. This is all fucking great, the party, the champagne, the interest, but I always thought that I would make it on my own. I never imagined I would need to fuck my way to the top."

I hear her breathe in sharply. "You don't mean that, Ronan. Those words aren't worthy of you."

"I apologize. You didn't deserve that, but it's the truth, isn't it? If we hadn't fucked, I wouldn't be standing here right now talking about showing some of my work to Carl Brunswick. I'd still be a nobody who no one gives a shit about."

"I'd like to call it serendipity," she adds quietly. "But that isn't what's truly bothering you, at least not completely, is it?"

I'm silent for a moment, gazing at the rolling hills in front of us. "It's just that I always thought that I could make it on my own."

She grabs my face, making me look at her. "Ronan, listen carefully. As much as Carl loves me, he won't put his business or his reputation on the line because I'm sleeping with you. If he sees potential in your work, he'll give you a chance. If he doesn't, he'll tell you as much without apology. If you get to the top, it's not because of me, it's because of you."

I open my mouth to tell her that there wouldn't be a top without her, but she interrupts me. "Stop it, you stubborn man. Listen to what I'm saying. All I'm doing is giving you a little push in the right direction. Your talent will do the rest. Now stop it, and kiss me." She pulls my face closer to hers, our mouths almost touching. "Kiss me."

I'm still not convinced, but kiss her anyway. I seek solace from my thoughts in her mouth, needing her body and the relief that she can offer me in this moment. When we break apart, I grab her ass, so soft covered in silk, and grind my growing erection against her cunt. "Let's go to your bedroom."

"No, I can't leave my guests," she breathes, but her eyes dazed in lust say the contrary.

"I don't give a fuck. I want you and you want me. Or do you want me to take you right here in front of all your guests?"

Moaning, her breathing accelerates. "You wouldn't."

Thankful to be standing in a secluded area, I slide the straps of her dress off of her shoulders, exposing her tits and burying my face in them. "I would, and you know it."

I suck her nipples, rolling the tip with my tongue, biting, tasting. "Oh God."

"Save that for later, babe."

She laughs throatily, and it's like sex in my ears. "What am I going to do with you, Ronan?"

"Why, fuck me senseless, of course. Now let's go before we give everyone a show they won't forget."

As we're walking toward her bedroom, she asks, "Who was that girl you were talking to when you first got here?"

Ah. She *was* paying attention, after all. "No one important."

Inside her room, I tell her to go sit on the chair next to her bed.

"Why?"

"You'll see."

I kneel in front of her, pulling down her thong, and push her legs apart.

"Are you enjoying the party, Ronan?" she asks softly, her eyes closing as her head rolls back on the back of the chair. Her hands go to my hair, pulling me closer.

"Now I am," I say before I get lost in her taste on my tongue.

chapterfourteen.

THE NEXT MORNING, I call into the office and tell Gina that I won't be able to go to work today. Not that she needs me since Lawrence is still out of the country, and, apparently, Blaire requested Tony to be her assigned driver in the meantime. Good riddance, I think to myself even though the words sound hollow and untrue.

I come back to bed and watch a naked Rachel smile at me as she tries to cover herself with the sheet. "Did you get in trouble?"

I shake my head, our gazes connecting. "Drop the sheet. Let me see you."

She blushes, but allows the material to fall like running water down her naked body. Mesmerized, my eyes absorb the way her blonde hair covers her shoulders, the rosy color of her nipples, and the soft curves that make her so damn tempting. With Blaire still fucking with my mind, I seek solace in Rachel's body.

"Spread your legs," I murmur raspily.

Bashful and insecure, Rachel opens her legs gently while her eyes burn invitingly. I kneel in front of her, pumping my cock in my hand, wanting her again. "No. My boss is out of town, so it doesn't really matter."

"So you're a chauffeur during the day?" she asks, following the motion of my fist.

"Amongst other things."

She watches me as I lean over her, taking her hands in mine and putting them above her head. Her pupils widen with excitement as her lips part and I kiss her deeply, roughly. It's a needy kiss that leaves us both breathless and burning from the inside out. Dipping my head down, I bite her shoulder before capturing her tit in my mouth. She purrs in my ear as I tongue and suck her nipple until it's painfully hard.

Her back curving, she digs her feet on the mattress. "Please, Ronan …" There's a blush that's spreading from the crests of her cheeks down to her chest. I can see the fast rise of her chest and sense her desperation growing.

I smile against her skin. "What do you want?"

She shakes her head. "No, Ronan … I …"

"Show me," I say before biting her neck.

Rachel reaches down to touch me, wrapping my cock in her small hand. Arching, she begins to rub me against her pussy, wetting the head, making me shiver, driving us both mad. She places the swollen head in her entrance and grabs my ass, pulling me inside her snug, wet cunt and wraps her legs around my hips. She gasps and I groan when I'm deeply rooted in her pussy.

I keep my hold on her one wrist and begin to fuck her in slow and easy strokes, feeling the walls of her cunt tighten around me, stretching for me.

"What are you ..." she moans. *In.* "doing to me ..." *Out.* "I can't get enough of you ..." *In.* "And Carl's waiting ..." *Out.*

"He can wait. I'm having my breakfast."

Letting go of her hands, I prop myself up on my forearms and continue to thrust, sinking deeper each time and pulling out farther. My arms are shaking and her body is trembling underneath me. My vision blurs. Her whimpers get more desperate. The pace is hard and fast now. Demanding. Urgent. And only release will soothe the fever spreading in our bodies.

I stop moving, my entire frame shaking with the painful need to release. My cock still buried inside her, I prolong the torture and withhold our pleasure. She circles her hips desperately, seeking her own release.

"Ronan ... I can't take it anymore. I need to ..."

"Rub your clit, Rachel. Feel me inside your cunt."

Looking down to where we're connected as one, I see her touching herself, touching my cock covered in her— glistening with her need. I groan. Fucking losing it, I begin to pound into her again and again, pumping deeper and deeper, harder and harder. I hear the headboard slam against the wall, the mirror hung above the bed rattles angrily, and the bedsprings squeak loudly as her moans get louder and louder in my ear with each thrust.

"No more," she pleads, she begs. Her voice hoarse.

"Yes, more. And more. And more."

And I go harder and harder. The walls of her pussy begin to flutter around me. I cover her mouth with mine, swallowing her cries as I take us both over the edge, coming inside her.

Rachel and I watch Carl go over some of my photographs in the living room. We're standing in my small kitchen, waiting for him to decide my future. It's funny how life works sometimes. Just a couple of weeks ago, I thought that I had hit rock bottom. My life seemed to be in shambles. I had a dead-end job and a broken heart. Then I met Rachel, and now Carl Brunswick is in my apartment, sizing up my work.

Rachel bumps my shoulder with hers. "What are you thinking about? You're quiet."

I meet her gaze and grin. "Breakfast."

She smiles. Lost in memories from this morning, we don't hear Carl walk toward us until he's standing two feet away from us. "Ronan, my boy, Rachel wasn't wrong. You *are* very talented." He glances in Rachel's direction. "Are you all right, honey? You seem flushed."

"I-ah-it's just very warm in here. I'll be fine. Excuse me." Her eyes a soft, dazed blue. "I need to use the restroom." She starts heading there but stops after taking a few steps, realizing that she's not supposed to know where it is. "Ronan, is it this way?"

"Let me show you." I look at Carl who's smiling knowingly at us. "Excuse me."

I follow her and once we're out of Carl's sight, I push Rachel up against the wall, my bulge cradled in that soft, warm spot between her legs. I cup her ass possessively, caressing the roundness and lowering my head to hers. "Stop blushing or I'm going to have to take you again."

"No ... Carl is ..." She leans her head to the side, offering herself to me, and closes her eyes.

"I don't give a shit."

She laughs throatily. "Haven't you had enough? I can barely walk."

"No, Rachel." I press her lower body into mine, imprinting the outline of my cock on her fancy skirt, showering kisses on her neck, my lips grazing pearls, and the swell of her breasts rising above her shirt. Grinning, I say, "Not by a long shot."

"Ronan, please. Be serious." She swallows and grabs the back of my head, pulling me closer to her. Her words deny but her body eagerly welcomes me.

I push her straight, perfectly blown out hair out of the way, and begin to suck the back of her neck, marking her. "Oh God ... Yes, Ronan. Fine. Later."

I let her go and grin like a cocky motherfucker as I watch her walk away with shaky legs and burning eyes, heat spreading through her cheeks.

Back in the living room, I find Carl looking at another photograph. By the time he notices me, he places the picture down on the coffee table and walks back to the tiny kitchen. "You're a very talented young man. I'm truly surprised you've remained under the radar for so long."

"Thank you. I guess I never pursued anything too seriously. Life kept getting in the way." After I got into art school, Jackie got pregnant and needed my help. I put my dreams on the back burner, quit school, and got a job that paid okay money. We couldn't allow our grandparents to pay for everything. And then a couple years later, another chance came knocking on my door. Edgar got me in touch with an art dealer, who had seen a shoot that I did for a very obscure fashion magazine and liked what he saw. We set up an appointment to meet at his gallery the day before he was flying to Milan. On my way to the meeting, I got a call from school. Ollie had fallen from the monkey bars and broken his arm. Jackie was working and couldn't get out of work and our grandparents were away visiting friends in Florida. I called the art dealer and apologized. We never met.

"I see… A word of advice?"

"Yes?" I raise an eyebrow.

"Be gentle with her. She just got out of a nasty divorce."

Reclining against the fridge, I cross my arms on my chest. "We're just having fun."

He takes his glasses off and carefully polishes them with a handkerchief. "It's all fun and games until someone gets hurt, isn't it?"

"With all due respect, what Rachel and I choose to do is none of your business."

"Of course, but—"

"She's an adult, she knows what she's doing."

"I know she is, but do you?"

I scowl. "What do you mean?"

"I get the feeling that you're playing a very dangerous game, Ronan. One that will leave many people hurt. Do you know what I think?"

"Why don't you enlighten me?"

Carl stares at me, like he's able to see past all my walls. "I think that you're chasing more than fame here—something that Rachel and I can't give you. I could be wrong, but I rarely am."

At that moment, Rachel comes back into the room, forcing us to drop the subject. I make myself unclench my jaw so I can smile at Rachel, who's watching us carefully.

"What were you guys talking about? You seem so serious."

Staring at Carl, I take Rachel's hand in mine, raise it to my lips, and kiss it. "Nothing important."

"So what do you think, Carl?" She smiles at both of us. "Do you think that Ronan has what it takes to take the art world by storm?"

He clears his throat, but he can't erase the concern in his expression. Looking at Carl, I get the sense that part of him wants me to reject their help. In his silence, he's giving me a chance to do the right thing and walk away from Rachel, but I'm done doing the right thing. For once in my life, I want to think of me and only me.

I remain silent.

"I'm fairly certain that he will, Rachel. Question is," he turns to face me, "are you ready, my boy?"

So the charade is back on, and I'm not surprised. The thing is, even though I can see the concern and affection that Carl has for Rachel, he can't hide the greed behind his eyes. He wants me as much as Rachel wants me.

I shrug.

"I'll call my contacts at The New York Minute, The City, and Vanity. One of them will write a profile on you if I ask.

We need to start generating some buzz. Do you have anything else besides what you just showed me? Are you working on something else?"

I nod, giving him a brief idea of what I want to work on next.

"Oh! Ho, ho, ho, you rascal." He rubs his hands excitedly. "This is going to be magnificent."

They spend the rest of the hour going over details and mapping out each and every step in my road to success (or perdition). As their words become a meaningless buzz filling my kitchen, an image of my mom on her knees bandaging and kissing my father's weathered and callused hands flashes through my eyes.

"You work too hard, Noel. Look at your poor hands."

"Not at all. Stand up, Josephine. You know I don't like you kneeling on the floor. Don't think about my hands. I'm proud of them. They put a roof over us, clothe and feed our family. And that's enough for me."

"But—"

"But nothing, my love. I want to teach Ronan and Jackie that if you work hard day in and day out and never give up, everything is possible." He cups her face lovingly, staring into her eyes. "And that dreams do come true."

I shake my head. *What am I doing?*

"Wait. Hold up. I haven't said yes. I need to think about this."

Carl and Rachel stare at me as if all of a sudden I've sprouted two heads. Rachel places her palms flat on the countertop. "What do you mean *think about it*? I thought we went over this last night. Carl is offering you the chance of a lifetime. A chance people would kill for."

"I get that, but—"

Relentless, she ignores me. "He's willing to put his name on the line for you because he thinks you can go very far. Think about it, your face on the cover of magazines, articles written about you, interviews, parties, people clamoring for you and your art." She pauses. "You won't have to stand outside another Edgar Juarez exhibit as an insignificant guest. Next time, it will be *your* exhibit and people will be there for *you and only you.*"

Carl inspects his manicured nails. "She's right, Ronan. Dignity and pride won't get you out of"—he scans my apartment—"here."

I run my hands through my hair, wanting to pull it out. "I haven't said no. I just need time to think about it, okay? Give me a break."

Carl pats my shoulder. "We're just trying to help you. You make it seem as though you were selling your soul to the devil, my boy."

Why does it feel like I am?

Later, as we're being driven away in a black Escalade, Rachel reaches for my hand and asks, "What are you so afraid of?"

I look out the window and see a pair of blue eyes staring back at me.

"I'm a gold digger, you know? I fuck for money." She stares at me, a cruel smirk on her achingly beautiful face. *"And frankly, it doesn't look like you could ever pay my price."*

"Of getting what I want."

chapter fifteen.

Blaire

I'm SITTING AT MY VANITY, getting ready for tonight's masquerade party, when I hear the door open. Lifting my face, I see Lawrence's reflection as he walks into the room.

As I stare at him, so virile yet elegant and immaculate in his tuxedo and without a hair out of place, part of me grows inexplicably sad. All traces of my caring, sweet lover from a week ago are gone. And when our eyes meet in the mirror, and I'm able to look into them, I'm proved right. The fire, the need, the passion, and the playfulness that I saw briefly in those few lovely days are gone, and it makes me want to weep for their loss. His usual cool and detached veneer is back in place. There's something chilly in his gaze that wasn't there before.

Lawrence came back a few days ago and has barely spoken a word to me. He fucks me, takes pleasure in my body, but the banter—the intimacy—is gone. It begins and ends in his bed and in our shared breaths. Something has changed, and I can't explain exactly what.

I grip the handle of my brush harder. I hate the fact that his detachment bothers me, that his rejection hurts me—that it *matters* to me. *This* is what I signed up for. What *I* wanted. I know that. But I thought we had shared something special in the days before he left town. I thought that … well, I don't know what I thought. All I know is that things haven't been the same since he came back from his trip. I look at my reflection, frowning, as I finally admit to myself that I miss it—I miss *him*.

In the long, uncomfortable silence that ensues, Lawrence and I gaze at one another. I see not one glimmer of humor or emotion in his eyes. I turn to look at my flushed reflection in the mirror, hoping to hide my feelings from him.

"I'm about done," I say, reaching for my lipstick. I apply a shade of red that matches the red of my Valentino gown perfectly. I feel Lawrence coming up behind me before his cold hands land on my shoulders. It's hard to imagine that these are the same hands that have touched my body so knowingly and passionately. The thought fills me with inexplicable sadness.

"Lawrence … I …" *I'm going mad wondering what has changed between us? Did I imagine it all? Did I imagine the softness in your eyes, the tenderness in your touch? Did I imagine that, for one moment in time, we shared the beginning of something that I can't quite describe or understand, yet know deep in my heart that it was beautiful?* I want to be honest with him, but the coldness, the cool detachment in his gaze forbids it. I remind myself that what we have is just business. Nothing more. Nothing less.

"Yes?" He slowly caresses my collarbone. The movement is feather light and it makes me want to lean my back against his front.

I chicken out. "Oh, nothing. I forgot what I wanted to say."

Letting go of my neck, Lawrence places a jewelry case in front of me. "Open it," he orders in that voice of his that makes me weak in the knees.

I reach for the black case resting on top of the vanity table and do as told. Gasping in surprise, I stare at a very familiar piece of jewelry. "Could this be?" I raise my gaze to meet his in the mirror. "You didn't." I shake my head in disbelief. "You couldn't have."

"Of course I could, and I did." He reaches for the necklace lying on a bed of white silk and retrieves it. "Lift your hair, please."

Following his instructions, I watch Lawrence place the string of diamonds and rubies around my neck. I lift a hand and glide my fingers across the rows of gems shaped like a rose. It's the same necklace I was admiring at the Met's exhibit the night we met. He wasn't joking when he said that he could afford it. "Why?" I ask, meeting his gaze.

He shrugs nonchalantly.

"Thank you, but this is too much, Lawrence. Even for me."

"Well, that's a first." He looks at me with such cold contempt, I'm taken aback. I blush shamefully and hang my head low.

"No, don't hang your head. Look at me. I want to admire what I paid for."

Following his instruction, our gazes clash on the mirror. He raises a hand and traces with the back of his finger the bright color on my cheeks. "Modesty doesn't suit you, Blaire. After all, isn't this what you want from me?"

He lowers one of his hands into the plunging neckline of my dress. When his fingers come into contact with my skin, I shiver in fear … or maybe it's anticipation … or maybe it's excitement. But whatever it is, I can't deny the fact that I'm enslaved to his touch.

"Isn't it what you expect from me?" Lawrence continues.

I hold his hand on my chest, halting the trajectory of his fingers. "Cruelty doesn't suit you, Lawrence. But yes, that's all I want from you." I pause as I gather all my courage to lie to him. When I'm in control of my emotions, I smirk insolently. "What else is there to want besides your money?"

I aim to wound him with my words for they are the only tools that I have at the moment. And I don't miss, but then again, I rarely do. I see a flicker of emotion in those calm, icy green eyes of his. Good.

He smiles coldly. "There's the Blaire that I know. So full of hate and venom yet breathtakingly beautiful."

I let go of him and Lawrence continues to lower his hand down the opening of my dress. I observe the blink of his expensive Piaget watch, the length of his tuxedo, as his tanned hand traces a path down my sternum. "Watch us," he orders.

His hand goes lower and lower, not caring that the silk of my dress may rip. When he reaches the apex of my thighs, I can't help but spread my legs as Lawrence sinks a finger inside me. He watches me as he slowly adds another finger. I want to close my eyes but I can't—I won't. I want to see everything he's doing to me. Memorize it. Engrave it, so when I look back to this moment, I won't feel a trace of pain or sorrow or regret.

Lawrence withdraws his hand. He brings his fingers to his mouth, tasting me. Then he lowers his hand once more, entering me with three fingers this time, his saliva and my body's reaction to him lubricating his touch. My breath shortens as my pulse accelerates. I grip the edge of the table for balance and bite my lip to stop myself from moaning. I won't give him the pleasure of knowing what he does to me. He begins to pull them in and out, pumping savagely into me, making my head swirl in pleasure laced with pain. Or is it the other way around?

The sweet and pungent smell of sex fills the air. I can hear the wetness gathering in my pussy as he enters me with his punishing fingers, with his unforgiving, divine strokes. I feel him all the way to my core, carving his name in the marrow of my bones.

His thumb starts to rub my clit as he fucks me with his hand, hooking his fingers inside of me, hitting my G-spot deliciously. There's a fiery, hot blush spreading on the cheeks of the girl staring back at me; her eyes hazy with lust, his ablaze. His breathing accelerates and I ache with unfulfilled passion as he continues to finger fuck me to oblivion. My vision blurs. My body burns. I'm drowning. I'm flying. Everything sings. Everything explodes. And just like that, I come undone. I unravel. And it's fucking ecstasy.

When I'm lucid, I watch him withdraw his hand from my body. He raises it and traces my lips with his wet fingers.

"Open your mouth," he orders.

I ignore his demand and he forces his fingers past my lips, making me taste myself on him. Once he removes them from my mouth, he fists my hair in his hand, pulling my head back and making me look up at him. Hovering over me, he hisses angrily, "Taste what my fucking money can buy." Then, he leans down and presses his lips hard against mine.

With the kiss coming to an end, he lets me go and walks toward the door. Lawrence turns to look at me one last time. He looks composed and so fucking aloof. "I'll wait for you downstairs." He pauses. "You look beautiful in that dress."

"You like it?" I smile sweetly at him, feeling so cheap. "But I guess you should. It's something else your money bought." When he walks out of the room, I reach for the lipstick and finish applying the rouge on my lips.

Don't feel.

What did you expect? He's just another man.

The masquerade party is at the home of Alan Vanderhall, a family friend of Lawrence's. Located in Greenwich, the majestic estate is something you only see in movies. The house manages to leave me open-mouthed, even though it is smaller than Lawrence's mansion on Long Island. *Where the hell are all these rich people coming from?*

The road is illuminated with Japanese paper lanterns and the trees are wrapped in twinkling lights. It's a beautiful sight to behold.

By the time we make it inside the house, I think that I must be dreaming a bright, colorful, and rich dream. As

Lawrence removes my coat and hands it to the butler, I glance around the main hall, my eyes landing on crystal chandeliers shining like small constellations of stars, hundreds, no, thousands of flowers overflowing every nook and corner in the house, and an ocean of people hidden behind masks. There's some sort of magic flowing through the halls of the house that makes my heart beat with excitement.

Lawrence is wearing a full mask depicting a Chinese Dragon. It's a work of art with its colorful and intricate design. It puts my half mask of a black swan to shame, but then again, I doubt the existence of a man or woman who could obscure Lawrence's magnificence.

The crowd seems to stop talking as they turn toward the entrance to take a better look at us. I can barely hear the orchestra playing its music above the mad beating of my heart. I half expect him to walk away from me like Walker did at the Met when he places his hand on my lower back, firmly and possessively.

Looking up in surprise, I find Lawrence already staring at me with those deep green, inscrutable eyes of his. "Come," he orders. But when I hesitate, he adds more gently, "You don't have anything to be afraid of. You're with me. I won't let you go."

"I'm not scared," I lie, lifting my chin. I can tell that he doesn't believe me, and I hate the fact that he can see through my lies so easily.

His hand curves around my hip. "Come on, then. Show them what you're made of."

We stare at each other for a moment that seems to last an eternity. Giving in to his entreaty, I begin to walk with confidence. Regardless of his feelings toward me and what happened back at the townhouse, I'm sure of one thing: Lawrence means what he said. He won't let me go, and the thought makes me feel safe.

He introduces me to his lawyer, Ben Stanwood, a man with the loveliest honey-colored eyes I've ever seen and who's wearing a half mask depicting a panther. After we exchange some pleasantries, I excuse myself and go in search of a restroom.

On my way back, I see that Lawrence is occupied with a group of people. Giving him space, I go to the ballroom to watch couples dance to the music of the orchestra. There's a pillar to the side, hidden behind some high-top cocktail tables covered in white linen, offering the perfect view of the dance floor. I walk toward it and recline my back and head on the marble stone. I'm lost in thought, watching a man and a woman dance to a slow song when someone comes to stand next to me. I feel his warmth before I hear his voice, and my treacherous pulse accelerates. He reaches for my hand and intertwines our fingers tightly together. In this manner, we stand together in comfortable silence, enjoying the music. When the song comes to an end, there's a full, pregnant pause before he speaks.

"Dance with me?" he asks huskily. His question reminds me of another time when he uttered those same words, not so long ago. The memory makes my pulse spike.

I turn to face him, unable to refuse him. Lawrence removes our masks and leaves them on a nearby table. "This is better." He caresses my cheek so tenderly it makes my heart ache. "I can see you now."

He guides us to the middle of the dance floor, the crowd opening for us. My heart won't stop drumming in my chest. He places my trembling left hand on his shoulder, clasps my right one in his left, and brings his free hand to circle my waist tightly, closing the gap between us. This close, I can feel the heat of his body against mine, smell the champagne on his breath, see the way his eyes devour my face, the ice slowly melting and making them shine warmly once again.

When the orchestra starts to play the next piece, we begin to move and I'm lost to everything and every thought. It's magical and lovely. We're back in Coney Island. On the beach. In my bedroom. The week without him and what's been happening between us since he came back becomes an ugly nightmare.

Closing my eyes momentarily, I drift across the room in the arms of a man who's holding me as though I am something precious and worthy. It's a heady sensation. Opening my eyes, I find him looking at me. I feel like the most beautiful woman in the room, in the world. It's him I see. It's his hands, his body I feel. It's his smell that swirls in my head, inebriating my senses so full of him. This isn't the stranger from early in the evening. This is my Lawrence, the man who held me in his arms while I cried—my friend.

He leans down and places a gentle kiss on my forehead, so different from before, so full of something that I'm afraid to understand. "I'm sorry."

The way he's looking at me as his voice carries unsaid words spreads warmth in my chest, butterflies wildly ricocheting in my stomach. Maybe I'm a fool for believing him, but at this moment, I truly believe that he means it. Burying my face in his chest, I say, "I'm sorry, too."

He stops dancing. "Look at me, Blaire."

I lift my face as he cups my cheeks with both of his hands. Mesmerized by him, I raise my own and place them on top of his, asking softly, "What's changed, Lawrence?"

"There's no use. I've tried in vain to stifle my lo—" He pauses, his touch turning more possessive, more intense, more everything. "Don't you see—can't you see?" he entreats, deep passion vibrating in his voice.

Stunned, I shake my head. Lawrence smiles an achingly tender smile that makes me want to weep with its beauty. "I'm jealous of every man who looks at you. I'm jealous of every man who's touched you before me. I want you to be mine and only mine."

He leans down and presses his lips against mine, and in that one magical and thrilling kiss, Lawrence makes all the incessant noise inside me go away. My mind tells me that this is just another kiss of a man who doesn't have a heart, but my own tells me to listen to his silence, to feel and understand what his body is trying to say—but it cannot be …

He pulls away. "My darling love," he says hoarsely, "everything has changed."

In a daze, as though I am dreaming and the whole thing is happening to someone else, I manage to say, "Lawrence … I—"

I stop when out of the corner of my eye I see a man removing his mask. Normally, I wouldn't give him a second thought, but something about his air strikes me as familiar. Turning in his direction to get a better look, I see him talking to a blonde woman. After a moment that lasts forever, he smiles rakishly at her, lowers his face to the woman's neck and kisses her there. My heart stops beating at the sight of him and I feel as though I'm going to be sick—jealousy and hurt punching me in the stomach.

As his lips land on her pale skin, Ronan raises his gaze and looks directly into my eyes.

chapter sixteen.

"Is EVERYTHING ALL RIGHT? You look very pale."

"No, I'm okay. Don't worry ... I just ... excuse me." I let go of Lawrence and leave him standing on the dance floor as I rush out of the ballroom. I run past angry guests and waiters trying not to drop trays full of champagne and other delicacies. I run and don't stop until I'm outside the house and in the back garden away from Ronan, Lawrence, and the pain I'm drowning in.

Images of Ronan and that woman, his lips on her skin, kissing her intimately and knowingly, assault my mind. Dizzying jealousy hooks its sharp claws in my chest, making it close to impossible to see straight. I tell myself that I have no right to feel this way, that I chose to let him go, that it shouldn't matter to me that he's with her, but it doesn't work. My brain tells me to forget him yet my heart, my stupid, treacherous heart won't set me free of him.

Once I'm able to catch my breath, I slow down my pace and continue to walk for a couple of minutes, focusing on my surroundings. My high heels sink into the soft ground, the sound of the crunching grass the only indication of my existence out here. After a rainy afternoon, the air carries a lingering earthy scent mixed with that of autumn.

I stop when I reach a fountain concealed by a rose arbor, where the only light you can see is that of the silver moon. The music, a distant echo, tenderly strokes my senses like the autumn breeze strokes my skin. A gust of wind blows past me, making the leaves of the trees dance in the night, awakening me from my trance. I lift my face and stare at the sky, hoping the peace of my surroundings will quiet all the noise within me.

But it's pointless.

Weary, I cross my arms on my stomach and let my guard down for the first time since I saw Ronan. I'm bone tired and all I want to do is crawl up in a ball and cry.

I laugh bitterly. As much as I try to outrun that man, he won't let me.

I sigh and decide it's time to get back to the party. The urge to walk straight into Lawrence's arms seeking safety and affection takes over me. Guilt corrodes me, but all I can think of is being close to him, of being comforted by him and his spellbinding kisses.

I'm straightening my dress when I hear someone's footsteps. Thinking that it's Lawrence who followed me, I paste a fake smile on my face and turn around. "Sorry about before. I didn't mean to run out like that ... I just—"

"Hello, Blaire," a man says, leaving me hot and cold all at once.

I try to swallow but it feels as though my mouth is stuffed with cotton. "What are you doing here?"

My night companion steps into the moonlight, allowing me to see his achingly beautiful features. He looks like a different man dressed in a very expensive tuxedo.

Unreachable. His brown hair slicked back and perfectly shaven, he could pass as a stranger. And as he walks toward me, I notice that he seems more confident, too.

"Enjoying *your* world, Blaire," he says, smiling. I note that even his smile lacks the warmth that used to make my stomach flutter.

"Really? And how do you like it?"

He shrugs. "It's all right."

I know I should leave it alone, but I can't help myself. I must know. "I didn't know you were into older women." My eyes, starving for a sight of him, travel the length of his body. I see the expensive watch he's wearing, one that he couldn't have afforded on his own. "Are you fucking her for money?"

He smiles cockily. "Like I said, I'm enjoying your world and *everything* it entails."

I laugh, trying to hide how much he's hurting me. "Oh, how the mighty have fallen."

Ronan grabs a packet of Marlboros from the inside of his black coat, ostensibly undisturbed by my gibe. He takes out a cigarette, places it in between his lips, letting it hang loosely, and lights it up. After taking a long drag, he tips his head back and blows the smoke in the air. As I watch him do that, I suddenly realize that it isn't just his looks that have changed. *He* has changed. There's a reckless and confident air about him that wasn't there before. Something about him screams that he doesn't give a fuck what you think about him, all the while looking like pure sex.

"Don't you know smoking can kill you?" I reach for his cigarette, grab it, and bring it to my mouth, taking a drag. "I didn't know you smoked," I say and hand it back to him as I blow out the smoke.

His eyes meet mine as our fingers brush, the contact making me shiver. "There are worse ways to die."

Ronan takes me by surprise when he reaches for my necklace and caresses it, chuckling sarcastically. "*Nice*, Blaire."

I slap his hand away forcefully. "Don't touch me."

"Funny. I seem to remember a time when you used to beg me to do exactly just that."

"Did I? I have no recollection of it," I reply dismissively. Looking away from the hell burning in his eyes, I stare at the night. Wrapping my arms around me, I try to stop myself from reaching for him and touching him again, confessing to him that I do remember *everything*.

"Do you ever think about me? About us?" I hear him ask.

Every day and every night. You haunt me in my dreams and in every waking hour that I am without you. "No. What's there to think about?"

Ronan stands next to me, closing the space between us. Raising a hand, he rubs my lower lip with his thumb. The moment he touches me, I fight the instinct to close my eyes and get lost in his touch.

"What is it about you that drives me so fucking insane?" As his brown gaze holds me captive, his touch turns painful. "That won't set me free of you? Even when I'm fucking her and my cock is buried deep inside her cunt, you still manage to poison my thoughts."

"You're a pig," I say, pushing his hand away.

I don't want to be alone with him for another second, so I turn and begin to walk away. Before I take more than a few steps, Ronan grabs my left arm and twists it behind me as he pulls me flush against him, making me gasp. I struggle to break free but it's no use. I'm at his mercy, and he knows it. I'm butter in his hands.

Breathing hard, Ronan cups my tits. His touch is rough and meant to punish us both. "Does he fuck you as good as I did?"

His hand snakes down, touching me there, burying his fingers between my legs, past the resistance of my dress. "Does he eat your pussy as good as I did?"

"Stop it, Ronan," I beg, breathless and aching with passion and pain.

"I loved you, you know? But now I see you and I know that I wasted my time."

Battered by his words, I use the only defense that I have left—my body. Rubbing myself against him, I lower my free hand and rub his erection. "Then why is your cock so hard?" I purr.

He lets my arm go, putting some space between us. He seems cool and in control of the situation, but I *know* that deep down he's not as unaffected as he appears to be. "Because there's no denying you're a good fuck. Maybe that's all you were."

I slap him as hard as I can, leaving a red mark on his skin. He touches his right cheek and smiles. "The truth hurts, doesn't it, Blaire?"

I'm trembling from head to toe. "Go to hell, Ronan."

I begin to walk away when he grabs me by the arm and pulls me close to him again. "What? I don't get a good-bye kiss?" he hisses angrily in my ear, his warm breath sending chills down my spine.

My heart is beating so fast, it feels as though it's going to explode. This close to him, reality replaces my memories. His touch is once again real and it sears through me, making ashes of me. His familiar smell of man and Ronan fills my nostrils, inebriating my senses. He's here, in front of me, but he has never been more out of my reach. For a moment, I think to myself, *This is what living in hell must feel like.*

"What the—" I try to break free from his hold. "Let me go, Ronan."

"No." He tightens his grip. "Did you ever love me, Blaire? Or was I just another fucking game to you?"

"It doesn't matter. We're over, and I'm with Lawrence."

"Lies. Lies. Lies. Is that all you can come up with?"

I tug harder. "Fuck off."

He smiles cockily. "Gladly, but only after I do *this.*"

Ronan lets go of me, buries his hands in my hair, his fingers cradling the back of my skull, and pulls me toward him until our mouths clash aggressively. My body immediately reacts to him, to his touch, to his tongue, as a sense of having lost something and finding it again washes through me.

Yet it's a kiss full of hate and yearning.

It's fire on my lips, burning them, burning me to the ground.

It's a beautiful war.

And it feels like coming home.

Stunned and under his spell, I melt in the haven of his arms and let emotion override logic. Our tongues tangle in a passionate battle that demands total surrender from both of us, and for a short moment I give in, drugged by his taste, his essence, by *him*. I push myself closer to him as though I am trying to fuse our bodies into one, feeling a surrendering shudder rake through me, *or is it him?* And what a glorious torture it is. But then reality comes crashing down on me and I realize what I'm doing. What I'm allowing to happen. I move my arms between us, gather all my strength, and push him away from me, ending the kiss abruptly.

My chest rises and falls at rapid speed. I stare at a cool Ronan, who seems untouched by the kiss while I struggle to remain upright.

"You feel that, Blaire? *That's* the fucking truth. But keep lying to yourself, I don't give a fuck anymore."

I rub my lips with the back of my hand, trying to soothe the sting of his kiss, or maybe, I'm trying to rub it in deeper until it's engraved on my skin. In a moment of weakness, I crack. "You were supposed to be out of my life. You weren't supposed to be back messing everything up."

"But I am." He moves my hand away and rubs my lower lip. "So what are you going to do about it?"

"Nothing. I'm with Lawrence now."

At the mention of Lawrence, his expression darkens with hate. "I could've given you the world, Blaire. I fucking loved you."

Tears sting my eyes, pain settling deep within my chest. "No, you couldn't have. But Lawrence can."

Then I break into a run, seeking the solace of the party before I have a chance to make a fool of myself and beg him to take me back.

Ronan

I sag defeatedly against the trunk of a tree as she runs away from me. Shaken, I reach for my pack of cigarettes, open it, grab another one, and place it loosely between my lips. As I'm lighting it, I notice dispassionately how badly my hands are shaking. I bite my lip after taking a deep drag and blowing out the smoke. Hope and fear that the trace of her flavor is gone from my mouth blend as one, but I can still taste her and it's fucking torture.

Fuck.

When I make it back inside the house, I go in search of Rachel. I find her talking to Alan and Loretta Vanderhall, the smile on her lovely face stiff and unnatural. *Ah, she knows.*

Wrapping an arm around her waist, I whisper in her ear, "Want to get out of here?"

She places her hand on top of mine, nodding. As we walk toward the exit of the house, she says hollowly, "She's lovely, Ronan."

"Don't give her another thought. She's part of the past." I stare at her and grab her hand, bringing it to my lips and kissing it. "I'm looking at the future, and that's all that matters."

That next morning, I quit work and give Carl a call. My first interview will be with the Times magazine, and it's set to take place in two weeks.

I will forget you, Blaire. I will. I will conquer my love for you even if it costs me my own soul.

chapter seventeen.

Blaire

I MAKE MY WAY BACK to the party in search of Lawrence, except I don't want him to hold me anymore; the magical moment we shared on the dance floor forgotten. I don't have it in me to continue fooling myself, not when every fiber in my body is begging me to go back to the garden. Not when my skin still tingles with the memory of being in Ronan's arms after going so long without him.

The large trees surrounding the garden seem to be closing in on me, making me feel claustrophobic. I begin to walk faster toward the warm light of the house, a light that promises temporary shelter from all the darkness surrounding me. For a brief moment, I hope that my feet will carry me to a place where binding memories don't exist, where I can be free of my past. But then again, running away, or wanting to escape, won't solve a thing. It's not my past that holds me prisoner. It's my fucking heart.

I pause when I spot Lawrence. Sorrow for him, for us, fills me. My feet feel as though they are stuck to the ground. I take a few moments to compose myself and try to hide the tempest raging inside me behind the perfect façade. He lifts

163

his head and smiles that rare, earth-shattering smile of his as his gaze connects with mine. When I can't return the gesture, his disappears.

I'm so sorry, Lawrence. So sorry. I told you I was not worthy of anything good. I'm poison.

I look away from Lawrence, afraid that he will see through me. That's when I observe Ronan walking back from the garden. His face is set in a hard line but he remains as beautiful as ever, maybe even more so now because I know he isn't mine. I'm not the only woman in the room who notices him, either. Far from it actually. Desirous eyes everywhere follow his trajectory. His step is easy and sensual and so different from before. My mind tells me that he's the same man that made me believe in summertime and sunshine but as I stare at him, I know that man is gone and has been replaced by this stranger.

I want to scratch my eyes out when he wraps an arm around his companion's waist possessively and brings their bodies close together. The intimate gesture suggests that he knows every inch of her, and well. And the way she's watching him shows that she is, too, blinded by his light and everything that he is. My head spins while my chest contracts with such incapacitating pain that I find it hard to breathe.

Ronan ...
Yeah, babe?
What happens when this ends?
It won't.
It will. Everything ends.
I know it won't, and you know why?

I don't, but tell me. Make me believe, Ronan.

He takes my hand in his, uncurls my fingers, and places my palm on his chest. *You feel this, Blaire? It's yours and it will always be. That's why.*

Feeling faint, I place a hand on the wall next to me for support as the realization that I drove him away and into the arms of someone else assails me. It serves me right that he's moved on.

"You're making a fool of yourself. Stop staring at him," I hear Lawrence hiss angrily in my ear as he wraps his hand around my upper arm, his fingers constricting.

"Go away, Lawrence," I beg. "Please leave me alone."

"He came with someone else, Blaire. Let him go."

I watch Ronan and the blonde woman disappear in the crowd, draining the room of color. Crestfallen, I turn to face Lawrence, his expression unreadable once more. "What would you have me do? Deny my own heart?" I shake my head, laughing madly. "I can't. Not tonight."

He grabs me by the arms, his touch turning painful, fury flaring in his gaze. "I don't give a fuck what you want or what you do, but I won't be made a fool of."

"But you *are* a fool, Lawrence."

"Get your things. We're leaving now," he says quietly, a deadly tone in his voice.

I shake my head. "No."

"What are you going to do, Blaire? Go to that boy and beg him to take you back? And if he does, how long before his love for you chokes the life out of you? Before you feel trapped in his arms again? Sooner or later you'll come back to me, begging me to fuck you and offering me your body for my money." He pauses. "We've been there already, haven't we?"

"I won't. I can change," I say weakly.

"Frankly, I'm growing bored with you and your show of emotions. Come with me now and stop lying to yourself." When I hesitate, he extends his hand to me. "Come. We're beginning to draw attention to ourselves."

I stare at his hand as my heart and my head fight with one another. My head wins. I take his offered hand and go with him.

Lawrence is right. I can't change.

"I want to go to my apartment. I don't feel like spending the night at your place," I say after the car has been moving for a while.

"No."

"No, what?"

Lawrence is looking out the window and sitting as far away from me as possible. "You're not going back to your apartment tonight so get it out of your head."

"I said that I want to go back to my apartment and that's what I'm going to do. I don't need your permission." I'm about to press the button to lower the partition separating us from the driver and give him my instructions when Lawrence speaks.

"Careful, Blaire. I wouldn't do that if I were you."

Normally I wouldn't heed Lawrence's warning, but the dangerous edge to his voice and the energy he's radiating makes me stop. "What are you going to do? Force me to fuck you?" I spread my knees apart as I pull the skirt of my dress up, revealing my legs and bare pussy. "Why bother to go back to your house when you have all you need right here and now."

"Again, careful there, Blaire..."

"Or what? What are you going to do to me, oh mighty Lawrence?" I slide my dress off my shoulders, the fabric pooling around my waist and hips.

"You like what you see? Why don't you finish what you started before? It's yours." Naked from the neck down with only his diamond necklace against my skin glimmering in the dark, I smile insolently. "But no matter where and how you take me and all the gifts you shower me with, I won't ever be yours. I'm looking at you and it's him I want. It's him I'm thinking of. It's always been him."

I want him to get mad at me. Inflict pain on me. I want him to hate me, hit me, physically hurt me. Maybe then the guilt and pain breaking my chest will stop and numb me from the inside out.

He moves so fast that I have barely any time to realize what his intention is before he's over me and his hands enclose around my neck, making it hard to breathe. The venom of my soul has contaminated him.

I can't move. I'm at his mercy and some disturbing part of me rejoices in that fact. *Take away my will to say no, Lawrence. Make it easy for me to deny my own heart. Make it easy for me to hate myself. Please forgive me, Lawrence.*

"Don't mention him in my presence again," he warns, loosening his fingers.

I manage to laugh even as his fingers are wrapped dangerously close around my neck. "It doesn't matter. He's—"

Before I have a chance to finish my sentence, Lawrence covers my mouth with his. This kiss is as fatal as a bullet to the heart. It tears me open and makes me bleed. It's like dying a slow death each time his lips touch mine, but the masochist part of me wants that pain, that nothingness that he brings me. I shove him, kick him, and scratch him. I invite his wrath, his maddening fury. We struggle for dominance. My life in his hands, his pride in mine—both of us doomed.

Freeing one of his hands, he brings it down between us, pushing my legs apart as he unbuckles his belt, unzips his pants, pulls out his cock, and thrusts inside me. My vision begins to blur with the lack of oxygen as he moves aggressively, remorselessly in and out of me, but I love it. I wrap my legs around his waist, bringing him closer to me while my fingers go to his hair and pull violently. The anger is edged on his face. The degradation of my being in every swift and brutal thrust of his hips into me. And so help me, God, but I want him, need him with an animalistic hunger that scares me. He fucks me so good. He fucks me until he's marked every piece of me. I cry out in ecstasy spiked with pain when I come undone, an atomic bomb going off inside me as a frenzied Lawrence reaches his own temporary madness and spills himself inside me.

A second or an eternity passes by before Lawrence lets go of my neck and pulls out of me as though my skin were burning him. He pushes himself off of me and sags against the seat, a shudder running through his body. His face pale, he watches me with bleak eyes as I sit up and bring my hands to my neck and try to suck in as much air as possible. My lungs burn but my body sings with the memory of his cruel touch.

"That was very foolish of you, Blaire. Don't ever provoke me again." He runs a hand that shakes a little through his hair. "But if this is how you want to be treated, Blaire, so be it. I don't give a damn."

Once I'm dressed, I turn to gaze out the window and close my eyes as I feel my eyes burn with tears that won't fall.

What have I done?

A small, mocking voice inside my head answers my own question. *"What you're best at, of course. Destroying everything around you."*

I'm sitting on the cold, unmade bed as I watch the sunrise through the glass windows of Lawrence's bedroom. Clasping my arms tighter around my legs, I recline my head on my knees. As the rays cast their warm light on the floor and push the darkness away, I wish that I could disappear along with them. Maybe if I did, I wouldn't be able to poison and kill beautiful things anymore.

I think of Ronan and his sweet smile when I first met him, and then I see the man from last night. So cold. So hardened. So full of hate. And I know that it's my fault. I destroyed him and his beauty.

I think of Lawrence and how he looked at me and kissed me on the dance floor, offering himself to me. And what did I do? I took his offering and shattered it in my hands, feasting on his pain.

But the morning light has brought crystal clear clarity. And with it a slow, all-consuming realization that I can't continue living this kind of life, hurting the people who least deserve it—I can't. Lawrence deserves better. I know what I must do to atone for my sins, to purge the evil inside me once and for all. I close my eyes and bask in the peace of knowing that the end is near, even as I try to suppress the pain threatening to consume me from within.

I get dressed with the few clothes that Lawrence's money didn't buy and go in search of him. After we'd returned from the masquerade, he stormed off into his library while he instructed the staff of the house not to bother him for the rest of the night. Standing outside the room, I take a deep breath and open the door without bothering to knock. He lifts his head and looks in my direction. His gaze instantly finds me. It's a simple action but when our eyes lock and I'm able to see the naked pain in his, I feel the earth shake beneath my unsure feet.

I take an unsteady step toward him. "Lawrence ... I—"

"I must say that I'm surprised to find you still here. I would've imagined that you'd be on your knees doing what you do best with that boy by now." He puts the book in his hands down on the coffee table next to him. His lips flatten, his tone contemptuous. "What do you want?"

"I came to say good-bye. I'm leaving."

"Then leave. No one's stopping you."

Flinching, his words whip me raw, but I deserve his anger and hate. Shame paints red flags on my cheeks. "I know that anything I say right now won't be apology enough for the way I treated you last night." My throat suddenly feels constricted. "Of how I truly feel about you. But I'd like to explain why—"

"Enough!" He stands up and moves to stand by the window to look out onto the street, burying his hands in the front pockets of his pants. "I've had enough of your lies to last me a lifetime, Blaire. You don't have to put up an act for me anymore." He clenches his jaw, "And if it's your money you're worried about—don't give it another thought. It's yours. I don't want it."

"Lawrence, please. Listen to me," I beg, rushing toward him. With trembling feet, I close the space between us until I'm standing right behind him. "Won't you just look at me?"

"Why should I? Haven't you had enough?" I hear him say with utter scorn vibrating in his voice.

I step around Lawrence and force him to look at me. I pause momentarily at the sight of the pure hatred filling his eyes before forging on. "Lawrence, please … listen to me. I'm so sorry for everything. I've been so selfish." Wringing my hands, the emotions that have threatened to spill over since last night finally let loose and come crashing down, making the room swirl around me. Tears begin to fall down my cheeks, but I don't care. "I've hurt you—my dear friend— and it's tearing me apart. You're the last person who deserves this kind of treatment, and I can't do this anymore. I care too much for y—"

"Damn it!" He grabs me by the arms and begins to shake me forcefully, the bite of his fingers numbing. "Don't you get it? I'm done with your fucking lies!"

"I'm so sorry," I sob, "so sorry."

"Do not dare to apologize! I don't want your apologies." The hands that clutch my arms in an iron grip grow still. Leaning down until our faces meet, he hisses savagely, breathing as though it cost him every ounce of strength in his body, "I wanted you—you, Blaire! Can't you see? I fucking love you!"

His confession stuns me, leaving me speechless. Then Lawrence pulls me in an embrace that chokes the life out of me, but I let him because I want to stop breathing.

"To love you is to self-destruct, Blaire, but I seem unable to stop." The words are torn from his chest. I cry in his arms for everything that will never be and all the wrongs I've done, and the sorrow corroding me. I'm breaking at his feet, and it's only fair that I do.

With anger and frustration ruling his every move, Lawrence lowers his lips and begins to trail desperate, searing kisses across my face, tasting my tears and the pain hidden in them. I bury my hands in his hair, pulling him closer to me as his savage mouth continues to brand itself on my skin, the crest of my cheeks, my closed eyelids, everywhere he can reach. When my lips search for his, Lawrence yields momentarily, a tremor passing through his entire body.

I know that this is good-bye.

"Fuck!" he curses angrily. Abruptly, Lawrence pushes me away like I was burning him, his chest rising and falling rapidly. "Go! Leave and don't ever come back."

Standing by the door, I take one last look at the stoic man standing by the window. And as I stare at him, taking in his stormy features one last time, I finally understand what I've been too blind to see, what my heart has denied for so long. The truth becomes as clear as the morning sky and I can't deny it any longer. I love him. *I love him.* It's not the same love that I feel for Ronan, but it is just as overpowering and all-encompassing.

I pause with my hand on the doorknob and speak the one truth that I can give him. "I love you, Lawrence," my voice breaks.

He glances back and our eyes meet for what I know will be the last time, anger replaced by despair. "But not enough to stay." Lawrence turns to look straight ahead once more, dismissing me as an already forgotten thought.

"Good-bye, Blaire."

chapter **eighteen.**

Ronan

"Wake up, sleepy head!"

"Hmm ..." I reach out to touch the warm body that should be lying next to mine and find nothing but an empty pillow. "Come back to bed, Rachel."

"Not a chance. Open your eyes, Ronan!" she exclaims, her voice brimming with excitement.

I grab her by the waist and pull her on top of me, feeling her long legs straddle my waist as her laughter echoes in my ears. Opening my eyes, I find her staring at me with a big smile on her face. I lift a hand and stroke the side of her small, perfect tit covered in silk with the back of my fingers, enjoying the sensation of her body trembling under my touch.

"Now, *this* is a view to wake up to," I say, observing the tips of her hard nipples outline the cream material that covers them.

"You're insatiable," she teases. "But look!" She reaches for an item lying next to her and shows it to me. It turns out to be a magazine with my face stamped on it. The title of the cover claims me as the next prodigy in photography.

174

Excitedly, Rachel opens the magazine and flips the pages swiftly until she finds the article she's interested in. Giving me a saucy look, she clears her throat with aplomb and begins to read.

"Ronan Geraghty, the face of a Hollywood heartthrob with a one of a kind, rare talent: his lens. When I first heard rumblings that *the* Carl Brunswick, owner of the *very* exclusive and what is considered to be the Holy Grail of art galleries, The Jackson, had taken under his wing a new talent, my interest was immediately piqued." Rachel pauses to smile at me.

"The ability to impress Carl's discerning eye isn't an everyday occurrence. And when it does happen, you don't want to be the last one to find out—to miss what usually becomes a storm about to rage chaos in the art scene. And what sensual, daring chaos is Mr. Geraghty about to rage on us, his poor unsuspecting victims? I was invited to go inside his studio and take a first look at his work and what I'm sure will be the beginning of an illustrious career. The photographs are thought provoking, sensual to the point of almost being indecent, and every single one of them took my breath away ..."

Satisfied, Rachel places the article next to her leg. "You're going to be a star, Ronan. I can *feel* it. Look at them, losing their minds over you already."

I think of the woman who came to the studio that Carl provided and whose presence I forgot all about once I began to photograph the model posing for me, trying to capture her soul with the click of the camera.

"You think?" I ask, hating the uncertainty that tinges my voice.

"Without a doubt." Rachel leans forward, rubbing her chest against mine invitingly, before placing her mouth on mine and kissing me.

I snake my hands under her silk baby doll, finding her bare, and knead my fingers in the soft flesh of her ass. I start to move her back and forth, lazily grinding her hot, wet cunt against my growing cock.

Rachel ends the kiss with a frustrated groan and buries her face in the crook of my neck. "My God, you drive me crazy. I don't recognize myself when I'm with you. I want you too much."

I twist her hair in my hand, tug it back, and make her look at me, absorbing the lovely blush coating the crests of her cheeks. My heart remains silent, but I can't deny the fact that I like her, that my body hungers for her, and that I can't get enough of her. I need Rachel to soothe the pain and fill the emptiness threatening to swallow me whole.

"I want you, too. So damn much."

She bites her bottom lip while a shadow sweeps across her clear blue eyes, muting their color momentarily. I rub that same lip with my thumb, feeling its heat.

"What is it?"

"Tell me about her," she whispers.

I pause momentarily as Blaire's memory blinds me and I feel as though I am falling down a deep well where there's no escape. But I push past it until it's Rachel and her blonde hair and her body on mine that hold me to this place, to her.

"What would you like to know?"

"Are you still in love with her?"

"Right now," I grab the edges of the baby doll and pull it up over her ass, revealing her bare pussy to me, her flat stomach, and her perfect tits, "I am not." When Rachel is completely naked and trembling under my hands, I toss the fabric carelessly on the floor, reach for her hips, and guide her core toward my mouth. "Allow me to show you."

The article forgotten ...

Along with the woman I once loved.

chapter nineteen.

Blaire

THERE'S A KNOCK AT THE DOOR. *As I wake up, my eyes growing accustomed to my surroundings, I notice that this is my childhood bedroom. Confused, I push the duvet cover to the side and get out of bed. "Coming," I say as the banging grows louder. I open the door and find my mother standing in the hall, dressed in the same clothes that she had on the last time we saw each other years ago. It's like time has stopped moving and she hasn't aged. She's still as beautiful as the day I left home.*

"Mom? What are you doing here?"

She hands me an envelope without saying a word.

I take it and gaze down at the letters written on the white paper. "What is this?"

"Everything you have left of your father."

"What do you mean? Where is he?"

My mother spins on her feet and begins to walk away from me as fear clutches its ugly claws in my chest. "Mom! What do you mean? Where is Daddy?"

She stops somewhere down the hallway and turns to look at me, her eyes empty. "He's gone, Blaire. He's gone."

Devastating pain explodes inside me, shattering me from within. The room begins to spin, people, furniture, and various flying objects become a mass of swirling colors.

Then I'm in the arms of a man whose face I can't see. Every time I try to look at him, my sight becomes blurry and it prevents me from discovering his identity. His gentle touch is familiar, though, and it fills me with a sense of tenderness and love.

The man clasps me tighter to his chest without saying a word. His silence is more comforting than words could ever be. But it's his presence that means everything and gives me strength to continue breathing.

"My dad is dead," I whisper brokenly. "And I never got to say good-bye to him." I press a hand to the ache in my chest and wonder how someone can feel so much pain and be able to live through it, breathe through it.

He presses a kiss on my forehead. "Would you have wanted to?"

"I don't know ... I feel so lost."

"Go back home, Blaire. Go to him. Go to your mom," the man urges.

"I can't. I'm too late." I try to look at him again, but he begins to disappear as though his body is made of smoke. "No!" I shout hysterically, reaching for him but grasping nothing but air. "Don't leave me. Stay with me. I n-need you."

"Go back to them, Blaire. It's time to heal and to forgive ..."

I wake up suddenly, gasping for air as my heart races madly. My sight adjusts to the dark, and I half expect to find myself in my childhood bedroom, but the familiar furniture brings me back to the present. I get out of bed urgently and walk to the door, dreading who I'll find on the other side.

Nothing but my empty living room.

Relieved, I turn the lights on and go to the kitchen to pour myself something to drink. As I gulp the water down, images of my parents, of the man whose face I couldn't see, continue to flash in my eyes. Their voices grow louder and louder. I place the glass on the counter and cover my ears to tune them out, except it's no use. They shout like every fiber in my body is to go to them and set things right between us. It's the last thing that I thought I'd ever want but, in a startlingly lucid instant, it becomes as essential to me as my next breath. Suddenly gripped by a choking fear the dream might be true, I decide to go in search of answers back to where it all started.

But not before I take care of a few things here …

"Thank you so much for coming. You have no idea how much it means to me."

"Don't mention it." Elly wraps an arm around my shoulders as we stand in front of Lawrence's building. There was a time when I would have flinched from the close contact, but that was a lifetime ago. And today I need her and the quiet strength that she offers me in her one embrace more than ever.

"Do you feel better now?"

I think of what just happened, and my heart breaks all over again. "I don't, but at least he has his money back. I don't want it."

"His assistant was nice to you."

When we got to Lawrence's office, I expected to be removed from the premises immediately. Instead, Gina welcomed us and asked if there was anything she could help me with. I wanted to beg her to let me see Lawrence but I knew it was out of the question, so I'd handed her an envelope with a check for all the money he ever gave me and told her to tell Lawrence that it belonged to him.

"Thank you for everything that you've done for me, Gina. I really appreciate it. I know this is out of line, but can I ask you for one last favor?"

She hesitated. "Sure."

"Could you please tell him that I meant everything I said? He'll know what that means."

"He was there, Elly. I could feel him in the other room. I wish I could've seen him. Maybe ... maybe this time he would have let me explain."

"I don't think that's a good idea, at least not now. It's only been a couple of days. Maybe later ..."

I stare dully at the cars parked by the curb in front of us. "I hurt him badly, Elly."

I'm aware that I did the right thing by ending our relationship, but the knowledge hasn't diminished the pain one bit. If anything, the pain has gotten worse. Now that I've had time to look back and think about each and every moment that led to our good-bye, I can see that I have no one other than myself to blame. I was selfish and capricious. I took the blessed oblivion that Lawrence offered and soaked it in. I used him to forget and never stopped to think about his feelings. I believed him when he said that he only wanted my body, but refused to believe what his touch, his kisses, and the way he looked at me tried to convey.

I chose to ignore it all because it was safe and comforting.

And now look at the mess I've created.

"Well, Blaire, I would love to say that I told you so, but I'm pretty sure you already know that, so I won't go there. And as much as I hate that I'm about to sound like a motivational Pinterest quote, I think all you can do now is try and learn from your mistakes."

I feel a tap on my shoulder as I'm about to reply. Glancing back, my eyes widen when I take in the form of the person standing in front of me.

"Jackie?"

She crosses her arms across her chest. "So it's you, huh?"

"Excuse me?" I frown. "What do you mean?"

"Don't play stupid with me, Blaire. I'm not Ronan or Lawrence. I won't fall for your innocent act."

"Hey! Watch it," Elly interrupts, ready to pounce.

I place a hand on her arm and silently mouth the words that I got it. Then, I turn to look at Jackie once more.

"I work here." She nods in the direction of Lawrence's building. "I thought I saw you leave with Laurie a couple of weeks ago. I told myself that I was imagining things. But here you are, and suddenly everything makes sense."

"What makes sense?"

"Jesus, is this what they fell for?" She shakes her head. "Please, don't play innocent with me. It won't work. Tell me, how does it feel to break the heart of not only one good man but of two? Are you proud of yourself?"

As soon as the words leave her mouth, I'm punched in the face with the realization that Jackie is the same woman who Lawrence loved all those years ago. It all makes sense now. Ollie. Bradley. Jackie's confession in the kitchen about her past. Lawrence's description of her parents. All the pieces of the puzzle finally come together and it shakes me to the core.

"Jackie ... please, if you'll let me explain—"

"What? What could you possibly explain? I'm sorry but nothing that you do or say will justify in my eyes what you did to my brother. He loved you, Blaire. So much. And then you left him, and he hasn't been the same. I don't even recognize him. But that wasn't enough for you, was it?" She looks me up and down. "It never is for women like you. You had to hurt Lau—Lawrence, too."

Wincing, I raise a staying hand as I try to speak, but the words get stuck in my throat. "I'm sorry. I can't—"

"You know what, Blaire? In hindsight, I'm glad you're out of their lives. They'll be better off without you. Good-bye."

With her words ringing in my ears, I see Lawrence walk out of the building and meet Jackie by the revolving doors. He places his hand on the small of her back and they begin to walk in our direction. Our eyes meet briefly before he looks away from me and gets in an expensive car that I don't recognize, driven by a man who isn't Tony. It's as though he's purposefully erased all traces of me from his life.

I watch the car pull away as Elly's fingers intertwine with mine. "Make him look back at me, Elly. Make him …" my voice wavers. I let go of her hand and seek solace in her arms. "Make him come back."

"What will you do once you get there?" Elly asks, watching me from her place on the couch. "And would you stop that? You remind me of a caged hyena I once saw at the San Diego Zoo."

Sighing, I stop pacing the floor of her small living room and stand still. "I guess I'm going to go home and take it from there." I rub my arms as I gaze down and notice a faint pattern on her carpet from my shoes. "My mom might not even live there anymore."

"If she doesn't, what are you going to do?"

"I'm not sure. Ask around, I guess. And if that fails, come back home and get on with life. I need to find a job desperately. By the way, it's really nice of Alessandro to let me borrow his car."

Elly's attention seems to be caught by a stack of magazines lying on her coffee table. I stare at her as she swiftly leans forward, picking them all up in her arms, and heads toward her bedroom. When she comes out, she seems relieved and calm. The magazines are also missing.

"Sorry, what were you saying?"

I frown puzzled by her odd behavior. "What was in those magazines?"

Elly instantly looks away but not before I see the guilt in her eyes. Without giving her a chance to stop me, I walk to her bedroom in search of whatever she's hiding.

"Blaire, no. Wait!"

After a quick search, I end up finding the magazines hidden under her bed. I sit on the floor cross-legged and start going over the covers as my pulse accelerates, a bad feeling settling in the middle of my chest.

"It's not worth it," Elly murmurs sadly.

"What's not …"

My voice trails off like an unfinished thought as I discover what Elly didn't want me to see. Quickly as though my life depends on the speed of my fingers, I flip through the pages until I find Ronan's interview. My eyes consume the words written about him and when I'm done reading the article, I punish myself even further by looking at his pictures, memorizing each one of them. Like the one where he's with the blonde woman from the party. With an arm around her waist, Ronan is photographed whispering something in her ear that makes her laugh. Her name is Rachel. She's a socialite. The next photograph is of Ronan's profile as he stares out of a massive window. He looks more like the man that I knew and fell in love with on a dream-like summer, but it's just an illusion. My heart's desire playing me for a fool. He's gone.

"I didn't want you to see it. I thought that it would be better if you didn't."

"He's going to make it, Elly. I'm so happy for him."

"I'm not," she says gruffly.

Shaking my head, I trace the outline of his lips with trembling fingers. "No, don't say that. I ... I deserve it all. Elly, is there a limit to the pain one can feel?"

"I wish I knew, babe."

"Jackie's right. They're better off without me." I stare at his picture, the image blurry through my tears. "Anything ... I would give anything to " I press a hand to my chest as though I could stop it from shattering, but it's no use. I'm breaking into a thousand pieces, and the love I feel for them is the driving force.

"I can't. It hurts too much, Elly. I can't."

chapter twenty.

LONG AGO, I LEFT THIS PLACE *never* to return. I buried my heart somewhere in this house, along with its memories. I thought that I could escape from my own past and that it would never catch up to me, that I would always be two steps ahead.

But now I realize that I was a fool to believe that. The ghosts of my past haunt me whenever I look in the mirror. They walk with me. They sleep with me. They rule my every thought and every action. I thought I was free, yet now I see it was just a stupid illusion. I never stopped being the lonely girl who felt unworthy of love, who cried herself to sleep while praying to a deaf God to make her parents love her back. No, I don't think I ever truly left this house full of regrets and fears.

Chewing my bottom lip, I stare at the white Victorian house where I grew up. At the two perfectly matched flowerpots that border the faded red door and the navy blue shutters framing the windows. I'm not even sure what coming here will accomplish. All I know is that my dream still haunts me and I haven't been able to shake off the feeling that I need to be here.

Once I ring the doorbell, I fidget nervously, attempting to fix my clothes one last time. The lights of the porch come immediately on as a woman exclaims that she's coming.

She opens the door and gasps in surprise as her gaze lands on me. "Blaire?" She opens the door wider. "Is that you?"

"Hello, Mom," I say, surprised that my voice sounds so calm.

She stares at me silently and I think she's about to tell me to leave when she steps forward and embraces me in a hug so fierce I can almost feel the air disappearing from my lungs. It freezes me to the spot. I want to return her embrace but a part of me forbids it with rancor, while the other cries for her. So I stand still, unable to move.

After a moment, my mother pushes herself away from me. It seems like she wants to touch me again, but she won't. Her eyes rove over my face. "I thought I was never going to see you again."

I bury my hands in the back pockets of my black skinny jeans. "Me too."

My mom lowers her gaze, focusing on her hands. "It's been a long time."

"Yes, a very long time." The words hang between us just as the many lives that we have lived without each other. I wonder if she, too, remembers our good-bye as clearly as I do.

"My goodness, I've forgotten my manners." She looks up and smiles sadly at me. "Would you like to come in?"

"I—"

"Please?" she pleads.

When I was fourteen, I developed my first crush. His name was Brendan and he had a penchant for bathing himself in Aqua Di Gio. That year, I loved Aqua Di Gio. Brendan sat in front of me in Spanish class. I would close my eyes, lean in a little closer and breathe in his smell. I would picture us going to the movies. We would hold hands and he would pay for popcorn and soda. He would pretend to stretch his arms just so he could wrap an arm around my shoulders. It was lovely. It was unattainable. Brendan didn't know I existed. Brendan also had a crush on Paige. Somehow Paige discovered that I liked Brendan, and unbeknownst to me, she got him to ask me out to the movies, just like in my teenage dream. I showed up at the movie theater, heart beating fast. My first date with a boy. Brendan did show up, but he wasn't alone. He was with Paige. And boy, did they put on a show for me.

I grew to hate the smell of Aqua Di Gio.

Now, that cologne is forever associated with Brendan, the heartbreak of my first teenage crush, and Paige. So, yeah, I can't stand the smell.

And like Aqua Di Gio, this house bombards me with memories as I follow my mother into the living room, most of them painful. A part of me wants to run out the door, forgetting that I ever came.

But it's too late to turn back.

I sit down on a couch I don't recognize as I look around, my attention arrested by a picture of my parents. Together.

Older. I frown. My mom follows the direction of my gaze, walks toward the frame, and picks it up. She caresses the glass tenderly, her fingers stroking my father's face. The frown grows deeper. *Am I missing something here? Or am I falling down Alice's rabbit hole?*

When my mother looks back, she must see the perplexed expression on my face because she places the picture down and smiles sadly. "I love this picture."

"Um, yeah ... I can see that," I say but what I really want to ask is, why?

She stares at me for a short while, studying me. I want to fidget under her gaze, but I manage to sit still. "You're more beautiful than I remember," she murmurs softly.

"And does that bother you, Mom?" I reply, poison dripping off my every word.

She flinches as though I just slapped her. "I deserve that."

"No," I reply, angry with myself for being rude. "You didn't. I'm sorry."

My mom sits on the sofa across from me. "We used to do that, didn't we? Go for each other's throats? See who could slash deeper, hurt harder."

To avoid looking at her in the eye, I pretend to study my nails. "Doesn't matter now, does it?"

The silence that ensues is deafening. Our past shouts at us. Each and every memory raising its voice demands to be heard.

"What made you come back, Blaire?"

Swiftly, I raise my eyes, meeting her gaze. "I'm sorry it's an inconvenience for you." I stand up, getting myself ready to leave. "I should go. This was a bad idea."

My mom grips my hand, stopping me. "No, don't go. Not yet. I didn't mean it like that, Blaire."

I stare at her hand on my arm and remember the last time she ever touched me. It was a slap on the face. "When I was a little girl, all I ever wanted was to be held by you. To be loved by you. But that was then and this is now. Would you please remove your hand from my arm?"

She lets me go immediately, her eyes bearing naked pain. "We did you wrong, your father and I. My beautiful girl ... What did we do to you?"

I don't know whether to laugh in her face or throw myself down at her feet begging her to hug me and never let me go. Maybe both. Yes, definitely both. "You know what? I can't do this right now." I shake my head. "I need to think."

My mom doesn't stop me this time as she watches me grab my leather bag from the couch and stand on my feet. "How long will you be staying in town?"

"I don't know. I'm not sure."

"Where are you staying?"

"At the Wiltmore."

She stands up and walks over to me. As she approaches, I take the opportunity to notice the marks that time has left behind on her face. And time has been very kind to her. She's still as beautiful as I remember her. Regal. Though there's something very different about her. Something I can't pinpoint. *Softness?*

"Why don't you stay here? This is your home, after all," she adds quietly.

I reach for the car keys. "Thank you, but no. I think I need to be alone tonight."

"Would you like to do breakfast tomorrow?"

The refusal sits ready on my tongue, but I swallow it back. I came home in search of some closure, and closure I'm going to get. "Sure, I'd like that."

I'm about to cross the threshold when my mom asks me to stop. I glance back, our eyes connecting. "You know what I regret the most, Blaire?" Her question comes out as a whisper.

"Yes?" I ask stiffly.

"When I left that first time, you were a little girl of barely six. You came running toward me, tears streaking down your pretty face. You hugged my waist so tightly as you begged me between sobs to take you with me, not to leave you behind. I watched you and felt my heart break. I regret not taking you in my arms and staying for you. But I couldn't live with your father for another day. It was killing me."

Anger boils inside me. *Now she tells me that? Now? Twenty years too fucking late, Mom.* "You know, Mom, have you ever stopped to think what it felt like to me—to your *daughter*—to watch her mother walk out of the house suitcase in hand, not even bothering to look back at her? What about me, Mom? Did it not matter to you that my heart was breaking, too?" My voice is rising, but I don't give a shit. "You left Daddy and me behind. And Daddy only got worse after that."

My mom's beautiful blue eyes glaze over with tears. "I'm sorry, Blaire. I'm so sorry. I wish that I could go back in time and do it all over again."

The fight gone out of me, I stare at my mom numbly. "I'm not sure that I can."

The next morning, I meet with my mom at a small, quaint diner. She's waiting for me when I arrive. At first, things are very tense. She doesn't say much and neither do I. We sit staring at our hands or out the window, always avoiding each other's eyes. The pain is still too tangible. The wounds that never quite healed bleed once more.

She breaks the silence. "Would you like more coffee?"

I look down at my mug, realizing for the first time that it's empty. "Sure."

She gets the attention of our waitress and asks for a refill. As the waitress brings the coffee pot over, my mom takes my hand in hers. I find myself torn between wanting to keep it there, relishing the feel of my hand in hers, or withdrawing it.

I keep it there.

"Blaire ... there's something that you need to know."

I lift my face and our gazes meet. The tone of her voice rings warning bells in my head. "Yes? Does it have to do with Dad?"

She nods, squeezing my hand gently. "Your dad passed away two years ago."

The restaurant begins to spin around me. I feel faint as everything becomes blurry. There's an explosion of pain followed by utter grief and sorrow. *I am too late, then.*

"How did he die?" I manage to ask through the pain.

"It was a massive heart attack," my mom says sadly.

"Were ..." I pause, trying to swallow through the pain. "Were you with him?"

She nods. Then my mom, the woman who I always thought to be the strongest of all, the most beautiful of all, the most heartless of all, breaks down and cries. Sobs are torn from her chest as if someone is ripping them out, as she covers her face with her hands and gives into grief.

Instinctively, my heart tells me to go to her, to lend her my support. However, a lifetime full of hurt and memories stands between us, making me remain seated in my spot as my mom crumbles in front of me. But as I stare at her, a broken woman, my heart wins. Standing up quickly, I move out of my side of the booth and slide into hers. I enfold her in my arms.

My mom's arms come around me, pulling me closer to her. "He's gone, Blaire ... he's gone," she cries. Minutes pass. When my mom is calmer, she lets me go and dries her face with a paper napkin. "There's so much that I have to tell you about your father and me."

"That picture ..."

She blows her nose. "Yes, that was your daddy. Somehow after everything that happened, we both found our way back. We got married for a second time. We tried to look for you. Your dad even went to New York City, but no one knew where you went. You didn't stay in touch with anyone from here." She reaches for her bag, taking out a letter and hands it to me. "He wrote this for you after he had the first attack. I think a part of him always knew you would come back."

I stare at the envelope in my hand. "Thank you."

My mom then takes my hand in hers. "Sweetie, your father and I had a very complicated relationship. We loved

194

each other to the point of madness, but that love also drove us apart. It was much too intense. You are an adult now, so you must know that relationships aren't cut and dry. There's so much beauty in a marriage, but there can also be so much pain. You were our blessing, our love, what kept us together far longer than expected."

I look down as tears fill my eyes, her words wounding and healing.

"It wasn't your fault that we couldn't stay together. We loved you, Blaire. But we were too selfish and self-absorbed to show you. Blaire, look at me," she urges me tenderly. When I do, she raises a hand to caresses my cheek with the back of her hand. "I can't do anything about the past. If I could, I would, but I can't. It's too late for that. But what I can do is ask you for your forgiveness and if you can't give me that just yet, I beg you to find it in your heart to give me the chance to try and earn it."

As my mom awaits my answer, I feel as though I'm waking from a dream. I will never have closure with my dad. He died without knowing that I loved him. And here I have an opportunity not to repeat the same mistake with my mother. Sometimes people walk out of your life never to return, and all you have left are bitter memories and what ifs. And though you try to move on and forget them, they become regrets that cut deeper than the sharpest knife, slashing you over and over again.

"You don't have to give me an answer now, sweetie. Why don't you read your father's letter? Take some time. And when you're ready, I'll be there for you."

Once we say good-bye, I drive back to my hotel. After taking a shower, doing my nails, reading, doing anything and everything to avoid my father's letter, I finally find the courage to take it in my hands, open the envelope, and read it.

My dear Blaire,

If you're reading this letter, it's because I'm too late.

My life has been a string full of regrets. Not walking you to school. Not taking you to the park more often. Not making you laugh. Not telling you that I loved you enough. But my biggest regret is not being able to watch you grow and become the wonderful woman that I know you must be.

I wish you were with us now so you could see who we have become. Your mom gave me one of the best presents I could wish for: her forgiveness. She did it because she says the past doesn't exist anymore and it's all about who we are now. And she's right, Blaire. Don't ever let the demons of your past tarnish your present.

I'm so sorry for being such a lousy father to you, Blaire—my sweet blue-eyed angel. My shining star.

In my sober moments, it was you who made my life not seem such a waste. And in my alcohol induced moments, it was you who I lamented.

I love you, my child.

Always,
Your father.

Gripping the letter tightly to my chest, I cry for the girl I was and for the family we could've been. I cry because I never got to tell my dad that, in my eyes, he was never a failure. And I cry because that little girl still loves him so much and he died without knowing it.

chapter **twenty-one**.

MY MOM OPENS THE DOOR and smiles brightly when she sees me. "You came."

"Yes," I smile, too. "I want to try, Mom."

All my life has been a collection of decisions ruled by fear: fear of getting hurt, fear of feeling too much, fear of loving, fear of allowing people to get close.

Fear.

Fear.

Fear.

I once thought I had broken free of it, but I was just fooling myself.

I'm done running.

It's time to face the music.

And hopefully, time to heal, too.

chapter **twenty-two.**

"WOW ... THIS PLACE IS INSANE," I say, following Elly around the house. She's giving me a tour of Alessandro's sky lodge in Vermont. We're now on the main floor that features an open living area and a ridiculous floor to ceiling stone fireplace, framed by bay windows. I stop walking and absorb the view of the mountains against a bright blue sky.

"The view is something else," Elly says.

"Yep. The whole place is amazing, Elly." I move to sit on a large cream-colored couch. I grab a comfortable looking throw pillow, hugging it to my chest, and meet Elly's eyes. "Thanks for inviting me."

Elly sits down next to me. She reaches for my hand and laces our fingers. "How are you doing?"

I focus on the fire burning in the hearth, thinking back to the last few weeks of my life and the peace that I found by letting go of all my anger and resentment—the peace that I found in forgiving, and accepting forgiveness in return.

"I once made a promise to myself that I would never love again because it made me weak. I decided to ignore my heart and let my brain rule every decision that I made, so I hid behind money and its comforts. I knew money couldn't buy happiness, but it could make my life pretty comfortable—

shroud it with glittering safety. I see now that I was mistaken. I mean, don't get me wrong—money is important. But it isn't everything." I turn to face her and smile sadly, thinking of my father's letter. "Love can be many things. Cruel. Exhilarating. Deceitful. Jealous. Hateful. But at its purest form, love can be redeeming—forgiving." My voice falters, but I continue past the rock stuck in my throat, "Love can heal, Elly."

She squeezes my hand. "That's beautiful."

I wipe a tear off my cheek with the sleeve of my sweater. "Ugh … I hate this," I say, sniffing. "Lately, everything seems to set me off. And once I get going, I can't stop crying."

Elly laughs, the sound musical. "Aww, the ice in your heart is thawing."

"Shut up." I roll my eyes as a smile tugs the corners of my lips. "It freaking sucks." We stare at each other and burst out laughing. Once we've calmed down, I grab the pillow sitting on my lap and throw it at her, missing her head by an inch. "What would I do without you?"

"You'd be lost without me." She pretends to shudder. "But tell me … how are you doing? You know, with Ronan and Lawrence."

How can I explain to Elly what happened in the past few weeks when I barely understand it myself? I laugh because I went through life protecting my heart, making sure that I never gave power to anyone, but I ended up falling in love not once, but twice.

"It sucks. The pain is still too raw. Too fresh. But I've had some time to think about it, I guess."

"And?"

"It's hard to explain. Because how can you explain loving two men at the same time?"

"Only you would go from not falling in love at all to falling for two guys at once."

I laugh. "It's karma at its best." I bite my lip. "With Ronan, he came into my world and tilted it upside down. I didn't have a chance against him—he stole my heart. And it didn't happen like that with Lawrence. No, what I feel for Lawrence doesn't have a beginning or an end. What started as a distraction turned into something beautiful that can't be named or explained or measured. Each of them owns different parts of me."

"That sucks, my friend. Too bad that this isn't some kind of fun ménage book where you get to keep both."

That makes me laugh. "Yep, and now I don't have either."

"Screw them. We'll get you a nice rebound. As long as you promise me that you won't go self-sabotaging another relationship of yours, we should be good."

We're laughing when Alessandro comes into the house with his hands full of groceries. We get up and go help him, the subject dropped.

It is now past midnight and I'm still awake. After tossing and turning for countless hours with sleep evading me, I push the sheets to the side and get up. I walk over to the window and drag the curtain to the side, allowing the moon to fill the room with silvery light. Worrying my lip, I mull over Elly's words.

"Yeah ... self-sabotage would be putting it mildly," I whisper into an empty room.

I decide to go for a walk to calm down after we're done with breakfast. I'm jumpy and exhausted after a sleepless night and I feel like I'm going to lose my mind if I remain indoors for another second. I put my jacket on, open the back door, and walk out of the house.

Shivering, I stop on the wooden deck. The majestic view and the tranquility of my surroundings steal my breath away and invigorate me. As I climb down the stairs, I remember Alessandro mentioning the existence of a creek behind the house. I make up my mind to go in search of it.

Upon my return, there's laughter coming from inside the lodge. The rest of the guests must have arrived. I'm about to open the door when I hear someone approaching the house from my left. Instinctively, I turn my head in that direction, and the air is sucked out of my lungs. The tall form of the man approaches me, completely unaware of my existence. As my eyes devour him, taking in his familiar features, the scruff covering his jaw and framing his luscious lips, the endearing (and mega-hot) way that he looks wearing a navy blue beanie ...

I know with complete certainty that he's the only man for me.

And even though he shares my love with another, I will only belong body and soul to this man. I just pray that I'm not too late.

I let go of the doorknob and spin on my feet until I'm facing the direction that he's coming from. I take a deep breath like it were my last and throw caution to the wind, gambling my heart away. "Hello, Ronan."

Ronan stops dead in his tracks the moment he hears my voice, a rainbow of emotions flashing in his eyes as our gazes meet.

"What are you doing here?" he utters with so much hate it stuns me momentarily. "*Fucking* Elly."

Flinching, I move toward him. "I—"

The door opens then and a woman whose face I could never forget walks out. Her arm brushes past mine as she goes to him. She extends both of her jeweled hands for Ronan to take. "There you are. I was beginning to wonder what happened to you."

Ronan places two overnight bags on the floor before taking her hands in his and pulling her toward him. He pretends that I don't exist as he smiles a slow, seductive smile. "Missing me already?"

Rachel laughs airily, and it consumes me with jealousy. *God, even her fucking laughter is graceful.* She says something to him, but I can't hear past the ringing in my ears. Suddenly feeling dizzy, I recline my back on the wall behind me.

Letting her go, Ronan laces his fingers with her, picks up the bags with his free hand, and walks inside the house. As they pass me by, Ronan's eyes lock with mine and I see nothing in them but hard indifference. "Excuse us," he addresses me in a voice so cold it freezes me from the inside out.

When they disappear inside the house, I lean my head back and close my eyes.

And there's your answer, Blaire.

You are late.

Too fucking late.

chapter twenty-three.

"I'M SO SORRY, BLAIRE. I had no idea that Alessandro had invited them," Elly pleads sorrowfully.

"It's okay, Elly." I look up from the chopping board, tightening my hold on the knife. I try my best to smile. "It's not your fault that I behaved like an asshole in the past and now I'm finally getting what I deserve. Anyway, how did he manage to get them here? I didn't know that you guys knew him outside the one time that he drove you?"

She explains to me how she ran into him at Rachel's party and how they struck up a conversation. At the mention of her name, I feel bile rising in my stomach, but my desperation to know about him outweighs my unjustified dislike for that woman. "Alessandro told me that he ran into Ronan at a bar in SoHo last weekend and invited him to come up. He had no idea that you guys had a history. God, I was so mad at him when I saw them walk in."

"Poor man." I resume chopping the garlic cloves, pretending to pay particular and meticulous attention to what I'm doing. "Hope you weren't too hard on him."

"Eh, he'll survive," Elly says saucily.

I chuckle ruefully.

Elly takes a sip of wine and then swirls the liquid in her glass, seemingly waging her next statement. "Blaire ... I don't think he's over you."

"Don't say that," I whisper but my heart begins to beat so loudly I can barely hear my own thoughts through it.

An image of Ronan and Rachel hanging out by the fire, laughing, his arms around her waist, her hand buried in the back pocket of his jeans as they chatted with Elly and Alessandro and the rest of the guests flashes in my mind. I could have had that if I hadn't been a fool, but now Ronan is with Rachel and there's nothing I can do.

"You're wrong, Elly." I place the knife on the counter and turn to face her. "He hates me."

"I'm not so sure about that. He's lying to himself, Blaire. I can feel it. Whenever he thinks that no one is looking, he follows your every move. He can't take his eyes off you."

"Stop it, Elly," I plead, going mad. *Stop giving me hope.* "He brought Rachel. He's obviously with her."

"Just because they're fucking doesn't mean that they're in love." Elly chews her bottom lip. "But I've got to admit that I'm not sure what to do about her."

"Nothing!"

She raises a staying hand. "He seems to be into her, I'll give you that, but he doesn't look at her the way he looks at you."

"And how is that?" I ask softly, barely able to get the words out.

"Seriously, Blaire. I can't believe how blind you are. The man looks at you as though you are the center of his universe. It's obvious that he's mad as fuck, but—"

"Please let it go, Elly," I beg. "Sometimes things can't be fixed."

She purses her lips. "I thought you were done with lies."

"I am. But denial," I reach for her glass, take a large gulp, and hand it back to her, "is the only thing holding me together since he arrived. Come on, let's cook."

I tell Elly to go set the table up and that I'll finish cooking. I'm not sure how good it will taste, but how hard is it to cook meat sauce and boil spaghetti? Once the timer goes off, I drain the pasta and transfer it to a plate. I'm looking for the olive oil when I sense him behind me. I freeze on the spot the moment we come into contact.

"Where's Lawrence?"

I shiver, feeling his large body pressed behind me. I swallow and shake my head, the fear of being alone with him, of being caught by someone walking into the kitchen, and of wanting him so much makes me dizzy. I place both of my hands on the countertop for support.

"I—we're not together anymore," I breathe.

Slowly, he places both of his hands on top of mine, caging me between his arms. "Did he get bored of you?" he drawls.

"No ..." I know I should turn around and walk away from Ronan, breaking his spell on me, but it's impossible. He owns me even after all this time. "It's not like that. I just couldn't do it anymore. I l—"

"Quiet." He pushes me against the countertop, the edge digging into my stomach. "I can't think when I'm around you," he hisses.

"There's so much that I have to explain ..."

207

"What do you want from me?" he whispers harshly in my ear. "Why is it every time I think I'm moving on and things seem to be going well, you come back into my life and fuck with everything? Reminding me of what I can't have?"

Cursing, he presses his lips on my jaw and begins to trace a path down my throat and up my neck, raising goose bumps all over my body. Fear mingles with excitement. Yearning with reality. Want with need.

He thrusts his fingers past the waistline of my jeans and underwear, finding me. "But I don't give a fuck anymore." He begins an assault on all my senses with his touch, making me moan with pleasure. "Always so responsive. Did you react to him like this, huh?"

It's the emotionless way that he speaks to me and how cold his voice sounds that breaks the hypnotic hold that he has over me. It's as though he's here physically, touching me, making me his, punishing me while his heart remains untouched. I push myself away from the counter and spin on my feet until we're staring at each other.

"What's wrong with you?" I wrap my arms around me to stop myself from shaking, feeling so dirty. "What's fucking wrong with me?"

He chuckles amusingly.

"You were never this cruel, Ronan," I cry.

The laughter leaves his face and it's replaced by a quiet fury that burns in his eyes. He leans down until our mouths almost touch and our breaths fuse as one. "You. You are what is wrong with me," He lifts a hand about to touch me, but pulls it back, clenching it into a fist. "I want to know how to live without you," he utters angrily, his brown gaze stormy. "But I don't fucking know how."

I take a step forward about to reach for him. "Ronan ..."

"I thought that I saw him walk in here ..." Elly says as loud as possible, alerting us to their approach.

Ronan and I both put as much space between us as we see Rachel and Elly enter the kitchen. Unable to look at them, I excuse myself and leave the room in a hurry, without taking another glance.

Ronan

"It's a beautiful night."

I glance back to find Rachel reclined against the doorframe, looking perfect in a cream cashmere turtleneck and trousers of the same color. I command my fucking heart to beat, to feel something, anything at the sight of her beautiful face, but it does nothing. It remains as calm as it always has been.

"Yeah." I put out my cigarette and lean on the wooden handrail. "Come here, beautiful."

"The house is so quiet." Rachel steps onto the porch and walks straight into my arms, hugging my torso. "It seems we're the only two people who didn't go to the bar after dinner."

I run a hand over her back, feeling her slight tremble under my touch. "Did you want to go? We can probably still catch up with them."

Rachel shakes her head, rubbing her cheek on my chest. "You smell so good."

I kiss the top of her head and will myself to stop thinking about Blaire. *Damn it to hell. Rachel deserves better than this.*

After a pause Rachel says quietly, "We had fun, didn't we?" I wrap her in my arms and tighten my hold on her, understanding what she means.

"I thought that you had moved on, but you haven't. I don't love you, Ronan, but I *am* falling for you. And for that reason, I'm walking away." She places a soft kiss on my neck. "I can't do this again. Not so soon after my divorce."

"I'm sorry, Rachel."

"Don't apologize," her voice cracks, "because if you do, it will mean that what we shared was a mistake, and it wasn't. It was beautiful." She lets me go, straightens, and pats my chest. "Just as you are."

My hands go to her hips, gripping her soft curves. "I wish that I could—"

"Love me?" She smiles a small, rueful smile that doesn't reach her eyes. "No, my beautiful, blind man ... you couldn't have. Not when you never stopped belonging to her."

I clench my jaw, hating myself because it's true. As much as I try to deny my own heart, it's no use. Blaire owns me. I thought that I had a choice to forget her, to live without her, but I was just fooling myself. To do so would be like asking the sun to stop rising at dawn. Impossible. Yet the consuming need to hurt her as much as she hurt me runs rampant within me, obliterating any tenderness for her left in my heart. The thirst to tear her apart with my fingers and feast on her blood is the fuel that has kept me going all this time. Because if I'm being honest with myself, she's the reason why I accepted Rachel and Carl's help. Why I gave up my foolish dreams of someday making it on my own and took the easy way out. She's the reason behind every choice that I've made to bring me to this point.

"Ronan ... if you love her, and it's obvious that you do, why don't you go after her?"

I look away from her blue eyes that seem able to get past every barrier that I have erected. "I can't."

How can I explain to her that my hunger for revenge outweighs my useless love for a woman who never wanted it? But it doesn't matter. Life has finally smiled my way by placing Blaire in my path, and I will make her pay.

She urges me to look at her again. "There's the stubborn streak that I love so much. But be careful or it will be your downfall."

"I don't deserve you, Rachel. I've done you wrong."

"No, don't say that, Ronan. I'm a big girl, and I knew what I was getting myself into from the beginning. Am I hurt?" She shrugs. "Maybe a little. But you're worth it. So worth it. And I'll recover. I know that now." She touches her chest.

"You know, when I met you, I felt like there was ice inside me, but it's gone. It isn't there anymore. You've reminded me of what it feels like to make love, to laugh, to feel beautiful and desirable. Thanks to you, I feel like myself again."

I lean down and kiss her for what will never be.

When we pull apart, she strokes my shoulder and smiles too brightly, her gaze glistening with unshed tears. "I better go. I sent for a driver a couple of hours ago and he just got here." Rachel heads toward the door and stops when she's almost reached it. She turns her head and looks me in the eye. "Life is too fleeting, Ronan. Make sure you don't waste any more of it."

chapter twenty-four.

Blaire

TONIGHT AS I SAT IN A booth surrounded by people, watching them laughing, drinking—having a good time—I couldn't bring myself to join in the fun, to pretend that everything was all right. Emotionally and physically tired, I decided to come back to the house.

Locking the door behind me, I place Alessandro's car keys in the dish on the wooden table by the entrance and go to my bedroom. Elly wanted to come with me but I told her to stay behind and hang out with her friends. She was probably worried that I would run into Ronan and Rachel.

I push the thought of them together in bed out of my mind as quickly as it comes. *Definitely not going there.* Once I'm inside my room, I recline my back against the door and close my eyes, losing myself in the silence and its accompanying calm.

"You win."

I open my eyes swiftly and look in the direction of his voice. As my sight grows accustomed to the dark, I recognize Ronan's form sitting in the accent chair by the window, the moonlight illuminating his face. Unable to speak, I watch as he rises and strolls toward me.

"Let's hear what you have to say."

I remain silent, incapable of uttering a coherent thought.

"What happened?" he asks, sarcasm dripping from his words. "You were so eager to explain things earlier. Well, now's your chance."

"No ..." I protest weakly. I clear my voice and summon all the strength that I possess to deny him and do the right thing. "There's no point now. Go back to Rachel."

"Rachel's gone—it's over between us. It's just you and me. Are you happy now?"

When he's standing an inch away from me, it takes every ounce of willpower I own not to fall down to his feet asking him to forgive me. "I'm not happy, Ronan. How could I be after everything that I've done?"

"I see." He chuckles, running a hand through his hair. "So this is your act now? Save it for another unsuspecting bastard, Blaire. You don't need to put on a show for me. I've already told you that you won. I'm here, yeah?"

My heart is ready to burst with combating emotions—hope, fear, sorrow, and love blend as one. But the loudest is my love for the man who I tried unsuccessfully to forget. And it's that fierce love that propels me to move forward and reach for him. Gone is the fear that someday he will hurt me or leave me. Gone are the thoughts that our love won't be enough. All that matters is to finally hold him in my arms without anyone else between us.

"It's not an act, Ronan."

"I told you to save it." He raises a staying hand. "I see the way that you look at me … I'm here to fuck you and get it over with."

"You don't mean that." I dare to get a little closer to him. Lifting a hand, I watch him suck in a deep breath as I caress the crests of his cheeks with the back of my hand, I allow myself to feel an emotion that I haven't in a long time.

And it's wonderful.

And it's madness.

It's the sweetest hope, and it unfurls with each beat of my heart spreading like a wildfire throughout me. "Why are you really here, Ronan?"

His gaze penetrates mine, and I get lost in a sea of amber. "Why am I here?" he repeats forcefully. "Because I can't fucking pretend when I'm around you. How can I when you're embedded in me—in my damn soul. I'm here because I can't help it. I need you even when you tear me apart." Even in the darkness, his eyes burn me to ashes while his words give me life.

Ronan cups my face with both of his hands, holding me his slave, his touch in turns unforgiving and possessive. "I told myself that I should walk away, that I should forget you, that you're not worth it."

"And did it work?" I ask softly.

"No. I'm here, after all. Wanting you more than ever and it's fucking killing me." He tightens his grip. "I hate you for making me love you, and I hate myself because I can't stop."

Our eyes remain locked as I remove his hands gently from my face and begin to shower them with slow, revering kisses. *Please forgive me.* Kiss. *It's always been you.* Kiss. *Can you feel it?* Kiss. *Come back to me. Come back to me.*

Come back to me.

Defeated, Ronan groans and pulls me in a tight embrace, and it feels like I've finally come home. Our time apart melts into a meaningless nothing.

"Tell me that you want me to go," he pleads, his voice hoarse with emotion.

"I can't." I pull him closer to me. "Not that."

"Why not?" The words are torn from his chest.

"Because I can't lie to you." I raise my eyes to look at him, offering myself to him. "You cruel man, I don't want you to leave me."

"Then I'll stay."

"Undress."

He stands by the foot of the bed as I take off my clothes, watching me remove every layer that covers my body. Hesitant and nervous, I feel like we're back in my bedroom about to make love for the first time on that never-forgotten lovely summer evening. By the time I'm completely naked, he undresses as well and comes to stand in front of me.

"Lie on the bed."

His voice suddenly so devoid of emotion sends a chill running down my spine, but I ignore it. My desire to make him understand that I am his and only his blinds me to everything, even the odd light flashing in his gaze.

When I'm lying on the bed, he moves to stand between my legs, grabs me by the hips, dragging me forward so my feet touch the floor, and spreads my thighs apart. It's crude and detached. Part of me knows that he's punishing me for what I've done to him, so I let him and hope that this is what he must do before he can forgive me. Without preparing me for his invasion, Ronan pushes forward until he's deep inside me. I cry out in pain while losing my mind in the sweetest agony of feeling him inside me after so long, of being this close once again. Breathing heavily, he stops all movement as a tremor runs down his entire body. The anger edged on his face should scare me, but all that matters, all I care is giving myself to Ronan.

His chest rises and falls in a labored rhythm while his arms tremble as he holds himself above me. "Blaire, I—" his voice breaks.

"Shh …" I reach for him, enveloping him in my arms, and pull him toward me until our bodies become one, willing my love for him to show him the way back to me.

"I love you, Ronan."

He tries to pull away from me then, but I don't let him. "Don't," he murmurs harshly. "Don't say that."

We struggle but I continue to hold onto him as though my whole life depends on this moment, feeling every muscle in his body shake like a rolling earthquake under my hands. "I love you," I repeat. I caress his skin, showering him with kisses as I try to make him understand with my touch what he won't accept with my words. "I love you. I love you. I love you."

The fight gone out of him, Ronan finally gives into me. And when he does, it is a storm full of thunder and wind and rain. It shakes. It vibrates. It rumbles deep within us. Howling …

Breaking …

Healing …

Tearing us both apart so our kisses, our shared breaths, the feel of him moving deep inside me, and his heart beating against mine can put us back together for every month, and every week, and every day, and every hour, and every minute, and every second that we weren't together. It's the holy communion of our bodies.

"Please forgive me, Ronan." I pull him closer to me, tightening my legs around his waist, trying to swallow him into my body, fuse his soul with mine, but it's not close enough. It will never be. He begins to pound into me.

Hard …

Painful …

Agonizing …

He's not making love to me. He's trying to possess me, to brand himself in me with each thrust. And through it all, I tell him how much I love him, hoping that I can break each and every single barrier between us. Lawrence. Rachel. All the unnecessary hurt.

Jealousy …

Anger …

Betrayal …

Lies …

Deceit …

It all fades to nothing.

Throwing his head back, Ronan pulls out of me, coming on my stomach as a shout is torn from deep within him. After cleaning myself in the bathroom, I come back to bed and find him lying flat on his stomach, his hair messy and eyes closed. I go to him, my heart swelling with happiness and love. Without saying a word, he pulls me in, enveloping me in a fierce embrace, and we fall asleep. As I'm closing my eyes, drifting away, I finally understand what true happiness is.

This moment.

In his arms.

I wake up feeling exuberant and ridiculously happy. The delicious soreness between my legs reminds me of all the times Ronan took me last night with an incessant passion and need that burned so brightly I'm surprised the place didn't crumble down to ashes. With a smile on my lips I reach for him, but my hands come back empty. I open my eyes and discover that he isn't in bed anymore. Sitting up, I find him sitting in the same accent chair watching me closely. He's already showered and dressed in a red plaid shirt and jeans. The moment my gaze lands on him, my heart jumpstarts again.

I cover myself with a sheet, suddenly feeling shy. "Good morning."

Silently, Ronan stands up and comes to stand at the foot of the bed, his handsome face inscrutable. Hard. The expressionless way he's staring at me as though I'm an unwanted vision sends a chill running down my spine, but I tell myself that it's just my overly tired imagination. This is the same man who made me his over and over again all through the night while he held me tight and never let go.

He takes out his wallet from the back pocket of his jeans, opens it, and pulls out some bills. Frowning, I'm about to ask him what that money is for when he throws it carelessly on the bed. My heart sinks as the green paper slowly floats like feathers onto the mattress.

"What's this?" I manage to ask.

"Isn't this how it usually goes?" He puts his wallet away while his gaze roves over me dispassionately. "I'm paying for your services. I seem to remember that you once told me that I couldn't afford you. Well, now I can."

No. No. No. No.

Gripping the sheet close to my chest as if it were a lifeline, I tell myself that I'm dreaming and I'll soon wake up to find that this has been a horrible nightmare. But as I stare at the man in front of me, feeling my barely healed heart shatter all over again, I realize that last night was a beautiful dream and this is my cruel reality.

"It can't be ..." I bring my hands to my temples, feeling lightheaded. "I don't think I heard you right."

"But you did, Blaire. I hope you're not naïve enough to think that what happened last night had anything to do with love," he says with a detached calm. "I would be a fool to fall for you again. And if I may say so, your act is getting to be quite desperate. You don't have to pretend to love me to get me to fuck you. It's obvious that I want you. And that you want me now because I'm no longer a nobody, my ambitious and greedy Blaire."

I'm unraveling into nothingness. I fell in love with Ronan the same way that you watch fireworks light up the sky. It was unexpected and breathtaking. My eternal midnight was suddenly full of glittering sparks that together rivaled the brightest of stars. He filled it with his powerful light, illuminating my world in beautiful colors. And last night, the sky didn't just glow—it burned like the most brilliant sun. But as his words slice me open and deeply, the light goes out, leaving me in total, blinding darkness once again.

"I think you should go," I say numbly.

When he's by the door, his back to me, I hear myself say, "Wait."

He looks back, raising an eyebrow, appearing bored. "Yes?"

"I wish with all of my heart that I could stop loving you."

Suddenly, a long forgotten memory of another good-bye similar to this, with another man, and a much younger girl flashes through the eyes of my mind. Matthew Callahan's voice telling me that one day I would fall in love with a man, and he hoped he would break my heart. Then I would know what kind of pain I was able to inflict.

"If that is all ..." he drawls.

I turn to the side and close my eyes, waiting for him to leave. The moment I hear the click of the door, I bite down hard on my lip to stop a sob from escaping, as burning tears streak down my face.

chapter twenty-five.

Ronan

I DECIDED LONG AGO that I would rise in a world that had no place for the likes of me and conquer it with my hands, watching them lose their poor, pathetic minds over a nobody like me—their diamond in the rough. I sold my soul and surrounded myself with people who once spurned me just so I could forget Blaire.

Last night when I took her in my arms and sunk in the wonderful abyss of her body, I felt my resolution waver for the first time in a very long time. I thought that maybe we could start all over again, leaving all the bullshit behind, allowing my love—my madness—for her to be the bread to sustain us and give us life. But even as my heart urged me to give into her siren song, a voice so loud, so jarring, told me not to be a fool and fall for her lies again.

She was with me because Lawrence didn't want her in his life. She wanted me now because I had something to give her that I didn't before. That same voice told me I'd come too far to just throw it all away for a brief yet alluring dream that was just that—a dream. So as I stared at Blaire, my emotions at war, I woke up and came to my senses. I stop packing my bag momentarily to look out the window as an image of Blaire flashes through my mind. The raw pain in her eyes as I threw the money at her. Clenching my jaw, I tell myself that it was only an act, just like her false admission of love. A new wave of hate and repulsion washes over me, clearing my mind. Once upon a time, I would have given anything to hear her say those words, but they mean nothing to me now. They are empty. Useless. She doesn't love me. She loves no one but herself. Shortly after I'm done packing, there's a knock on the door. Opening it, I find Elly waiting for me on the other side.

"I hope you're happy with yourself," she says.

I cock an eyebrow. "What do you mean?"

"She's gone." Elly shakes her head, placing her hands on her hips.

"Ran back to Lawrence, didn't she?" I sneer, willing myself to not feel one fucking thing. "Well, that didn't take her long."

"You're such an asshole." Elly takes a step forward, closing the gap between us, unafraid of me. "She broke things off with Lawrence."

"Did she now?"

"Yes, she's not going back to him."

"I highly doubt it happened that way. Lawrence probably got bored of her and dumped her." I turn on my heel to walk toward my suitcase lying on the bed. "But I don't give a fuck anymore. She can do whatever she wants."

"My God, you're blind. And I'm so stupid ... I thought that maybe—"

I glance back, our eyes locking. "What? That we would make up and live happily ever after? Please, Elly, don't be so fucking naïve. That ship sailed a long, long time ago."

"You know what? Maybe it's better this way. You're not the man she fell in love with—you can't be. I barely know you, but I'm sure that she doesn't need you in her life."

I throw my head back and laugh, though the sound is empty just like everything inside me. Hollow without her. "No, that man is gone. She never loved me, Elly."

"But she did!"

"Oh, yeah? Then why did she run? Why did she break my fucking heart when all I wanted was to love her, to be with her? I didn't want for much. All I wanted was Blaire. You know why she's back? She's back because I'm no longer a poor nobody."

"Wait, no," she interrupts, stunned. "You got it all wrong. All wrong, Ronan. Didn't she tell you? Damn it, Blaire. Why didn't you—" Elly says outwardly talking to herself. Focusing on me once more, she closes the space between us in a hurry, placing an entreating hand on my arm. "You got it all wrong, Ronan. So wrong."

Pushing her hand away, I turn away from her and the deceiving light in her eye. "Save it, Elly. We're done. I think you should go. Or better yet, I'm out."

She reaches for me once again, making me look at her. "*No*. You're going to listen to what I have to say once and for all. I'm done watching both of you waste your time and hurt each other for nothing. Blaire left you the first time because she didn't think that she was good enough for you."

"Please. She broke up with me because I didn't have any money. She chose Lawrence over me because of his deep pockets. She's a fucking gold digger," I spit the words like venom.

"*No*. She fell in love with you, Ronan. Head over heels in love. You were the first man to make her want it all. Everything. Love. A relationship. Forever. During that summer, Blaire glowed. She was happy for the first time in her life. I didn't know your name, but I knew it was because of you."

I shake my head, sitting down on the bed as her words fight to get past the wall inside me. "That can't be." I raise my gaze to meet hers. "You're lying to me."

"No, I'm not. And you know it. Deep down you must know it's true. But what did you expect from a girl who all her life thought she was unworthy of love, who was uncomfortable with a simple hug? It was too much for her, Ronan. Listen, I'm not excusing her behavior. She should've spoken to you. But she did the only thing that she knew. She ran. She lied to you because she knew that if she made you hate her, she could walk away from you. Otherwise, she wouldn't have been able to leave you."

My heart begins to pump hard. Images of our short summer together, the masquerade, and of last night— especially last night—come crashing down on me. They were real.

Real.

"It wasn't a lie then," I mutter hoarsely, shaken to the core. "Last night when she ..." Closing my eyes tightly, I feel sick to my stomach. "What have I done?"

She wasn't only offering her body to me. She was offering her love to me. And I knew it. I'd felt it. But I let my thirst for vengeance get in the way.

"You've let your pride get in the way, Ronan. Besides, I saw you with Rachel and I've read the articles about your career. You're the last person who should judge her."

Defeated, I open my eyes and focus on Elly. "I've been a fucking fool."

"Both of you have. But listen to what I'm saying. She loves you. It's always been you. So why the fuck are you still here? *Go after her.*"

I was brought into this world but I never understood why. Why me and not someone else? Why was I here when there was nothing special about me? I was just another guy trying to get by. But as Elly's words smash the walls around me, leaving me naked—defenseless—giving me a new hope that pulsates with every beating of my undeserving heart, I realize why.

Getting up, I go to the door. When I'm about to cross the threshold, I hear Elly ask, "Changed your mind?"

I glance back, smiling ruefully. "I pity your enemies, Elly. You're a formidable adversary. Now if you'll excuse me, I must go after my woman."

She grins. "Took you long enough."

chapter twenty-six.

Blaire

AFTER ARRIVING AT PENN STATION from Vermont, I take a cab and head back to my apartment. I lean my head back on the seat and close my eyes, allowing the familiar noises of the city to lull me into relaxation. In a moment of weakness, I think of last night and this morning, but I bury the thought as fast as it appears. I'm not ready to go there yet, because if I do, I might not be able to take another step without falling apart.

Once I'm out of out of the cab and inside my apartment, I drop my bags in my room and go to the kitchen in search of food. As soon as my eyes land on the green bottle of champagne, Lawrence's seductive smile flashes through my mind. Shit. Even my home is haunted by memories of them. But what did I expect? Unable to remain here for another moment, I shut the door as quickly as possible, get my stuff, and head out.

It's dark by the time I reach the Bethesda Fountain, the moon and the stars hidden behind fast moving clouds that glow silver in the night. The air is electric like right before a storm. I sit in the same spot where I met Ronan, so many

227

memories and lives ago. I enjoy the cold weather. It helps to clear my head. I'm not really sure why I came here other than to torture myself some more, but here I am.

As I look around the empty park, absorbing the way the street lamps bathe my surroundings in amber light, the first drop of rain lands on my skin, followed by more. Each lands simultaneously on different parts of my body. Closing my eyes, I place my hands behind me. I lean back on my palms and lift my face to the sky as I welcome the sensation of the droplets kissing my skin. I should go home, or seek shelter under the terrace, but I remain seated. Maybe a part of me wishes that the rain could wash away all my sins along with the dirt covering the stones of the fountain, purifying me. Or maybe I stay put because it was in this place where my life began and ended, and it is here where I should say good-bye and bury my short-lived dreams of a life with Ronan.

All of a sudden the sky opens up and it begins to rain heavily. Lightning illuminates the dark sky momentarily in a white light before the sound of thunder rumbles nearby. Wet to the bone and freezing, I'm about to move when the outline of a man appears to my right. As he approaches me, closing the space between us, I recognize him immediately. I would know him anywhere. Fire burns in my chest as I get up and begin to walk away from him as fast as my feet will allow.

"Blaire! Wait!" he shouts.

My treacherous heart urges me to stop at the sound of his voice. But I won't listen to it. Not right now. I pick up the pace, beginning to run blindly. It doesn't matter where I go as long as it's far away from him. My feet slip on the wet ground as my vision blurs. The pain is much too strong. I'm being consumed by it.

Taking me by surprise, Ronan grips my arm and turns me to face him, slamming my body against his. Thunder and lightning continue to strike over and over again, illuminating his features. The wind has picked up speed, too. We both breathe heavily as desperation courses through our veins. But it's his eyes that hold me hostage.

"Let go of me, you bastard!" I yell, hitting him on his chest as tears fall down my face. "Haven't you had enough?"

"No."

Ronan wraps me in his arms as he closes the space between our mouths. I turn my face to the side, looking away from him and the hurt embedded in his features, hurt that is a direct reflection of mine.

"Don't be scared of my touch," he begs urgently near my ear. "Don't take this from me. Kiss me, Blaire. *Kiss me.*"

I shake my head, continuing to push him away. "No, Ronan. I can't. It hurts."

"I know, baby. It hurts too fucking much." He lets go of me and cups my face, making me look at him through the rain. "Let me take the pain away," he whispers hoarsely.

"Please." He leans over and silences me with his mouth. Defeated, I give in. To him, to the feel of his arms around me again, to his persuasive tongue, and to his eyes full of tenderness.

Kisses that clear my mind of everything but him.
He crawls deep inside my skin.
He's the fire on my tongue.
Is it heaven or is it hell?

I think it must be both.

Because he's here with me.

Wrapped in his arms, I open my eyes slowly and focus on his glorious face once more.

"Blaire, Blaire." He tightens his grip. "I know I've fucked up. I was angry and drowning in hate and jealousy. Wanting you and not being able to have you drove me mad. I've done many things that I'm not proud of, but loving you is not one of them. I love you. So damn much. And there hasn't been a day when I haven't." I clutch his arms as a sob escapes my mouth.

"You're my reason to exist, Blaire. I am nothing without you. Say that you love me again," Ronan pleads. "I need to hear you say it."

I love you.

Just a few short syllables. Three simple words that separately mean nothing, but together mean hope, life, beauty—everything that is worth living for. Words are easily said and easily forgotten. They can make you whole, breathe life into you.

They can destroy you.

"You stupid, stupid man," I say shakily. After so long, we've finally found each other. "I was afraid to love you because I knew that it would destroy me, but living without you is like dying a slow death each day that I wake up and you aren't with me."

"I know. I felt it, too. Every day and every second without you. But I'm here now and I'm not going anywhere."

There's so much that has happened between us. Maybe we'll be able to let it go and put it behind us, maybe we won't. But right now he's here with me. And that's all that matters.

"Take me somewhere, Ronan. Make it all go away."

We ride a cab to a hotel in silence. We don't touch each other. There's no need. The connection between us has never been stronger. It's electrifying. If I closed my eyes, I would know that he was sitting next to me. I would feel him everywhere he went. He could change his appearance, change his name, become someone else, and my soul would continue to recognize him. My Ronan.

He reaches for my hand, intertwining our fingers. "Are you okay?"

I lick my lips. "Yes."

There are no nerves. No fear. No what ifs. For the first time since I can remember, it feels right. It feels like I am right where I belong—next to him.

In an unspoken agreement, we go to a hotel where there aren't any memories of others. It's a place where we can start anew. I laugh when he checks us in as newlyweds. Mr. and Mrs. Klein. Hidden meanings behind our stolen glances. *I want you. Make me yours. You're mine. Always.* Euphoria vibrates through every pore of my body. My senses hum, coming alive whenever we touch accidentally. Oh, sweet anticipation.

We stand inside the small, dark room. Our shared and labored breaths are the only sound that you can hear. He takes a step toward me. I take a step toward him. We come together. Ronan and I undress each other slowly, taking our time, discarding the wet clothes on the floor until there's no barrier between us. Skin against skin, his hands on my waist draw me closer to him. But it's not close enough. It will never be.

Our hands caress and relearn, their touch tender and forgiving—healing. My fingers slide over his skin, his nipples pebbling under my touch. Slowly, Ronan dips his head and kisses me. It's tender at first, then angry, then tender again. We kiss and kiss and kiss until our lips are sore and we're left breathless.

Ronan whispers my name over and over again like a litany, bringing us closer together, marking me as his own. *Blaire, Blaire, Blaire, Blaire, Blaire, Blaire ...* He calls for me, and every part of me surrenders to him. And together, we fly so high.

Ronan grips my shoulders and turns us both around to face a full-length mirror hanging on the wall. In the reflection of the glass, there's a man whose beauty makes me want to weep for its perfection. His skin is light caramel. His body is made for worshipping.

"We belong together," he says, his voice husky with passion. "You hear me?"

I watch him snake a hand down my body while he dips his head and kisses the curve of my neck before biting it. Our gazes meet in the mirror as his fingers cup my tits, rubbing and tugging my nipples. I gasp and recline my head back on his shoulder, seeing him fight for control as he continues his indecent exploration of my body. Reaching behind me, I wrap a hand on his erection. I curl my fingers around his hard cock and begin to stroke him, feeling the hot heat of his hardness slide through my palm.

I grip him harder making him moan. "Take me."

Losing the little control that he has left, Ronan pushes me forward until my front is touching the glass. I stare at his reflection in the mirror as he grips my hand holding his dick and makes us both rub the head against my pussy, spreading its folds, and rubbing my clit.

"No more," I beg, guiding him toward my entrance. "I need you inside me."

Ronan places a hand on the small of my back, urging me to bend at the waist. I let go of his cock and place my hands in front of me for support. I'm a slave at his feet. Blood rushes to my head. My pussy is dripping wet with want as he nudges my thighs to open wider for him. "Fuck," he curses long and slow, impaling me with one deep, fierce thrust.

And it's paradise.

He slowly pulls back, and when he's almost all the way out, he thrusts forward again and again and again. Each thrust is more aggressive than the last, more demanding.

"I want to hear you say those words," he orders harshly, pounding harder, faster. "Say it, Blaire."

I lift my ass higher to give him better access. "I love you."

"Say it again."

"I love you," I moan.

He fucks me incessantly, dominating me with his body, with his hands, with everything that he is. And I give him every piece of me, surrendering my soul and myself to him. "Again." His voice shakes.

"I love you," I repeat, watching as tears begin to roll down his chiseled cheeks.

"Again."

"I love you, Ronan."

"You're mine, do you hear?" He grips my hips forcefully, pumping in and out of me, bringing me closer to the edge. "Give me a thousand lives and a thousand eternities, and I would still find you and make you mine. Always."

"Ronan … I …" I close my eyes and come undone. Ronan groans, finding his own release, as I feel a warm rush spreading deep inside me, filling me completely.

I wake up sometime in the middle of the night. Fear grips my chest when I discover that Ronan isn't lying next to me. As my sight grows accustomed to the dark, I find his naked form sitting on a chair and looking out the window. Apprehension runs through my veins, making me doubt my next step. But a small voice inside me urges me to go to him.

Looking around for something to wrap myself in, I locate his discarded shirt on the floor and put it on. He glances back and sees me. He reaches for my hand and pulls me into his lap so I'm sitting astride his legs. Ronan then grasps my thighs under the shirt and tugs me forward, bridging the space between us. In this position, I can feel his thick cock spreading the lips of my pussy apart, warmth gathering at my core.

A hot blush coats my cheeks as I lower my gaze and begin to trace the outlines of the tattoos adorning his carved torso. *How devastatingly beautiful you are.* Ronan places a hand behind my neck and gently pulls me toward him. Closing my eyes, I rest my cheek on his chest as he runs his fingers through my hair. The beating of his heart soothes me. His touch hypnotizes me.

"What made you go to Central Park?"

"I went to your apartment first, but you weren't there. I didn't know what to do or where you were, so I ended up going there."

"Why?"

"I guess it's because it reminds me of you."

Happiness swells within me, making me float. More minutes pass in comfortable silence.

"I need to know, Blaire," he says hoarsely, fear embedded in his words.

I tilt my head back and stare into his warm brown eyes that show me his soul. "What is it?"

"I saw the two of you at the masquerade ..."

"Oh." I bite my lip.

"Do you," he pauses, "do you love him?" The question is torn from him. I can almost taste the blood it draws from him on my tongue.

I think of everything that we've been through to finally get to this moment; all the heartache, the lies, and the deceit. I wish that I could explain to Ronan that I don't love Lawrence the way that I love him. That a small part of me, the one who loves another man, will always mourn for him. But I'm finally with Ronan to whom I belong body and soul. I remain silent, unable to lie to him.

Sometimes what is not said is answer enough.

"I see …" A cloud of sadness crosses his eyes before closing them.

"Did you love her?"

He looks at me again. "I don't think so. I liked her a lot, Blaire. I liked being with her, we had fun together, and the sex took my mind off of you. She helped me when the dark was so fucking dark I couldn't see …"

His response is like a dagger to my heart, but it would be naïve to think that we're the same two people who fell in love during an idyllic summer. We've both lived many lives since then, lives that have changed us. But at the core, I hope that our love for one another remains just as strong as it was before. That it can glue us back together.

"You feel this?" I place my hands on his shoulders as I begin to rub myself against him. "It's yours. Only yours." I kiss his jaw, each corner of his lips, his mouth. "I wish I could tell you what you want to hear, but I can't." Groaning, Ronan holds me by the waist as I undulate my hips over his growing erection. It swells and throbs for me. "All we can do is move on. Together."

I cup his cheek as Ronan grabs his cock in his hand, pulling me forward with the other, and enters me in one swift, deep thrust. Moaning, I close my eyes momentarily at the feel of him moving inside me. So hard. So thick. "I know that too much has happened and it has changed us, but together we will get through it. I *know* it."

Ronan thrusts upwards. "Are you thinking about him now?"

"No, baby." I caress the crest of his cheek. "I'm not."

We fuck then. It's angry and fast. Bruising. It is as though he's trying to fuck Lawrence's memory out of me, out of the room, out of my heart until it's only him I feel inside, around me, everywhere. He brands himself on me, in me, claiming me as his once again.

And I let him. I give him everything that he wants.

When we're finished, he picks me up and carries me back to bed. His arms, strong like corded steel, come around me from behind, pulling me closer to him. We lie down in silence as our breathing slows down.

"I talked to Elly."

I stroke the skin of his arm, smiling. "So that's why you came after me, huh? And here I thought it was because you couldn't live without me," I tease.

"I can't live without you, Blaire," he states before nuzzling my neck. "But tell me why?"

"Why did I leave?" I sigh while I tell myself that he has every right to know, and the only way that we will have a chance at making it is to finally be honest with him. "I hope you're not sleepy because it's a *long* story."

"I'm not going anywhere." He reaches for my hand, squeezing it. It's such a small gesture, but it makes me feel like I'm not alone.

"Where should I start? There's so much to tell."

"Start at the beginning, babe."

And I do. I tell him everything about my childhood, my life in New York City and all the men that came before him, why I left him, and what happened after that with Lawrence and my parents. There are no more barriers and walls left around us.

After I pour my heart out for what seems like hours, I'm embarrassed to even look at him. There's no scarier feeling than opening yourself to someone, exposing every ugly and flawed piece of you, and hoping that they will love you, despite it all.

"You know, all my life I thought that it was my fault that my parents fought. That if I behaved like the perfect child, they would stay together, love each other and me. But I know now that it had nothing to do with me or with the love that they felt for me. The realization is …" I swallow, trying to soothe the ache in my chest. "Freeing."

Letting me go, Ronan grabs me by my shoulder and turns me to face him. "Hey, hey," he says gently. "Don't hide from me, baby. Come here." He embraces me in a hug so tight it's hard to breathe. "Listen to me, Blaire … every sharp corner, every single scar that you have is mine to love. And I will help you heal because I'm a selfish bastard and I need you in my life to be complete."

"I don't deserve you." My heart swells. I shake my head. "I'm not worthy of you."

"Here, babe." Placing a hand under my chin, he tips it up and makes me look at him. "We both made mistakes. I just wish I had fought harder for you. I shouldn't have let you walk away from me so easily."

"But I said all those things …"

"They wouldn't have mattered." He moves to lie on his back, bringing me with him. Ronan stares at the ceiling as he caresses my naked back with his fingers. If I were a cat, I would purr. "You know … in a way, I'm glad that I met Rachel and Carl. Because without them, I wouldn't understand how easy it is to get carried away into a world where every luxury, every whim, and desire is within reach. I wouldn't understand how easy it is to be seduced by their lifestyle."

He sighs. "I liked it, Blaire. I loved the adoration I saw in their eyes, people wanting to know me, how easy it all seemed. So now you see I'm not perfect. Far fucking from it, actually."

"But you *are* talented, Ronan. I've seen some of your photographs and I read the article. The reporter seemed very impressed."

He smiles ruefully. "Am I? I guess we'll find out soon. My first exhibit is next week."

I kiss his chest. "It's going to be a smashing hit."

"Blaire?"

"Yes?"

He's quiet for a moment. "If you could have one wish, what would it be?"

I caress the left side of his face, staring at him. *You.* "I'm good. What about you?"

He tucks a strand of hair behind my ear and dips his head to kiss the top of my head. "I would steal you, take you somewhere where no one knows us and start all over again."

"Could I open a bookstore?" I ask, making him laugh.

"Yes, babe. You could do whatever you wanted." Smiling crookedly, he adds, "As long as I got to do whatever I wanted to you at night."

"Steal me away then." I grin against his skin, thinking how easy it is to dream. "But go on. I like this."

"There wouldn't be a Lawrence—"

"Or Rachel," I add.

"Or Rachel," he repeats, chuckling.

"And what would our names be?"

He raises an eyebrow, answering drolly. But he can't hide the amusement sparkling in his lovely eyes. "I'm surprised at you, Mrs. Klein."

I giggle as I move away from him, kneeling on the bed with his body between my legs. Lifting my left hand, I say, "I don't see a ring, do you?"

Ronan reaches for the notepad with the logo of the hotel lying on the nightstand. After he rips a page off, he rolls it into a long, thin line. Taking my hand in his, he ties the piece of paper around my ring finger as though it is the real thing.

"There," he says smugly. "What were you saying now, Mrs. Klein?"

I close my hand with the paper ring, making a tight fist, and press it against my chest. Ronan's boyishly handsome features blur as I try to speak, but the words get stuck in my throat. A river of emotions rushes through me, dragging me down, making it impossible to breathe.

Sitting up, Ronan reaches for my hand and kisses it tenderly. "Let's run away together, Blaire. Let's leave it all behind us. It will be just you and me, babe. Starting all over again with nothing coming between us." He grins. "And maybe down the road, you can make an honest man out of me and marry my sorry ass."

My lips tremble. "Ronan ..."

"Why does it have to be a wish or a dream?" he whispers huskily, burying his hands in my hair, his long fingers cradling the back of my head. "Why can't it be a reality?"

I place my hands on top of his. Dispassionately, I notice that they are trembling too. "You don't mean it—"

"I do. I want to spend the rest of my life with you, Blaire. I want to watch your belly swell with my babies inside you. I want to wake up every morning and fall asleep each night with you next to me. I once told you that one day you were going to let me love you and I was never going to let you go, that I would love you as if it were the only thing I was meant to do. Nothing has changed." He kisses my nose before resting his forehead against mine. "One lifetime wouldn't be enough when I'm with you."

"Is this really happening?"

Cupping my face, Ronan wipes the tears rolling down my cheeks. "It has to, babe," he murmurs so softly, so tenderly, it makes my heart ache with love. "Tomorrow morning we go to JFK and our new life. Making love, living, laughing. We won't have much at first, but I'll find work with my camera and provide for you."

The picture he paints is so lovely, so perfect, I can almost see us living it. He would leave in the morning after making slow love to me. I would dress, run my hands over my stomach feeling a small bump full with life, and then I would walk to my bookstore. Life would be sweet. We wouldn't have much, but we would be happy.

The old me would think I'm stupid to even consider it. She would say that love would eventually die when we didn't have enough money in the bank to pay the bills. Sex would be replaced by obligations. Laughter by the buzz of the television. And maybe that old Blaire is right, but I also know the old Blaire wasn't happy. She had money and security. Yet her heart remained empty.

No ... I'm done listening to her. Life becomes beautiful when we learn to appreciate what we have and be thankful for it. Life becomes beautiful when we stop coveting things we don't have and are grateful for what we *do* have. Life is beautiful when we *choose* to make it beautiful.

Mistaking my silence for hesitation, he adds, "It won't be what you're used to, I know, but—"

"Shh." I place a finger on his lips, silencing him. "Those things don't matter to me anymore." Frowning, I think of a hiccup that could potentially mar our happiness. "But what about your exhibit? You're about to get your big break, Ronan. You can't leave now."

He wraps a hand around my neck possessively as he bends forward and begins to trail kisses on my neck, my jaw, my shoulder; making me tremble with hunger for him. "I don't care about it. Carl can keep the photographs and the money. I don't want any of it. I want to try doing it without their help—the right way. I want to be proud of what I've achieved, babe. And I can't be proud of what feels like was handed to me because of—"

"Rachel," I finish for him.

He nods, kissing my neck. "It's all a big reminder of a life without you."

I place my hands on his shoulders for support as a moan escapes my mouth. "You make me want to be selfish and agree to your plan ..." Ronan begins to roll his hips against me, sliding his cock between my pussy, lighting me on fucking fire.

"But it would be unfair to you," I moan, closing my eyes. "What if we waited until after your exhibit?"

"Don't," he breathes huskily. He licks his thumb and lowers it between us, rubbing my clit and making the room swirl, my senses coming alive with his touch. My body sings for him.

"It's my choice, Blaire. Everything I did, I did for you. And now that you're mine, I don't give a fuck about anything else. We'll make it on our own. Your bookstore and my camera." His smiling eyes gaze into mine as he grins cockily at me. "So what do you say, Mrs. Klein?"

Kissing his nose, happiness bubbles deep inside me. It makes me want to get up and run naked in the street, throw my head back, and shout that he's mine. It's all a beautiful dream, and it might be foolish to believe it, to want it so much, but we'll figure it out. There's no other choice for us.

"Yes," I say slowly. "Yes," I laugh. "Yes," I cry. "Yes. Always and forever, yes."

He makes love to me then. Slowly. Tenderly. Passionately. He worships me with his mouth, with his hands while his body tortures me with never ending pleasure. Moans cease to be moans. Kisses cease to be kisses. Thrusts cease to be thrusts. We transcend to a point where our bodies are not only joined together, but it is our souls that mate with one another, creating life.

It's magic.

And our new beginning.

With a towel wrapped around my torso, I walk out of the bathroom while applying lotion to my skin. I smile at the sight of Ronan. He's propped against the headboard and dozing off. I'm not surprised he's tired. The man's sexual appetite is unquenchable. Not that I'm complaining. Far from it, actually.

When I reach the foot of the bed, he opens his eyes focusing on me. The way he's staring at me like he wants to devour every inch of my body makes me feel a little reckless. Adventurous. I place the small bottle of lotion on the bed.

"How was your nap?" I ask, running my fingers through my wet hair.

"Lonely."

"Poor baby," I pout. "Would you like me to try and make you feel better?"

"You could try," he teases.

Leisurely, I reach for the bath towel wrapped around my torso and remove it, exposing every inch and curve of me to his wondering eye. Ronan watches me closely. His caramel gaze, sparkling with lust, roves over my figure.

"Like what you see?" I tease.

"Not sure. Why don't you come a little closer so I can take a better look?"

"Oh yeah?" I get on the bed and crawl toward him, taking my time as I close the space between us. I straddle his lap, rocking my pussy on his cock. "Well, what's the verdict?"

"Let's see …" Ronan grabs me by the hips, his long fingers gripping my ass firmly, and pulls me forward until I'm kneeling over his face. I reach for the headboard for support and look down as my breathing accelerates.

"Perfect," he says, his voice as thick as smoke. Smiling sinfully, his eyes are on me when his fingers spread my folds apart and his thumb begins to rub me in small circles. "Fucking perfect."

He plays my body like a damn maestro. I bite down hard on my lower lip the moment he drags his tongue along my soaked pussy. He breathes me in, his hot breath caressing my thighs as his hands move me against his eager mouth.

"And so damn sweet."

My body trembles. I grind my hips against his tongue as he goes wild. Licking. Sucking. Killing me. I look behind us. He's fisting his cock. Up and down. Up and down. Hypnotizing me. I bring a hand to my mouth, running my tongue over my palm and fingers to wet them. Twisting around, I push his hand away and wrap mine around his dick, pumping it in my fist, feeling him throb for me. It's magic and wildness.

Ronan's groans cut the silence in the room. I smirk as I let him go and move to kneel with my legs on either side of his body, hovering over him. I'm slick and so wet. I begin to rub myself on his hardness; back and forth, coating him with my juices as I glide my hands over my torso and tits, touching my nipples and pinching them until they are painfully hard.

The head of his cock spreads my lips and caresses my clit over and over again, lighting me like a match. When his hardness is glistening with my need, I move slightly back. "I want to taste you," I say huskily, before leaning down and running my tongue over him, tasting myself on him. Then I suck the tip of the head while he shudders and mutters my name.

I lift my eyes and meet his as I hold him in my hand, feeling the veins pulsate in my palm before I take him all in. I want to be choked by him, to feel his thickness fill my mouth completely, and make me gag.

Moaning, Ronan places a hand on the back of my head and pushes me down to take him deeper as he begins to pump into my mouth, fucking it hard and fast. My eyes fill with tears as I try not to gag. I pull him out, my chest rising and falling at speed. I wipe my chin with the back of my hand while trying to catch my breath.

"Time to fuck," I say. But Ronan surprises me when he flips me over, making me land on my stomach, and moves to straddle me.

"Yes, babe, time to fuck." Gripping my ass in his hands, he palms my cheeks. Spanking me once, twice, before he spreads them open. He places his cock right at my entrance, sinking shallowly, teasing me, making me beg.

Oh God, yes. Shuddering, I close my eyes. "Put it in me."

He dips his head low and rains kisses down my spine as his cock begins to fuck the crack of my ass. "Show me where you want me," he breathes against my skin, before biting my shoulder so hard I cry out.

Reaching behind me, I take his wet hardness and guide him toward my entrance. "Now, Ronan. I'm going crazy," I breathe heavily.

"Always and forever mine," he utters, passion flowing from his voice and through his movements. And then he enters me in one deep, forceful plunge that makes the headboard slam against the wall. I gasp, not knowing whether to cry in pain or scream in ecstasy. It doesn't matter.

It's much too beautiful to care. His cock slides in and out of me. It's slow at first but the intensity of his thrusts can't be denied. I feel them from the top of my head to the tip of my toes, and everywhere in between.

Then, out of nowhere, he stops moving. Desperation flows through me as I move my hips in circles, seeking my own pleasure with him still inside me, but it isn't enough—I need him to take me. "Ronan ... what are you doing to me? Please fuck me," I beg.

He grabs me by the hair, pulling me back, and leans over my shoulder. He begins to move ever so slightly, his thrusts shallow.

Taunting ...

Devastating ...

I roll my hips, seeking that blissful pressure. "Say you belong to me," he orders, his breathing labored.

"I do," I moan deliriously, pushing back.

He tugs harder. "You do *what*?"

"God, I'm yours," I whimper, shuddering. "I belong to you."

Growling, he lets go of my hair as his hands come up from behind me and he wraps them around my neck, pulling me toward him as his cock enters me more deeply. And then he loses all control and fucks me to Nirvana and beyond. It's brutal, violent even, but I love it. I'm coming so hard I see stars. Ronan finds his release soon after me as a ragged groan is torn from his chest. I feel him tremble above me as he lays his head on my back, shuddering.

After a few seconds pass, Ronan squeezes my ass while he runs his nose along the curve of my neck. "Mmm. You smell like you just got fucked, Mrs. Klein. And it pleases me very much."

Too tired to move, I close my eyes and laugh. "You better let me sleep now. Your sex slave needs rest."

"Not a chance," he says thickly.

"I need an hour."

"Twenty minutes."

"Thirty."

"Fifteen," he murmurs seductively against my skin, his tongue trailing a magic path along my shoulders up to my neck and behind my ear.

"Aren't you tired?" I ask, but it comes out more like a moan. His mouth and tongue are doing *very* wicked things to my neck. "Okay, fine." I shudder. "You win. Ten minutes. Happy?"

"Blaire?" he asks, his voice a low rasp.

"Yes?"

"I love you."

I smile. *I love you, too.*

Sometime in the early afternoon the next day, we stand outside the hotel about to go our separate ways. Both of us need to pack, say good-bye to family and friends, and we have to let our landlords know that we will be terminating our respective leases. My stomach is full of butterflies and my body is blissfully sore. It's such a high to be together that nothing else matters. *Tomorrow.*

I wrap my arms around Ronan's waist, holding him tight, and tilt my head back to take a better look at him. My gaze devours the mouth that knows every secret that my body has to offer, the jaw covered in scruff that has tickled me in more than one forbidden place. But it's his eyes, the color of chocolate and honey swirling together, that hold me captive.

I smile with lips that are swollen from our kisses. "I can't believe that we're going to do it."

"Are you afraid?"

"No. Not at all."

"Eight p.m. tonight. And then forever," he murmurs tenderly.

We agree to meet back here at that time and spend the night in the same hotel room. Tomorrow morning, we'll take a cab to JFK Airport, and get on the first flight leaving. The thought makes my heart beat faster, excitement rushing through me. I want to burst with happiness.

"Kiss me," I say.

Ronan buries his fingers in my hair, tugging it slightly, and lowers his face to mine. The warmth of his breath caresses my skin.

He smiles, biting my lower lip. "No."

I mirror his smile. "Kiss me."

"Nope." Ronan laughs. He kisses my temple before leaning his forehead on mine, our noses touching. *God, how can I feel so much love for this man?* "Trust me, Blaire. I want to kiss you, too. But once I start, I won't be able to stop. And we both have a very busy day ahead of us."

I grin. "It's not my fault you can't control yourself, Mr. Klein."

Ronan raises an eyebrow, the corner of his mouth tilting in a crooked smile. "And whose fault is that, Mrs. Klein?" He pauses, his gaze hungrily roving over my face. "Oh, fuck it. Come here, babe."

His mouth is on mine, swallowing me, breathing life into me with his lips. I feel him so deep in my soul, I tremble with love.

"Happy?" he asks when the kiss comes to an end.

I nod, smiling smugly. "I do love getting my way, you know?"

"You'll pay for that later. But before I forget," he says, pulling something out of his back pocket. "I have something that belongs to you."

I gasp, covering my mouth with a hand when I see what he's holding. Ronan reaches for my wrist. "Here, let me put it on you."

With a trembling hand, I touch the Hello Kitty watch he gave me all those months ago. "You kept it? After all this time?"

He runs his fingers through his hair, nodding.

"Why?" I ask dazedly.

"I couldn't get rid of it. It meant too much," he says softly.

I close the space between us and hug him once more. "Tomorrow can't come soon enough."

"I know, babe. I know. But in just a few hours we'll be back together, and everything will be all right."

I hold onto him tighter, drawing him closer into my arms, suddenly afraid to let him go. Life can't be this perfect, can it?

"Promise?"

"Promise."

I'm packing my suitcases, trying to figure out what to take with me, when my doorbell rings. I walk to the door, frowning as I go because I'm not expecting anyone. Elly is still in Vermont, so I have no idea who it could be. My heart freezes when I peek into the peephole and see who's standing on the other side. Dread settles in the pit of my stomach as I unlock my door as fast as possible and open it.

chapter twenty-seven.

"MAY I COME IN? WE NEED TO TALK," Jackie says, her expression inscrutable.

I tuck in some hair behind my ear, nervous. And with good reason. Besides her expression right now, which isn't the friendliest, I haven't forgotten our last meeting. "Um ... sure, come on in."

Jackie walks past me and into my apartment. I close the door behind me and watch her inspect my place. Her head moves this way and the other as she takes in the expensive furniture and the décor. All evidence of the person I used to be. Things that a hostess salary could never pay for.

She turns to look at me, dislike embedded in her face. "So this is what Lawrence paid for?"

That's a hit below the belt. One that I didn't expect from her in my own home. And one that hurts because of how true it rings. My instincts shout at me to hit back and draw blood, but I bite my tongue. I take a calming breath, reminding myself that she's Ronan's sister. And that she has every right to be angry.

"If you came to insult me, I think it's better if you leave now. I love your brother and I don't want to say something I'll regret."

Jackie ignores my request, blatantly daring me with her eyes. Crossing her arms, she reclines her hip against the back of my couch. "Oh, cry me a *fucking* river, Blaire. Listen, I will make this visit short and sweet because it's obvious that there's no lost love between us."

I hold on to the back of an accent chair for support, gripping it so hard my fingers grow numb. I try my best to appear calm while there's a storm brewing inside me. "Go ahead, then," I say, surprised at how blasé I manage to sound.

"When I first met you, I warned you that if you were just passing the time with Ronan, you should end it. No one would've been hurt. Not really, anyway. You obviously didn't listen to me. And why should you when it's usually all about Blaire, isn't it? So you kept dating my brother and he kept falling harder for you," she pauses, roving over my figure with so much scorn. "Then, one day my brother came over to visit Ollie, and I couldn't recognize the broken man who stood in front of me. My brother was gone, replaced by someone I didn't know."

She shakes her head, staring at the floor. "I couldn't figure out what happened to him, but when he stopped talking about you and pretty much forbade everyone in the family to even mention your name, I had a good idea of what must've gone down." She raises her gaze to meet mine. "What happened? Did you realize that he couldn't afford your going rate and Lawrence could?"

It all happens in a blur. One moment I'm by the chair, and in the next I'm standing in front of her, my hand stinging while she holds her cheek. "I'm sorry," I say, taking a step back and almost tripping on the rug. "I'm so sorry."

"Save it," she sneers. "I'm going to cut to the chase. I came here to ask you to please leave my brother alone. He came to say good-bye to Ollie earlier because apparently he's going away on a trip. When I told him that he couldn't leave just now, not when the exhibit is next week, you know what he said? That he didn't care about it anymore. He had that look in his eye. The one he had over the summer."

"What would you like me to do, Jackie?" I whisper dully.

"I don't have to spell it out for you, Blaire. You're smart. *Think.* My brother is on the brink of making it *big.* Huge. Are you really willing to let him sacrifice it all for you? Let him go, Blaire. I don't care if you have to break his heart again. Eventually, he'll get over the pain and love again."

"No." I shake my head frantically, feeling dizzy. "Anything but that, please. I love him … I love him. He has a plan …"

"What's his plan, Blaire? Throw it all away for love and go back to dead-end jobs? Back to doing things beneath his talent?"

She takes a step closer to me. "This is his moment, Blaire. If he lets this go, there's a big possibility it will never happen again. Can you live with that on your conscience? If you have one, that is."

I hang my head low and stare at the floor through eyes swimming with tears.

"And can you promise me you won't leave him again when things get tough? You already broke his heart once, Blaire, and it almost destroyed him. Can you promise me that you won't do it again?"

"I won't leave him again. I promise you. And I have changed—"

"If you have, then why are we having this discussion? Are you trying to convince me or yourself that you are worth more than Ronan's future?"

I walk to the window and stare at the skyline with unseen eyes. *Where has all the light gone?* With my back facing Jackie, I hug myself as though I could ward off myself from the truth in her words, from the pain that they inflict, but it's of no use. She's right. I'm being selfish by agreeing to his plan. "Even if I lie to him—" My voice falters, but I pull myself together. "He won't believe me. He won't let me go. Not this time."

"*Make* him believe you, Blaire. I'm sure you'll think of something."

"Why is happiness always so fleeting?"

"I'm sorry. Did you say something?"

"Nothing important," I say numbly, tightening my arms around me, suddenly very cold. *Hold it together, Blaire. Just for a few minutes longer.* "I think you should go."

She's silent for a moment. "Can I count on your word that you'll leave my brother alone?"

I can't answer that. The words get stuck in my throat, in my heart, in the core of my soul. My chest implodes with pain.

"Listen, Blaire," I hear her say, and for once there are no traces of dislike in her voice. Only resignation and defeat. "This has been his dream since he was a little boy. Don't let him give it all up for a few months away playing house with you." She places an envelope on my coffee table. "This is an invitation to his exhibition at The Jackson next week. Take a look at it and maybe then you'll know what is the right thing to do."

I look back and watch as the door closes behind Jackie before taking the invitation in my hands.

Suddenly an idea comes over me that fills me with a brief but dazzling hope. Maybe it doesn't have to be this way. Maybe …

Without stopping to think, I pick up my phone and give Ronan a call. He answers right away.

"What's up, babe? Finished packing?"

"Not yet. Ronan … I was thinking, maybe we shouldn't go just yet. What's another week? We could stay for your exhibit and then—"

He sighs. "Babe, I thought we already went over this."

"But—"

"No. I don't want any of it. I want you. Just you. Anyway, I just got to Carl's. I've got to go. I'll see you at the hotel. Love you."

After hanging up, I stare numbly at the elegant writing on the expensive paper. As Jackie's words beat me down over and over again, I think of Ronan and our future together. I know that Ronan said that he doesn't care about the exhibit and how close he is to achieving his dream, but will he still feel the same way when he's starting all over again, struggling between jobs? Could I look Ronan in the eye and live with myself knowing that I stopped his career because I was selfish?

I've lived all my life thinking about no one but myself. My needs and my wants. I never once stopped to consider the consequences of my actions. And because of that, I've hurt so many people.

But I can't do that anymore.

Least of all to Ronan.

I love him too much to let him sacrifice his dreams for me.

I stand by the door and take one last look at my apartment. Every memory, happy and sad and somewhere in between, will remain behind. I need them to stay here, if I am to survive the next few hours, the next few days, the next few months, the next few years—the rest of my life. I must try. I must try for him.

I press a hand to my chest, making sure that my heart is still beating. It feels broken past remedy. But it does. It beats. It beats for him.

It always will.

Ronan

About an hour late, I arrive at the hotel. It took a little longer than I expected to explain to Carl that I wasn't going to be part of the exhibit. The man wasn't happy. But he mellowed when I mentioned that he could keep all the photographs and sell them for however much money he wanted. As I was leaving, he told me that I was a fool to throw it all away for a woman. I laughed, not at him, but because life was so fucking sweet. I looked him in the eye and said that I would rather be a fool than to live a life without her in it, and then I left.

I run to the room. I can't be bothered with patience. Not when my body is vibrating with energy—with love for the woman waiting for me behind those doors. Happiness, need, and the yearning to be reunited with her propel my every step.

I get off the elevator in a rush, bumping into an older lady who appears to be my grandmother's age. Once I apologize, I impulsively take her by the arms and waltz with her, making her smile and blush rosily as we glide across the hallway. I'm so damn happy, I want the entire world to share the moment with me. I twirl her slowly as we both laugh. She calls me a crazy boy. I tell her that I am crazy—crazy for a woman.

"Oh my goodness," she says, fanning herself. "It's been many, many years since I last danced with a handsome stranger such as yourself."

"The pleasure is all mine, ma'am," I say, letting her go, and smile shamelessly. "Now if you excuse me," I take her hand in mine, bowing over it, and kiss it. "My woman is waiting for me."

I open the door expecting to find Blaire reading in bed. Instead, I'm met with a room bathed in darkness. *Odd.* Frowning, I reach for the switch and turn the lights on. The bed is empty and so is the room. "Blaire? Are you here, babe?" I ask, heading to the bathroom. Maybe she's taking a shower. She isn't in there either.

Slowly, I walk back and look around for any signs that Blaire was even here. As I'm scanning the furniture, there's a knock at the door. Relief floods me, making me dizzy. There she is. She was just running late. *Like me.*

There's a man dressed in the hotel uniform staring at me. "Mr. Geraghty?"

"Yes?"

"A lady dropped this letter for you. She asked me to give it to you personally."

I shove him to the side and swiftly step outside. "Is she here? Where is she?" Panic rises inside me. No … this can't be happening. Not again.

"Where is she, man?" My voice sounds desperate. "Where is she?"

"She left, sir." He swallows, measuring his next words. "I helped her get in a cab."

My ears begin to ring as I retrieve the letter from his hands. After tipping him, I close the door and attempt to open the envelope. It takes me a few tries because my hands won't stop shaking. Cursing, I close my eyes tight and breathe deeply.

Ronan,

I want to lie to you and tell you that I don't love you and that we can't be together anymore to make this easier for both of us, but I can't. You deserve more than that. You deserve my honesty.

I love you so much it hurts. It hurts not to be there with you right now. It hurts to know that our dream won't ever come true. And it hurts because I finally had you just to lose you all over again. My love for you is the only thing that is pure in this tarnished body of mine. And I refuse to taint it with my selfishness. It is because of that love that I'm letting you go, my eternal summer.

I'm setting you free.

I can't let you sacrifice your career for me, Ronan. Not when you're so close to achieving everything that you've dreamed of.

You were meant to soar, to be adored.

You deserve all the success that you have coming your way, and the last thing you need is someone like me holding you back. Our short-lived daydream painted such beauty, such hope, but I would never forgive myself if you gave it all up to be with me. Eventually, you would grow to resent me, maybe even hate me, and I wouldn't be able to live with myself if you did.

I hate to say good-bye to you like this, but I'm weak. I don't think I would be able to let you go if I saw you again. I would fist fight through the pain and all the righteous reasoning to keep you close to me.

Maybe one day we'll meet again, but if we don't, know that I will always be waiting for you in that place between sleep and lucidity where dreams come alive. That's where our love will always exist.

Don't look for me, please. Move on. Live. Love again.

Yours always and forever.
Blaire.

Something falls out, catching my attention. Bending down, I pick up Blaire's paper ring. I grip it tight in my fist as I sit down on the bed and will myself to feel something. Anything. But there's nothing left inside me.

It is all gone.

chapter **twenty-eight**.

Blaire

Two months after...

NUMB.

How can I go on?
Will I ever be able to?

chapter twenty-nine.

Blaire

Six months after …

THERE'S A FOG THAT HAS settled around me. Grief holds me back and I can't break past it. I panic. I breathe in and exhale. Tell myself that it will get better. *It must.* So I keep walking, with my arms outstretched, hoping to eventually find my way.

chapter thirty.

Blaire

A few years later ...

"HOW ARE YOU DOING?" my mom asks on the phone. "Are you excited?"

I throw the rest of my breakfast away and wipe the counter of my small kitchen clean. Gripping my cell tighter, I smile. "You have no idea. I can't believe that I'm going to Paris in a few days."

"Don't forget to buy a nice gift for Joanna and Jacob, honey."

"Already got it, Mom. And I also called them yesterday to thank them for giving me the job."

A couple years ago, heartbroken and unsure of what to do with my life, I went back home and spent the rest of the winter and spring with my mom. It wasn't easy at first, but every single argument was worth it in the end. Together we found forgiveness and eventually love.

As the days turned into weeks and weeks turned into months, I came to the realization that somehow, unbeknownst to me, a part of my core had changed. My mom had told me that if I wanted change, it had to start from within, and she was right.

I couldn't go back to sleeping with men for money. The thought alone made me sick. There was a time when I could have given my body to a man who I didn't love. He would finish, I would go home, sore between the legs, numb, my pride in shreds and with a bank account full of money. I wasn't happy. However, I was safe. But how could I go back after everything that I had shared with Ronan and when every part of me still belonged to him? It was unthinkable.

Change doesn't happen overnight. But the hunger, the thirst to make something of myself bloomed like a flower in early spring. And suddenly the barren landscape that my life morphed into wasn't so barren anymore. That's when I decided to go back to New York City, enroll in school, and get my art degree.

It hasn't been easy. Far from it. But for once in my life I can say that I'm proud of myself. Learning to forgive and love myself came later ... and that took a lot more work than I expected. It's no easy feat to let go of a lifetime full of hang-ups. It's a daily battle.

"Are you sure that Elly's husband won't mind you staying in their apartment while you work there?" my mom asks, concern embedded in her voice.

I pick up my bag and keys, locking the door behind me. "Nope. Alessandro is the sweetest man. He told me that his parents own another apartment that they can always stay at. It doesn't matter, anyway. I'm hoping to save enough money working at Joanna and Jacob's art gallery to be able to afford my own place."

"Well, that's good."

We chat some more about what my plans are for the rest of my belongings that I can't bring with me to Paris, and the cute barista who took me out on a third date the other night. When she asks me if he spent the night over at my apartment, I decide to quickly end the conversation. We've grown extremely close, but I'm definitely *not* going there with my mom. Besides, how could I explain to her that yes, he did come back and it felt lovely to be touched again, to be wanted, to be kissed. But the moment I tried to be physically intimate with a man for the first time in years, I panicked and broke down in tears. Poor Phoenix—cute barista, actually, mega-hot barista, who happens to make a killer latte—just held me in his arms, rocking a massive and very painful erection while I cried.

I give my head a little shake, feeling myself blush with embarrassment. *Yeah*, I was definitely *not* going there with my mom.

Getting off the train, I make my way to the deli outside my subway stop and buy flowers. I take my iPhone out of my purse, check the time, making sure that I'm not running late for work, and then walk into the coffee shop next door. I spot Phoenix immediately. It's impossible to miss him— tallest guy around, tatted, and drop-dead gorgeous. His electric blue gaze lands on me as soon as I walk in. I blush under his roving and appreciative eye.

He walks toward me, cocky smile in place, as he pushes some of his black hair away from his face. "Mornin', gorgeous. I didn't expect to see you today."

I laugh. "You should have more faith in me."

"I do, that's why I haven't stopped asking you out for the past two years."

"Two years." I scrunch up my nose. "It really has been *that* long?" I do the math in my head and grimace. He's right. Thing is, for most of my life I had always been in a relationship with a man, or dependent on one. I didn't know what being single was. I didn't know who I was outside of a relationship, and it felt nice to get to know myself.

"Yep." He leans down to kiss me on the cheek, but his mouth lands on the corner of my lips. I tell you. He's smooth. "Anyway, I figured you needed some space after the other night."

"Here," I say, handing him the flowers I just bought. "My apology."

He cocks an eyebrow. "Well, this is a first. No one has ever bought me flowers before."

I place a hand on top of his arm. "Do you have a few minutes? I need to talk to you."

He turns to look behind us, toward the counter where a very pretty and dainty girl with blue hair is preparing some drinks. "Winter, I'll be back in a few. Give me a shout if you need me."

When we step outside the coffee shop, he reclines his back on the wall while he crosses his muscled arms across his even more muscled chest. "All right, gorgeous. What is it?"

I stare at the pavement, noticing that my shoes have seen better days. "I just wanted to explain to you what happened back ... you know ... the other night."

"Blaire," the teasing tone in his voice is gone, "you don't have to explain anything to me. We got carried away and you weren't ready. End of story. Now, question is when do we get to try again?" he asks cheekily.

"Seriously?"

He grins. "Can't fault a man for tryin'."

"You're a brave man for even thinking about it, Phoenix. I pretty much lost it. Like, total psycho move."

He chuckles, and even the chuckle is sexy, but that's Phoenix for you. "Can't promise you that one day I'll look back to that night and think of it as one of my fondest memories."

"You're too much." I laugh. "So am I forgiven?"

"Always. But can I just say something?"

"Go ahead."

"Eventually you're going to have to let his memory go, Blaire. You're young, smart, beautiful, and so much fuckin' fun. A memory won't warm your bed at night. Not like I could anyway."

Phoenix is right. I know that, and that's why I finally agreed to go out with him. But what happens when your heart is deaf to reason and blind to every man who isn't a world-renowned photographer with brown eyes?

"I know, Phoenix." I take his arm in mine, patting his hand, and walk inside the coffee shop. "I'm trying, I promise."

"Every time I see an article written about how fucking talented he is, my hands itch to punch his pretty face," he says angrily.

"Don't say that. I'm proud of him." His success makes the pain worthwhile. I recline my head on his arm since I'm too short to reach his shoulder. A long time ago, the mention of his name alone would have been like a knife to the heart. Not a day goes by when it doesn't hurt, but at least I can look at his pictures and read about him without falling apart. "I'm going to miss you, Phoenix."

"I'm going to miss you, too, Blaire."

Back at work, I'm folding some dress shirts in the men's department when a customer asks me to look up a sweater in a particular size. I take the item from his hands and head to the register. Distracted with my mind in Paris, I bump into a solid chest.

"Beg your pardon," I apologize as I look up, beginning to move away.

The moment my eyes land on the man standing in front of me, I swear my heart stops beating momentarily. The world feels as though it stops spinning, and everything hangs in complete stillness.

"Blaire?"

Weak in the knees, I feel like I'm about to pass out. "Hello, Lawrence."

chapter **thirty-one.**

Lawrence

STANDING IN FRONT OF ME is the woman who still haunts me in my dreams.

"Hello. I see that some things haven't changed," I say, attempting to smile but even that smile tastes bitter on my tongue.

She flinches as a blush rich in color spreads across her porcelain skin. Blaire, enchantress and tormentor, remains so beautiful even after all this time. "Actually, I work here."

Surprised at her response, I begin to notice small changes in her appearance that at first didn't register in my mind. Her long black hair is out of place, her clothes a little shabby, the color faded, and a pink watch on her wrist. But it's the soft light in her eyes that arrests my attention. The hard, cynical look is missing.

And she takes my breath away.

Gone is the girl with the embittered smile that never quite reached her eyes. There's no hardness left in her womanly body. She's a stranger who is far lovelier than her counterpart ever was.

"Forgive me for assuming that—"

"No need to apologize, Lawrence." She lowers her gaze to the floor, depriving me of seeing her face. It makes me want to rage, to take her in my arms and beg her not to ever look away from me again. I've gone so long without it already.

"You haven't forgiven me, have you?" she asks sadly, the words almost whispered.

Instinctively, I reach out to touch her but stop myself just in time. I lower my hand, burying it in my pocket. "The past belongs in the past." *I've forgiven you, but I haven't been able to forget you.*

She remains silent.

"Have lunch with me." The words come out unbidden from somewhere deep inside me as I stare at her profile, willing her to make eye contact with me.

She looks up then. Her eyes widen in surprise. "I can't."

I'm a fucking fool. What did I expect? That she would come running into my arms? "I see … Well, it was great seeing you. I better go—"

"But I can do dinner," she adds quickly.

Blaire

I arrive at a small Italian restaurant of Lawrence's choice. There can't be more than ten tables. I stand on my tiptoes and look for him, finding him sitting all the way at the back, away from the crowd. When our eyes connect, we both smile at the same time. He stands as I make my way to him.

Even after all this time, my heart still skips a beat at the sight of his rare smiles.

Lawrence places a hand on the small of my back as he leans in and kisses my cheek. The moment his mouth comes into contact with my skin, a shiver runs down my spine. Funny how my body hasn't forgotten what it's like to be touched by him.

"Sorry I'm late ... I had to unpack some of my suitcases to find something decent to wear."

A waiter comes over to take my coat, but Lawrence dismisses him. "Allow me." His fingers brush my bare shoulders as he helps me. He takes the chair in front of me and pulls it out. "You look beautiful," he says, his voice a caress as I sit down.

"Thank you." Suddenly feeling extremely nervous, I reach for the menu and go over it. It gives me the perfect excuse not to look him in the eye.

He pulls the menu away, his hand settling on top of mine. "Don't be afraid, Blaire. Not of me," he adds huskily.

Swiftly, I lift my eyes and meet his stare. "It's not that ... I'm nervous."

"Why?"

I focus on his tanned hand on mine, and it's turns out to be a mistake. Because as I do, memories of how intimately that hand has touched me, how well it knows every part of my body, flood my mind. "Why am I nervous, he asks?" I repeat incredulously. "Do you really have to ask?"

He has the decency to laugh. "Why don't we order some wine first, and then you can tell me the reason behind the suitcases?"

"I'd like that."

Over dinner, I begin to loosen up around him, even though he watches me in a way that makes me flush under his gaze. We discuss my plans in Paris, and his work. School. New projects. Life. The future. We talk about everything and nothing at all, always avoiding Ronan and the past. Always avoiding our last encounter.

Soon we fall back into the old ways where he reclines his back on the chair twirling the red wine in his glass while I do most of the chatting. In no time, we're back to being dear friends.

While taking a sip, I seize the opportunity to admire him unabashedly. Time hasn't changed Lawrence Rothschild. No. He's as lethally attractive as the first moment I set eyes on him. Every pore, every atom in his body is wired with virility.

There's a small smile on his face that makes the corners of his eyes crinkle attractively. "In some ways, you're the same."

I raise an eyebrow, placing the wine glass down on the table. "You mean I still don't have a clue when to shut up?"

He chuckles wryly. "And in other ways, you're very different. What's changed, Blaire?" he asks softly.

"Everything." I trace the white tablecloth with the pads of my fingers. "You know, I don't have much anymore, but I'm happy. Everything I own, I've earned by working on my two feet. And it's the best feeling in the world. I look at myself in the mirror each morning and I'm not ashamed." I raise my face and smile.

"I'm finally free, Lawrence. For once, when I look in the mirror, I like the person who's staring back at me. Don't get me wrong. I still like pretty things, but my existence and self-worth do not revolve around them. I don't have to hide behind them, either."

Lawrence reaches for my hand, lacing our fingers tightly together. He doesn't say a word. He doesn't have to. His touch is enough. "Where's Ronan, Blaire? Why isn't he with you?"

I attempt to smile, but I can't hide the pain from Lawrence. "Some things aren't meant to be."

"Don't I know it?" Lawrence adds quietly.

I lift his hand, raise it to my mouth, and kiss it. "I'm so sorry for everything, Lawrence. Even after all this time, it still hurts to know that I caused you so much pain. You didn't deserve any of it. I didn't—"

"There's no room for logic when the heart is involved. To love is to lose all sense of reason." He stares straight ahead, his mind far away. "Before you came into my life, I thought that I couldn't love again, that my life was as good as it was going to get. But you made me want more. Need more. You did hurt me, but you also awoke something in me that had lain dormant for years."

"What's that?"

Lawrence trains his eyes on me, a rueful gleam illuminating his green gaze. "Shall we call it the need to love and be loved in return?"

Later in the evening, we're standing outside the restaurant. The summer breeze is warm against my skin and makes strands of my hair fly wildly in different directions. As we look at each other silently, sadness fills me from within, sorrow gripping my heart with its sharp nails. A gut feeling tells me that this is the last time that we'll see each other, and I'm not ready for that.

A knot forms in my stomach. "So is this good-bye?"

He stares at me and without saying a word, I already know the answer. I can see it in his eyes.

"Lawrence, I—"

"Don't say it, Blaire. Don't say something that you'll regret."

My eyes absorb the man standing in front of me, memorizing his features so dear to my heart. "I regret many things that happened between us, but I won't ever regret you, Lawrence. Not you," I add softly.

I love you.

Taking a step forward, I close the space between us. I place my hands on his shoulders, stand on my tiptoes, and kiss his cheek. I shut my eyes momentarily and breathe him in, losing myself in the past. Meeting him at the Met. Going to his estate for the first time. The taste of his kisses. The feel of his arms around me. The laughter. The friendship. Yes, most of all, the friendship. My friend. My lover.

As I'm moving away, I whisper in his ear, "I'll always remember Coney Island."

He doesn't touch me. He doesn't reach for me. My blood runs cold. It's unfair to be this close to him, yet still so far.

"Good-bye, Blaire. Be kind to Parisian men and their hearts."

I take a step back and begin to walk away from Lawrence. My feet are shaky. *Don't look back, Blaire. Don't. Let him go.*

When I reach the curb of the street, I hear Lawrence call out my name. I'm about to turn in the direction of his voice when his hand grips my arm, spinning me around, and he pulls me flush against his chest. Burying his fingers in my hair, his hands cradling my head, he dips his head and presses his mouth to mine.

A kaleidoscope of emotions burst inside me, stunning me with their intensity. And as he steals my breath away with a bruising kiss that makes every nerve in my body come alive, I see a different life flash by. Lawrence standing by the altar, his smiling eyes trained on me. Lawrence and I at the beach chasing two little boys who look just like him, their laughter, our laughter, filling my ears, creating music. Making love by the fireplace, slow, needy. It's a beautiful life.

As he deepens the kiss, his tongue seeking mine, I allow myself to be swept away by him and the beautiful portrait in my mind. And for a short magic moment, somewhere between the past and the present, I yearn for that life. But deep down, I'm aware that it can never be. Not when my heart knows that Ronan is alive somewhere in this world.

Breathless and shaken, I bury my head in his chest while my arms go around his waist. I hold onto him tightly as I fight through the pain of finding him just to lose him all over again. *Why is doing the right thing always so hard?*

"My love, my darling, not a day goes by when I don't remember," he murmurs hoarsely. "But it's time for me to let you go."

Even after all these years, I know that I will always love Ronan with all my heart. I surrendered it to him willingly that night by the Bethesda Fountain. But as I watch Lawrence disappear into the crowd, I realize that he's taken away with him a small part of me that I will never get back, leaving a hole in my chest that no man and no love will ever be able to replace. It will always belong to Lawrence.

But I'm not afraid of the pain anymore.

Nor do I have to run.

If my life, and losing Ronan and Lawrence have taught me anything about myself, it's that I'm a survivor. I'm strong because I've been weak. I have sharp edges because I've been broken. Through all the neglect of my childhood, the pain, the fear, the heartache, and the lonely days and even lonelier nights, I remain standing.

And no matter what storms life continues to throw my way, I know now that I have the strength within me to weather them all.

So if my story ends with no knight in shining armor in sight, I'm okay with it because I don't need one to save me.

I have myself.

And that's good enough for me.

epilogue.

Ronan

"HERE YOU ARE, the man of the hour!"

"Hey, Jackie."

"Why are you hiding from all your guests? This party is insane."

I turn in the direction of my sister's voice, our eyes locking. "I couldn't stand the noise."

"Well, I'm celebrating. All your photographs sold out within the hour, Ronan. Again." She leans against the wall and takes a sip of champagne from a crystal flute. "I'm so proud of you, but I've got to say that I can't get used to seeing them losing their minds over my little brother. It's trippy."

I bury my hands in the front pockets of my slacks as I stare at a photograph hanging on the wall, willing myself to feel some sort of excitement or enthusiasm, but it's of no use. There's nothing inside me. She took it all with her, leaving the ghost of a man behind.

Sometimes I see her in the curves of a naked woman lying on my bed or in the color of bluebells in the spring. Even after all this time, the smell of rain still reminds me of her. She's everywhere and nowhere. Between heaven and hell. Her memory raises me high just so reality can slam me down—she's gone. Every day and every night the chains inside my soul rattle with her name, calling out for her to set me free.

She told me to forget her, to move on, to love again. But I wish she could have told me how to do those things. How can I live a life without her in it when she's as much a part of me as I am her?

"What's wrong, Ronan?" Jackie asks quietly.

"Nothing's wrong. Let it go." The words sound empty in my ears.

"I think you're lying to me. You aren't happy, Ronan. I can't remember the last time I saw you smile."

"What's there to smile about, Jackie?"

Her brown eyes, the same color as mine, spark with light. "Your success!" She spreads her arms, signaling my spacious SoHo flat. "Your life. Everything that you have accomplished on your own. I mean, take a look at this place. It's ridiculous."

Yes, I've achieved success beyond my wildest imagination and without the help of anyone, but it means nothing to me. Nothing has for a very long time. Soon after Blaire left, I threw my body and soul into my work. I created to fill the gaping hole inside me. It didn't work. However, it took my mind off of the fucking pain that was threatening to break me in two each and every day without her.

I was selling my photographs in the subway one day when a man stopped and asked me if I had taken them. Turns out he was the curator of a very famous New York museum. The rest is history.

"I better get back to my guests," I say smoothly.

She grips my arm and stops me from taking another step. "It's because of her, isn't it?"

I slant a wry look at her, raising an eyebrow. "I don't understand what you mean."

"I thought that I was doing the right thing by keeping her away from you—"

"What do you mean, Jackie?" The small hairs on my arms stand on end. My heart begins to pump hard. "Who did you keep away from me?"

"Blaire." She hangs her head as her shoulders crumple in shame. "I went to see her the day you came to say good-bye to Ollie. I only had your best interest at heart ..."

Barely keeping my control in check, I turn to face my sister, holding her by the arms. My hands are trembling. "What did you do, Jackie?" I whisper harshly. "What the fuck are you talking about?"

"Oh, Ronan ... I ..." She looks up at me. "There's so much that I have to explain."

Blaire

"Au revoir," I say as I watch the couple leave the gallery. Their bank account took a hit, but their home is going to look fabulous. It's been a couple of months since I moved to Paris and things couldn't be better. Jacob and Joanna have been a pleasure to live with and work for, and I'm in love with the city. The architecture, the culture, the fashion, the food (oh my God, the food!), the art and the people are all breathtaking. Every day I fall a little bit more in love with it all.

I sigh, giving my head a tiny shake, and go back to my desk and get back to work. I'm going over some paperwork when I hear the glass doors open and close behind me. Smiling, I turn around to greet the new customer.

As my eyes land on him, my smile freezes and I feel the air knocked out of me. Blinking repeatedly, I absorb his achingly beautiful features, but it's his eyes that hold me captive and their slave.

"Hello, Mrs. Klein," he says huskily, his voice full of tenderness.

"What—" I grip the desk, feeling like I'm about to faint. "What are you doing here?"

"Elly told me where to find you." He closes the space between us, detaches my fingers from the desk, and takes me in his arms. My knees give out, too weak to hold me straight, but he holds me tight in his embrace as he caresses my wet cheek.

"I came to get what's mine. Besides, you forgot something." He takes my hand in his and places the paper ring on my finger, *right where it belongs*. Then he smiles into my eyes and the world suddenly makes sense once again.

"Always and forever and over a thousand eternities, mine."

The End

acknowledgements.

I WANT TO THANK MY HUSBAND and my family for loving me and supporting me through it all. I love you more than words can ever describe.

Next I would like to thank each and every single person that helped me in creating Sweetest Venom—my very special and kick-ass group of beta readers. Without your help and feedback this book would have never been completed. Your unfailing dedication to these characters and your wisdom were my guiding light. Luna, Jx, Priscilla, Rosalinda, Kathy, Rachel, Megan, Melissa, Mint, Milasy, Tennille, Deana, Kelley—SV wouldn't be what it is without you! You guys are not only my team, but you are my friends. I love you, girls.

Luna and Jx, thank you SO much for your friendship, support, and help. You kept me on track when I wanted to give up. And you were there for me when I was racing toward the end. I don't know how I would've done it all without you. You guys rock my world. I love you!

Penelope, my P, I don't know what I would do without your friendship and your guidance. Seriously. I love you, woman.

Claire, #soulsisters. #darksideisalwaysbetter #loveyou #givemeOliverandIllgiveyouLaw

Corinne, one day I promise to listen to all the amazing advice that you give me. LOL. Love you!

Priscilla, thank you for your friendship. I'm very lucky to have it.

Rosalinda, your feedback regarding Blaire's past was indispensable to the story. Thank you so much for everything that you did and for your friendship.

Melissa, Megan, and Mint, we DID it!!! WE DID IT! We met about four years ago. We bonded over our love for books, and the rest is history. You were the first three people who read my first draft of Easy Virtue back when it was all a big dream of mine. And you have been with me ever since. Thank you!

Kathy N., thank you so much for listening to me vent about my characters every other week. <3 You're the best.

Jennifer, my beautiful, generous, caring, patient, and very talented editor, thank you so much for being there for me and for dealing with my crazy. I may have written Sweetest Venom, but it was your work and magic that made it readable and enjoyable. Thank you so much!

Ryn, I want to thank you for perfecting SV with your proofreading services. Also, thank you so much for squeezing me in. You rocked!

Kassi, you're a rock star. Thank you so much for making SV pretty and for answering all my questions and meeting my crazy deadlines. I'd be dead without you. <3

TRSOR Lisa and Milasy, thank you so much for putting up with my crazy, your friendship, and for your help, my friends. I don't know where I would be without your support. You organized a kick-ass cover reveal and blog tour. Love you, girls <3

BIG, BIG SHOUT OUT to my girls in the EV Discussion and Spoiler group. You guys have made that place something really special. Here is to hoping SV gives us as many hours of discussion as Arsen and EV did. MAD LOVE TO YOU ALL!

I want to give a special shout out to all the bloggers and individuals that helped spread the word about my work. No one would know about my novel if it weren't for your help. I would be nothing without your help. Thank you for believing in me (again) and in Sweetest Venom. I'm so lucky and very grateful to have you in my life.

To FYW, thank you for all your help! Liquidate that! ;)

BBFT, best group ever!

Thank you to all my family and friends for putting up with me and for always being there for me. I know I'm forgetting someone and if I do know that I'm truly sorry. I love all the encouraging words, the lovely words from every single person that has stopped by my page and said hello. I love every single one of you.

This book would not be anything without the support and love from all of you. Thank *you* so, so much.

OTHER BOOKS BY MIA ASHER

Easy Virtue
Arsen

Available at:
Amazon
Barnes and Noble
iTunes
Kobo

Made in the USA
San Bernardino, CA
27 July 2016